What Reader
ROGER N
OCCAM'S RAZOR

"First rate! In the tradition of medical thrillers typified by Robin Cook, Dr. Newman strings the reader along shamelessly, virtually forcing the reader to pull an all-nighter!"—*Dr. Jeff Thurston, author of Death of Compassion, and 1000 Questions About Your Pregnancy.*

"Occam's Razor" [is}like a true crime confessional. It's a wild and gratifying ride, y'all, well worth your money and time."—*Roger Pinckney, author of Reefer Moon, Little Glory and Blow the Man Down.*

"...a thriller involving the misuse of governmental power as it threatens to destroy the lives of a patient and her physician working in an academic medical center in Charleston. The world described in this riveting page turner is absolutely real—and you will love having visited it."—*Richard L. Berkowitz, Maternal Fetal Medicine, Columbia University.*

"...a gripping thriller, a passionate love story and a hero's journey that will keep the pages turning and have you cheering by the end. Newman combines his intimate knowledge of hospital life with the South Carolina Low Country swamps and beaches and the narrow streets of Charleston to create a setting that is as alive as his characters—told through the magnetic voice of a man who loves and doubts and ultimately triumphs—an against-the-grain hero and a guy next door. I hope to see much more of Drs. Murphy and Newman in the future!"—*Taylor Polites, author of The Rebel Wife.*

OCCAM'S RAZOR

ROGER NEWMAN

Moonshine Cove Publishing, LLC
Abbeville, South Carolina U.S.A.

ISBN: 978-1-937327-47-7
Library of Congress Control Number: 2014943132
Copyright © 2014 by Roger Newman

Book interior and cover design by Moonshine Cove; cover illustration by Ginny Canady, used with permission.

ABOUT THE AUTHOR

Roger Newman, M.D. is a nationally known leader in Ob-Gyn; selected as one of the "Best Doctors in America" by Woodward and White for the past two decades. He has  been a Section Chair for the American Congress of Obstetricians and Gynecologists and an editor for the *American Journal of Obstetrics and Gynecology.* Dr. Newman was the national president of the Society for Maternal-Fetal Medicine and served five years on the Scientific Advisory Board for the NIH-NICHD Maternal-Fetal Medicine Network. He has written more than 120 peer-reviewed scientific publications and almost 20 book chapters. Dr. Newman is considered an expert on the care of women with twins or triplets. He has written the multiple gestation chapters in most of the major Ob-Gyn textbooks and has co-authored a book entitled *Multifetal Pregnancy: A Handbook for the Care of the Pregnant Patient.*

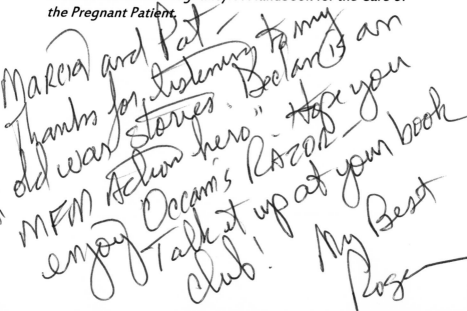

OCCAM'S RAZOR

CHICAGO O'HARE

There aren't many direct flights into or out of Charleston, South Carolina, but Chicago O'Hare is one of them. That was the only easy thing about the boards. Each December, young obstetricians and gynecologists embark on a mid-winter hadj to Chicago. They brave bone-chilling cold and lip-splitting wind on their pilgrimage. It is a holy expedition to take one final oral board examination in a drab, bargain-rate room at the Chicago Westin. The oral boards are medicine's version of poker's "all in." After losing most of their youth to medical training, hundreds of thirty-something Ob-Gyns flock to Chicago to face one last challenge before their final coronation as the hot-shots they believe themselves to be. Failure not only jeopardizes tangible things like hospital privileges, job opportunities and salary offers, but more importantly, the sense of infallibility and certainty of judgment that allows them to make the clinical decisions he or she must make each day.

The road to Chicago was much the same for me as the other examinees. I was among the minority of my South Carolina high school classmates who decided there were greater horizons in life than just being a Tiger or a Gamecock. I left for college in New Jersey and majored in pre-med. I'd be lying if I said it was a calling. It was mostly lack of imagination. Pre-med seemed to be the registration line with the most obvious connection to later employment. I worried sometimes about the utilitarian nature of my career choice. Not able to afford a private, out of state medical school, I returned home to the Medical University of South Carolina in Charleston. MUSC is the oldest publicly supported medical school in the South and one of the oldest in the nation. Unfortunately, despite her seniority, MUSC was Cinderella to her regional sisters, the University of North Carolina and the University of Virginia Medical Schools. MUSC's malediction is an ever-present institutional inferiority complex. Charleston's unofficial motto always was, "Too poor to paint; too proud to whitewash." The price was right, however, and there was never a shortage of poverty or disease. After medical school, I decided to stay in Charleston for a residency in Obstetrics and Gynecology.

Following residency, I took advantage of what I was sure would be my last opportunity to travel. I moved to California for two years, extending my training in the relatively new subspecialty of Maternal-Fetal Medicine at the University of California, San Francisco. After two professionally phenomenal, but financially crushing years in San Francisco, Declan Forest Murphy M.D. returned to MUSC to join the faculty as an Assistant Professor of Obstetrics and Gynecology. It was from Charleston that I had made my plane reservations to Chicago for one final oral examination.

The oral examinations were notorious for their ability to lay a good man low. Still, I felt positive about how things had gone. I had successfully defended my case list, and I didn't think they had tripped me up on any of the hypothetical cases. After a couple of pints of Guinness to decompress in the Westin lobby bar, I grabbed a taxi to O'Hare. It was a clear and crisp day, which is the most you can ask of Chicago in December.

O'Hare airport was humming, as it always is, but all the flights appeared to be on time. After the beers at the Westin, and almost two hours until my flight, I thought it wiser to walk past the terminal bars and find something to eat instead. I took a tour through the food court which was depressing. In the back corner I saw the Billy Goat Tavern. Having never missed a showing of Saturday Night Live, I had to pay homage.

I found an empty bar stool and table, and wiped the salt and water rings off the Formica top with my sleeve. My cheeseburger was wrapped in greasy wax paper and was extraordinarily bad. I was satisfied that I had enjoyed the entire Billy Goat experience. Unfortunately, there was still time to kill. I started to replay the entire morning's examination in my head, but quickly realized I was making a huge mistake. I had been confident I had avoided any major blunders, but the more I ruminated, the more I spiraled down to darker, more confusing stratums where I found no solace; only apprehension and anxiety.

The unsettling part of the oral board examination is the absence of any feedback from your examiners. We all expect feedback, no matter what kind of work we do. We're like puppies. When we do well, we expect to be patted on the head. When we pee on the carpet, we expect a swat on the butt. During the oral examination, the questions come one on top of the other, with no verbal or non-verbal cues as to whether you're on the right track. Many questions are based on hypothetical patients and build on your previous answer. If you make an incorrect diagnosis early on, or begin with the wrong initial treatment, you can build a house of cards that will ultimately collapse on itself. You can spend five minutes entangling yourself in a web of missteps without ever realizing it. An emotionless spider sits across the table and waits for you to tire from the struggle. The more you replayed the examination in your head, the more opportunities you recognized to have wandered off beaten path. I needed to think about something else.

Two college girls wearing DePaul sweatshirts sat at the table next to me. It seemed early in December for Christmas break, but maybe not. A distinguished older man in a very expensive suit and attaché case sat at the table to my right. I imagined he was probably an ambassador returning to Washington DC with vital diplomatic documents. I paused for a second to consider how long I had been training to be an Ob-Gyn. I had started medical school in 1970 when Tricky Dick still had us all fooled. Gerald Ford stepped in for Nixon one month after I started my residency in 1974, and I finished residency in '78 with Jimmy Carter. When I came back east from California in 1980 so did Ronnie Reagan. Now it was December 1983, and I was on my fourth administration. I better have passed that god damn test.

As I scanned the food court my attention was drawn to a curly-headed blond girl, probably 5 or 6 years old. She was waiting in line with her mother for a fruit smoothie. What caught my eye were her tiny ruby slippers, just like Dorothy's, which sparkled every time she took a step or shifted her weight. She was delightfully entertaining; dancing in place to music only children hear. As her mother ordered the smoothies, the sparkling red slippers drifted farther away into the center of the food court.

Only peripherally did I notice the presence of a pair of grimy white Converse All-Stars. The All- Stars, partially obscured by wide- whale brown corduroys, too long and dirt encrusted in the back, moved closer.

Then, in an instant, the sparkling ruby slippers were gone.

The snatch didn't create as much as a ripple among the sea of people in the food court. It was so smooth it was unbelievable. The little girl's slippers suddenly came off the floor, and then she and the Converse All-Stars with dirty corduroys were gone. Mom was still paying for two smoothies. What I had just seen was disorienting. Had the girl with the ruby slippers really disappeared? There were so many people much closer than I, but no one else seemed concerned. Maybe the little girl was still there and just blocked from my vision? Were the brown corduroys a family member? If so, where were they? Why hadn't momma raised any alarm? I probably sat there for twenty or thirty seconds, slack-jawed, trying to process what I had witnessed. Shit. I took off running toward the United Concourse.

The concourse was surprisingly empty. Thanks to a brief lull in the landing schedule, I had a good line of sight in both directions. I didn't see either the brown corduroys or the ruby slippers. I estimated how far someone could have gotten in thirty seconds. They seemed to have disappeared. I thought about shouting for help, but I couldn't think of what to say. The arrival area would be a dead end, so I started to run toward the terminal exit. I looked back one last time and my brain finally caught up with my heart rate. A men's room about twenty yards from the food court had a yellow plastic sign at the entrance, announcing in English and Spanish that it was closed for cleaning. Checking it out would cost me precious time, so it was a gamble, but it was where they had to be.

The sink area was clear except for an old black man jockeying a floor scrubber about twice his size. The urinal / toilet side looked empty too, but there was one closed stall. Beneath it, I saw the same dirty All-Stars and brown corduroys from the food court. I wasn't particularly scared. I could tell from his feet and the brief glimpse I had in the food court that this guy wasn't very imposing. At six foot four inches and 225 lbs. I wasn't concerned about him presenting a physical challenge. Still, I wasn't sure what to do next. I didn't want to hurt the little girl. Do I call him out? Do I kick in the door? Do I just wait for him to come out? My indecision wasn't a problem very long.

The toilet door opened. He stared at me, as surprised as I was. He wore a military surplus jacket and a Cubs hat that made me hesitate. I was pretty sure the guy leaving the food court wasn't wearing either a cap or a jacket. He had a green Army duffle bag slung over his left shoulder. His skin was waxy and he had the thin bloodless lips of a shut-in. The paleness of his skin contrasted starkly with the yellow-brown dinginess of his teeth. The stubble on his cheeks and chin couldn't hide the residue of what had been severe adolescent cystic acne. All I could think to say was, "Where is the little girl I saw you with?"

"Get the hell out of my way," he said, as he reached his right hand out toward my face with what looked like a wash cloth. I was probably only one of a handful of people in all of O'Hare who would recognize the smell of ether. I grabbed his wrist with my right hand and twisted it behind his back. My eyes fixed on his, long, tobacco-stained curling fingernails. He cussed me, and dropped the duffle off his left shoulder.

"You'd better let go of me or else I'm going to fuck you up."

"I asked you were the little girl was." As I waited for a response, I realized that the creep had dropped his free hand into his left hip pocket. He pulled out what looked like a switchblade. I had not considered the possibility of a weapon. Stupid. I twisted his arm until I could feel something pop. I didn't know if it was an elbow or a shoulder, but from his scream I could tell it was disabling. With my left hand I shoved his head into the side of the stall. As he bounced back off the side wall, I punched him as hard as I could in the solar plexus. The air rushed out of his lungs as his diaphragm contracted and I saw his eyes roll backwards as he fell to the floor. I stomped his left hand which was still holding the unopened blade. Multiple small bones cracked and I could feel them crumbling. The knife skittered away on the tile bathroom floor. Still flushed with adrenalin, I kicked him in the ribs, probably breaking several. I looked around and saw a terrified janitor. He had no idea who was the good guy and who was the bad. I yelled at him to go get the police, and he ran.

The douche bag was now groaning on the floor. He wasn't going anywhere. I grabbed his hair in order to turn him over. As I did, both his hair and his Cubs hat came off revealing a short red- headed buzz cut. His nose looked broken and was bleeding like a spigot. His eyes were open, but glazed and unrecognizing. He was still gasping for air and the blood and spittle were congealing at the corners of his mouth. He was no longer a threat to anyone. I unzipped the duffle and said a silent prayer. She was unconscious, but still breathing.

"Get down on the floor right now sir or I will put a hole through your brain," I heard shouted over my shoulder. The sound of a hammer cocking into place was more than enough to convince me of the sincerity of the promise.

"Okay, but the little girl needs medical attention."

O'HARE SECURITY

No good deed goes unpunished. I had been handcuffed to a desk somewhere in the bowels of O'Hare for almost three hours. It was an empty, heartless room that smelled of sweat and fear. I'd told my story to an endless stream of police beginning with Airport Security, then graduating to Chicago's finest, first in uniform then plain clothes. This new guy was a different breed. Everyone else slinked into the shadows when he entered the room. That seemed to be fine because he didn't bother to acknowledge their presence. I had given up on getting back to Charleston for office hours tomorrow.

"Dr. Murphy, my name is Special Agent Walter Konopacki. I'm with the FBI office here in Chicago. Do you have any idea what is going on here?"

Having just taken my oral boards I was acutely aware of the possibility of a trick question. "I know what I thought was happening. I thought I was witnessing an abduction. When he pulled out a switchblade I probably got a little too excited. At least, it looked like a switchblade. I shouldn't have kicked him in the ribs when he was down. I've already apologized for that. If he's the girl's first cousin I guess I'm in a shit-load of trouble, but I'd be willing to double-down on pervert if this were Vegas."

"Do you know who the little girl is?"

"No idea. Is she okay? "

"Yes. She's with her mother. Her name is Lily Rosen. Mean anything to you?"

"Should it?"

"Probably not," Konopacki said. "Her father is Martin Rosen. He is one of my bosses at the Department of Justice. On his behalf, let me apologize for how long it's taken for us to get everything sorted out. Let me find someone to un-cuff you."

For the first time since I had entered this holding area, there was finally enough oxygen. "That's the best thing I've heard all day. I was beginning to get a little nervous. Who was the guy in the bathroom?"

"I'm not at liberty to say, but I think we both already know that he was a bad guy and this wasn't his first rodeo. If you hadn't caught him, he would have been out of the airport with Lily in a couple of minutes. We would have never found her. Ransom wasn't what he was after."

"I don't feel so bad about kicking him in the ribs."

"Dr. Murphy, I know we've kept you here too long already, but Mrs. Rosen would like another moment of your time if you're willing."

" Of course."

Mrs. Lena Rosen entered the room a few minutes later. She was probably in her early 40s. I vaguely recognized her dress from the food court. Even with reddened, mascara- smeared eyes she was attractive. She carried herself with dignity despite what had to have been a confidence-shaking last several hours. Mrs. Rosen hugged me with surprising strength. She pulled back, but held me by the shoulders and looked straight into my eyes. "You saved my darling daughter's life and I'll never be able to thank you. I'm so sorry you were put in harm's way. But, I thank God you were there for my Lily when I wasn't." Then the tears began to flow.

I recognized the same guilt and grief that I'd seen many times before in pregnant women when we diagnose a fetal malformation. Uniquely, mothers assume immediate accountability for any misfortune or harm that befalls their children. "Mrs. Rosen, there's no need to beat yourself up. There wasn't anything you could have done. He was an experienced predator. I was watching Lily right as it happened. He grabbed her so fast it took me a minute to even realize what I was seeing. In fact, the only reason I was watching Lily was because of my fascination with her sparkling ruby slippers. Did you buy those for her?" As I had hoped, this brought a smile to her face.

"Yes, we got them for her at Halloween. She hasn't taken them off since."

"Well, that's why I was watching her. If she wasn't wearing those shoes, she wouldn't be back with you right now." The attempted kidnapping of her daughter was going to wrap Mrs. Rosen in tentacles of guilt. Prying them loose would take a long time. I hoped the ruby slippers would be the first step.

"Dr. Murphy, you stood between Lily and unspeakable evil. You're her guardian angel." She hugged me again, even more tightly, and kissed me on the cheek. "My husband will be arriving from Washington within the hour to thank you as well. We'll make sure you get home safely. I apologize that you've been detained so long. I have to go now to be with Lily. She is doing well, but is understandably upset and confused. They've taken her to the hospital for observation. You'll always be in our prayers."

"Well, please tell Lily that I'm sorry we didn't get to talk. I look forward to meeting her someday. And don't forget to tell her that I love her ruby slippers. She was right to never take them off. They're magic slippers. All she has to do is click her heels together three times, and all her dreams will come true."

Mrs. Rosen now smiled more brightly, "I will tell her all of that, exactly that." Then she turned, and left the room.

A couple of airport security guys brought me a Mountain Dew and a pack of Nabs. They lead me through an alarmed but silent door leading to a loading area. A black sedan and Special Agent Konopacki were waiting. The driver slammed the stick shift into drive and we took off across the tarmac. We had to be violating dozens of airport security rules, but Walter Konopacki had the look and manner of a man unconcerned by such matters. You never realize how large major airports are from inside the terminal. We drove a couple of miles before pulling up to an empty hangar at the far south end of the airport property.

Inside the open front end of the hangar were several worn couches and chairs. The coffee table was littered with old aviation and outdoorsmen magazines. Next to each couch were stand up ash tray porters that I hadn't seen since the sixties.

"Make yourself comfortable Dr. Murphy. Mr. Rosen will be here in about twenty minutes," Special Agent Konopacki said, as he and the driver stepped into a small office fitted into the corner of the hangar.

That's not going to be easy, I thought, but I said, "Okay."

Agent Konopacki returned a few minutes later, and we sat in awkward silence waiting for I wasn't sure what. About fifteen minutes later, the roar of a jet engine shattered the silence and crushed our eardrums. A sleek black Lear jet taxied toward the unworthy hangar. The jet rolled to a stop and shut down its engines. Special Agent Konopacki rose as the door opened and a well-dressed, serious- looking man emerged. Instinctively, I rose as well.

The man walked towards me without hesitation and extended his hand. "Dr. Murphy, I'm Martin Rosen. I'm very pleased to make your acquaintance."

"An impressive entrance." I replied.

"I work at the Justice Department in Washington. My wife and Lily were coming to visit for a long weekend. We were going to do some Christmas shopping. Little did we know, that you would give us the greatest Christmas gift we'll ever receive. The Attorney General insisted I take the Lear to get here as quickly as possible."

"Nice perk," I observed.

"Yes, I was very grateful. The worst thing about an appointment in Washington is not being there for your family. Thankfully, you were there for them in my place."

"Honestly sir, no thanks are necessary. The opportunity to put a twerp like that in jail is plenty satisfying."

"I heard you kicked the shit out of him," Rosen said, smiling broadly.

"Well, he started it."

"Hey, I'm not your mother. I'm disappointed that you didn't crack his skull open."

"It was all a little outside my daily routine. I might have gotten a bit jacked up."

"I can assure you that the Justice Department does not consider your efforts at law enforcement over-zealous." Rosen laughed. "Lena told me that you've missed your flight. I have to get to the hospital to be with Lena and Lily, but once we refuel the Lear and file the necessary paperwork, our pilot will fly you back to Charleston. It's the very least we can do. "

"Mr. Rosen, that's extremely generous, but it's already almost eleven and nothing can land in Charleston after midnight."

"Dr. Murphy, why don't you let me worry about that. There are a couple of Italian subs on board. In case you get thirsty, I have a nice bottle of Wild Turkey behind the bar. A U.S. Marshall named Hester McLeod will meet you in Charleston. He will take you wherever you need to go. That sound okay to you?"

"I'm a rummy actually, but anybody can hunt Wild Turkey," I said.

"I understand that you are a Gyno."

"Yes, sir. I was in Chicago for my oral board examinations."

"Well, after what you did for my Lily, I can't allow you to miss a delivery. Someone else's angel from heaven may need your protection. Travel safe, Dr. Murphy."

Thirty minutes later, I was ripping through the night sky enjoying some nice sipping bourbon and one of Blimpy's finest.

MEDICAL UNIVERSITY OF SOUTH CAROLINA – TWIN CLINIC

The juxtaposition was not lost on me. Wednesday had been a day I'd never experienced before. Now, it was a Thursday I'd experienced a thousand times. Same rooms, same nurses, same patients, same problems. When I returned from fellowship, people asked me what was the biggest difference between Charleston and San Francisco. They were surprised by all the similarities I found between the Holy City and Baghdad by the Bay. But to answer their question, I'd tell them the essential difference was that in San Francisco, every new idea is a good one until somebody proves it's bad. In Charleston, every new idea is a bad one until someone proves it's good. Things don't change very much in Charleston where the howitzers on the Battery are still pointed at Fort Sumter. Today was going to be another Thursday, just like every other Thursday. After Chicago, that was comforting.

Of all my clinical activities, I enjoy Twin Clinic the most. Obstetrical risks are all magnified in a multiple gestation. With the higher stakes presented by two babies, the challenge of Twin Clinic made it the most rewarding few hours of my week.

Male medical students ask me if it's possible for them to be successful as an Ob-Gyn. That's number one on my top ten list of stupid questions. It underestimates women, who are a thousand times more accepting of a male Ob-Gyn than men would be of a female urologist. I know there are women who can't bring themselves to see a male obstetrician, but it's not many. The women I was going to see today trusted my judgment, skill and discretion. Invariably, they asked if I would be in the office when they returned for their next visit.

To be a successful Ob-Gyn you have to love women. I love being around them. I love to listen to them. I love to share their joyful moments. Sometimes, not often, you are allowed a glimpse of their soul. A woman's soul is different than a man's. The things they value are more complex. Their souls are a deep reservoir of secrets. Women spend a much greater portion of their lives navigating around these secrets than do men. Only rarely, are the secrets revealed. You have to be paying attention or else you may miss the moment entirely.

Of course, none of this can be explained when buddies ask me how I can stand being an obstetrician-gynecologist. I give them my standard guy line, "I work there. I play there. If it was air-conditioned, I'd live there."

That was only a joke, however. It's professional suicide for a male obstetrician-gynecologist to shine up one of his patients. Women can smell the hound on a guy as easily as you can smell a skunk on your hound. Women can spend three minutes with a guy and size up his intentions as easily as checking the tire pressure. I've met very few guys with that type of intuition. Beyond that, your nurse will know. The receptionist will know. The jungle drums will start beating. By the next day, you have to sneak in the back door of the office because the looks in the waiting room are caustic. By the end of the week, you can't go to church or any of your favorite restaurants anymore. Once you cross the line, there isn't any coming back.

The female residents are a different story. I get a crush on almost every one. I can't help it, and I'm not sure how anybody could. If you spend all day, every day, with a smart, attractive, confident, and capable woman you're going to develop a crush. If you spend enough time with any woman, you'll find something fascinating about them. Admittedly, some residents make it tougher than others, but almost without exception, I'll discover something special about each of them. But infatuation is best kept to yourself. A resident dating a faculty member is not a mortal sin, like becoming involved with a patient, but it is a venial sin. Worse, it was cliché. As the faculty member, you'd always be a pitiful lecher, but for the resident, the stigma would be even worse. Flat-backing your way to the top is not well accepted within the resident group dynamic.

Although mindful of the need to be careful, I was not celibate. During residency, I moved in with Abby Brenner who was one of my co-residents. From our first day at the hospital, we enjoyed each other's company. We shared the same job, the same work hours, and the same sense of humor. We both loved playing basketball and we both loved Springsteen. I developed a bad crush on Abby during our internship year. By year two, moving in together seemed like the obvious thing. We took a lot of crap from our peers, but it worked. I didn't appreciate it at the time, but it was probably harder for Abby than it was for me. We lived together for the next three years.

We became social directors and organized most of the resident parties. Abby was small, but muscular, athletic and adventurous. We did wild things in wild places. We planned something for almost every free day we had. Two things we never did were talk about the future or hold hands. Abby made room for me in her heart. When the shit came down too hard at work, or I was too exhausted to do anything but stare at the ceiling, Abby would hold my head in her lap and rub my temples with her fingertips. She would call me "baby", and I would close my eyes. Those moments helped me get through residency more than I dare admit to myself. I honestly don't know if I gave Abby the same comfort.

Abby always knew she wanted to go home and practice in a small town. It was always assumed we would practice together. During our final year, however, I started talking about doing a fellowship in San Francisco. Although she didn't share it, Abby understood my passion for Maternal-Fetal Medicine and academics. I told I'd find a way to make it work, however, we both knew that my career choice was the antithesis of everything Abby wanted from life. There was zero chance of Abby coming with me to San Francisco, and less than zero chance that I was going to practice in rural South Carolina. When I matched to go to UCSF, we never once sparred about it. We both knew our time together was coming to an end. Neither of us wanted to spoil it by bickering.

The weeks leading up to the end of our residency had all the emotional depth of two college roommates going home for the summer. We had planned for months to go to a Springsteen concert at Gaillard Auditorium. Springsteen lyrics always seemed to verbalize what I found inexpressible. Springsteen concerts cleansed your soul of accumulated impurities. That night at Gaillard was especially draining. Springsteen forces you to confront the raw edge of your emotions. "*Racing in the Street*" narrated the drift that Abby and I were experiencing. Our relationship had started three years ago with all of the heat of a frontage road drag race. Now I could see the same wrinkles around Abby's eyes that Springsteen described and I knew that she cried herself to sleep some nights. I had damaged her and I prayed that someday, Abby and me could ride to the sea and wash these sins off our hands.

After the concert we went by Jimmy Dengates for a beer and got a booth in the back. I told Abby, "We've been living in a bubble for the past three years. All we had were each other and our work. It wasn't reality. Now we're both finally getting ready to really start our lives. Starting your own practice in your home town is everything you've ever wanted."

Abby smiled and spoke softly, "Don't minimize what we had. It was real to me. We'll both pay a steep price for our selfishness. I would've done almost anything to keep us together, but you asked me to give up my dreams. I think you knew what you were doing."

I didn't have an answer. Maybe Abby was right. I honestly believed I loved Abby, but maybe I didn't understand what love required. I had failed women in relationships before. Was my desire to pursue fellowship training honest, or was I a coyote willing to chew its own leg off to get out of a trap? Either way, when I chose to interview only on the West Coast, I was ending my relationship with Abby whether I wanted to admit it to myself or not.

That night we made love while Springsteen played on the stereo. Abby and I did not leave each other's side for the next two days. We pretended as hard as we could that what we had between ourselves wasn't crumbling , but it was. It was my fault. Why couldn't I be a hero for Abby the way I had been for Lily in Chicago? I was ashamed of my repeated failures to be heroic with the women in my personal life.

In today's Twin Clinic, I was working with Ellen Cates. She was a tall, waif-like resident with long, blond hair and skin the color of pearl. She was from a small town in the Pee Dee region of the state, but often seemed to be from some older, more antebellum time. Ellen had attended MUSC as a medical student , but seemed to have few friends and seldom dated as far as I knew. She spent her money on exotic vacations, which she went on alone. Ellen never dressed down and the expensive dresses she wore seemed anachronistic. Ellen moved without effort, gliding across the floor like a photonegative of Morticia Addams. She rarely spoke without being asked a direct question and, despite being a third year, was not very close with her co-residents. Most people recognized that Ellen Cates was damaged . I was certain that Ellen Cates carried more baggage than the rest of us would ever know. Ellen might also be one of the few residents I had never taken to task. Ellen set off a silent alarm. She was not a person who could be pushed.

All that said, I still enjoyed being in clinic with Ellen. She was bright and hard–working. Patients found comfort in her. Ellen could sense pain in others, and had empathic ability to take that pain onto herself. It's relatively easy to give when you have a lot. There is a nobility of the spirit when you give generously of yourself when you don't have that much to share. When Ellen told patients she understood, they believed that she did. Best of all, she worked quietly. After Chicago, the last thing I wanted was a lot of drama. Ellen registered very low on the drama meter.

Whenever you go away for a few days, you worry about what has happened to your patients during your absence. One of the twins I had been most worried about was still undelivered. Based on her cervical exam, I knew she was going to labor sometime soon. She had now made it to thirty-one weeks, and even if she did labor, both of her babies would make it. That good news was tempered by another woman carrying triplets who was only twenty-seven weeks gestation. Ellen described an eight-pound weight gain since last week. The mother was now spilling protein in her urine, along with significantly increased blood pressure. I lied and told the mother it might be nothing, but we needed to put her in the hospital to figure out what's going on. She pretended as well, and said she wasn't afraid. She was sure her blood pressure would come down if she could just get a good night's sleep. I hoped she was right, but knew she had pre-eclampsia and her triplets would make it worsen quickly. She would be lucky to make it through the weekend.

Otherwise it was a good day. Ellen and I saw several more interesting patients, including a woman near term whose presenting twin was breech. Ellen and I scheduled her for a Cesarean the following week which we would do together. We were also rewarded with some homemade chocolate chip cookies from a postpartum woman we saw just before lunch. As I left Twin Clinic, I wondered if Ellen enjoyed the day as much as I had. Life was painful for Ellen Cates, and I wondered how much joy she found in helping other women.

CANNON STREET YMCA

Dr. Jackson Brunson and I had been friends from the first day of medical school. Jack had chosen anesthesiology and we both stayed at MUSC for our residencies. He was still at MUSC when I came back from my fellowship. When we first met, I thought Jack was a stereotypical in-bred southern hotty-toddy with his pale blue eyes, recessive reddish-blond hair, horned rimmed glasses and seersucker Bermuda shorts. I wasn't even close. At six foot six and with a healthy mean streak, Jack was actually a rugged inside banger who had played basketball for Davidson. With Jack's inside presence and my outside shooting, plus a couple of other pretty good athletes in our class, we had a dominating intramural basketball team. We never lost after our freshman year. Late afternoon, while I was still in Twin Clinic, Jack paged to remind me that we had a game tonight.

The previous summer Jack had asked if I was interested in playing on a Charleston City League team. The whiteness of our team was unique in the neglected gyms of downtown Charleston. People were unpleasantly surprised when we finished second. The College of Charleston is an NAIA powerhouse and Coach John Kresse keeps his entire team together for summer league ball. They seldom took any prisoners, but we played them competitively in the championship game.

After more than a week of inactivity, I was excited to walk into the Cannon Street Y that evening to play some basketball. The North Charleston Rec Department

Hawks were already warming up. I wondered how many of the Hawks appreciated the historical significance of the building they were playing in.

In 1955, the Cannon Street YMCA Little League Baseball All-Stars won the downtown league championship and were invited to the district tournament. The eleven and twelve year-olds represented Charleston's first Little League for blacks. Even though they had been invited, the all-white teams at the district tournament refused to play the Cannon Y All-Stars.

Not knowing what to do, Little League Baseball declared them the district champions by forfeit and sent them on to the state tournament. Of course, nothing was any different in Columbia. It was okay for little white boys to get dirty and scuffed up, but their parents wouldn't let them compete with blacks on even terms. Again, the Cannon Y All-Stars were declared the winner by forfeit and they were sent to the regional tournament in Rome, Georgia. Jackie Robinson had already integrated major league baseball, but number forty-two was a long way from little league in the Deep South. The insult represented by the Cannon Y All-Stars was directly responsible for the birth of the lily-white Dixie Youth Baseball Congress. When the parents in Rome also refused to allow their delicate flowers to sully themselves, the Cannon YMCA All-Stars were crowned regional Champions. The Cannon Y All-Stars then boarded a bus headed for Williamsport, Pennsylvania, and the Little League World Series.

After weeks of doing the right thing from a distance, the good city elders of Williamsport and little league baseball finally blinked when a bus full of raggedy, but excited black boys from Charleston pulled into town. Revealing a heartbreaking lack of character, they decided that the Cannon Street YMCA All-Stars could stay as "guests" of the tournament, but couldn't compete. No one ever got to see how good William "Buck" Godfrey and his teammates were. They were the team that nobody would play. I was confident that not one guy on the North Charleston team knew that the Cannon Street Y was the home of the team that integrated little league baseball in the South.

While I knew this little bit of black history, it did not necessarily make me a welcome guest in the Cannon Y gym. Charleston's reputation for charm and Southern hospitality is a well-practiced veneer, overlaying longstanding racial hostility born of institutionalized racism. Anyone who denies that fact is either stupid or lying and beyond redemption. No one on our team had any illusions. We were going to play as hard as we could, but we were going to do it politely and respectfully. At least, that was the plan.

Our team's player-coach was Taylor Holmes. Taylor had been a great high school point guard and was still very hard to handle. He had played tennis in college and now did private instruction on Kiawah Island. Taylor had charisma and was a natural leader. He drove a metallic green Jaguar and knew everybody wherever we went. Best of all, he paid for drinks after all our games. If you wanted to call him, you had to look up his dog's name, Scooby, in the phone book. Taylor knew Jackson from high school, and Jack had told him about me.

Taylor had gotten us sponsored by Clarence McCants. At first, it was just funny. Later, we appreciated its genius. Clarence McCants was the best known black man in Charleston. His big, black smiling face was on TV about a dozen times each day, inviting people to come down to the Metropolitan Furniture Company at 501 King Street. There wasn't anybody in Charleston, white or black, who didn't know his nickname, Clarence "Don't Turn Nobody Down" McCants. Our jerseys had Clarence's face and nickname emblazoned on the front. Everybody loved them, and they gave us some small amount of credibility in the black gyms. Clarence wore thousand dollar suits, drove a black Lincoln Continental, and had never met a stranger. Clarence also possessed a well-earned reputation as a serious businessman. The last sentence of his signature commercial resonated with everyone. The narrator's voice intones with the slightest hint of menace, "We finance our own accounts." Being late with a payment to Clarence was not a smart financial move.

Everybody was here tonight and we had our best line-up. Besides Jack in the middle, myself on the wing and Taylor at the point, we had Langston Miles at shooting guard and James Earle Braxton at power forward. "Jeb" worked with Taylor at Kiawah where he was the human resources director. Jeb was taciturn at his most outgoing. I was confident that firing was more his human resources specialty than hiring. Jeb had been an All-SEC defensive tackle for Bear Bryant at Alabama. More remarkably, he played defensive tackle in the SEC at 6'4" and 230 lbs. In the fifteen or so years since finishing his football playing days he had not added a pound. Running into Jeb on the court was like smashing into a brick wall. When he played at Alabama he was on the last of Bear Bryant's all-white football teams. Jeb was a man who didn't invite conversation, but I did ask him once if it bothered him to play in the city league. His response was terse, "Doesn't bother me to play with blacks. Sam Cunningham explained integration to me a long time ago."

The only black guy on our team was Francis Bethea. He's only sixteen and technically shouldn't even be in the adult league. He had just transferred to Burke High School downtown, and, as a result, had to sit out a year. Since he couldn't play high school ball, he had come to the City Gym looking for a good league. The people in charge gave him permission to play in the adult league. After watching a couple of league games, he came to Taylor and asked if he could play with us. I always thought that was an unusual choice. Maybe he felt he would be a shoe-in for playing time, but I never asked him. Turned out, he was right. Francis is usually the first guy off the bench. Francis has a sweet jump shot and his slashing drives to the basket break down defenses, opening things up for shooters like myself.

North Charleston had a lot of quickness and pressed us effectively early in the game. Ultimately, though, the score began to get lopsided. You can't play zone against us. By the time they figured that out, Langston and I had torched them for about fifteen points apiece. Once they started chasing us, Jack and Jeb killed them inside.

There comes a point in a game when one team realizes they cannot win. That point gets testy when you're an all-black team losing to an almost all-white team in front of an all-black crowd in a historic black neighborhood gym. We had almost gotten away clean when Denny Williams got into a shoving match with one of the North Charleston guys late in the fourth quarter. Denny was a cracker from rural Barnwell County. He's a tough kid who plays basketball the same way he played football. He's aggressive and has a big mouth. We were usually happier when Denny didn't show up. Thankfully, the referee got things quickly under control with a double technical foul. Then the horn sounded and the scorekeeper signaled that Denny was disqualified with five fouls. We only had him with four.

Denny lost his mind. "What the fuck are you talking about? What is the matter with you people? Can't you count? I'm not going to sit because you learned math at Burke!"

Denny was out of control. We were going to be killed if he kept screaming at the woman behind the scorer's table. In short order, Denny received his second T and was ejected, but that only made Denny wilder. A group of about twenty people behind the scorekeeper were about to come onto the court. At that point, Jeb came up behind Denny and wrapped him in a bear hug that would have made a Kodiak proud. Jeb picked up the barrel-chested former football player and carried him kicking and screaming outside. Then, as calm and collected as I had ever seen him, Taylor walked over to the scorer's table. He held up the palm of his hand and addressed the crowd, "I apologize for my player. He's an ass-hole and will never play in this gym again. But nobody here wants to do anything we will all be sorry about tomorrow. Sit back down and let us finish these last two minutes."

It was an odd moment. I had never seen Taylor so demanding. His words were confident, almost stern. He wasn't asking the crowd to calm down; he was telling them to. And they did.

After the game, Taylor invited everyone over to Captain Harry's Blue Marlin Bar just off South Market Street for a couple of beers. David Bethany of the Killer Whales was scheduled to play an acoustic set. There was a rumor that Jimmy Buffett was going to drop by. The great thing about Captain Harry's Blue Marlin was that there was always a rumor Jimmy Buffett was going to drop by.

I decided to pass. Tomorrow was Friday which was my OR day. That shift started early.

MUSC PRE-ANESTHESIA CARE UNIT (PACU)

I wandered through the PACU a little after seven a.m. It was a bee-hive of activity as pre-op nurses and anesthesia residents prepared twenty patients for surgery. I saw Jack across the room and gave him a nod. I could immediately tell he had stayed at Captain Harry's longer than he'd intended. Personally, I'd take a hung-over Jack for my anesthesia before most of these other jokers.

I had a good schedule this morning. My first case was Salem Richardson. She was scheduled for a vaginal hysterectomy for non-invasive carcinoma of the cervix. The second case was a large left-sided pelvic mass which looked like a benign cystic teratoma. Gynecologists are obsessed with fruit. This tumor was the size of a cantaloupe. My third case was a forty-five year old woman with multiple uterine fibroids and excessive menses. She probably needed a hysterectomy, but was dead set against it. Instead, we were planning to do a multiple myomectomy. She was holding onto hopes a miracle pregnancy. I had no interest in taking those hopes away.

"Good morning, Ms. Richardson. Are you ready to go this morning? Any questions I haven't already answered for you?"

"None that I can think of, Dr. Murphy. I hope you're feeling good this morning."

"Well, now that you mention it, I'm a bit shaky. I've been this way several mornings since getting back from rehab. But don't worry, I keep some Vodka in my locker and just a couple of snorts will straighten those shakes right out. You know what they say, "Hair of the dog that bit ya."

Ms. Richardson laughed and for a moment the tension left her face. She was an attractive thirty-nine year-old city planner in the mayor's office. She was terrified because her mother had died of cervical cancer. I had reassured her several times already that surgery was going to be completely curative. After a quick recovery, she would return one hundred percent to her usual state of health. As an added bonus, I threw in a promise of no more periods. Ms. Richardson would soon be back to being a thorn in the side of the Charleston Board of Architectural Review.

"You shouldn't be saying things like that to people getting ready to go under the knife. You wouldn't want me to lose confidence in you?" Ms. Richardson said.

"Salem, you have no reason to be nervous. I'm totally committed to your case. I'm totally committed to everything I do. You know my motto, 'Rehab is for quitters.'" We both laughed.

We were interrupted by a nurse who wanted me to initial my pre-op orders. I asked Ms. Richardson who was with her, and she told me her husband was in the waiting area.

"The case will take about one-and-a-half hours. I'll speak with your husband as soon as we're finished. He'll be able to join you in post-op once you're fully awake. Sound okay?" Ms. Richardson nodded her assent. At that point, the anesthesiologist showed up and began preparing her for surgery.

After changing clothes, I met my surgical team in OR 17. My third year resident was Leighton Chase and my intern was Robert Parker Weaver. They had a medical student with them, but I didn't catch her name. I enjoyed operating with Leighton. She had also been a medical student at MUSC. I remembered being one of the few faculty who wanted to take her as a resident. Leighton was older than most of our other residents. She had spent several years waiting for her husband to find himself. He never did. After giving him several chances, she assigned him to child care and set out to become a doctor. She was mature and focused. A career as an obstetrician- gynecologist was her ticket out of a blue collar world. Her background also gave her insight that some of our more privileged residents lacked. She connected with women who had hitched their wagons to the wrong stars. Leighton was the embodiment of the American dream. She was going to succeed based on merit. All she needed was the opportunity. Plus, she had excellent surgical hands.

Robert Parker Weaver was another story. There is a long list of things I find interesting about women. On the other hand, it was a much shorter list for the guys. Since Parker had no interest in or knowledge of sports, we had little in common. Parker came from a tough background. He was the only child of a single mom who had never risen above subsistence in the slums of San Diego. While this kind of adversity had imbued caring and compassion into Leighton's character, it had only forged a hard shell around Parker Weaver.

Parker had fallen victim to the most common of character flaws, hubris. He viewed his success as a testament to his own personal charm and talent. Despite the lifelong support of his mother, mentors, teachers, the Reagents of the state of California and the Federal government, Parker had somehow come to the conclusion that he had been completely self-made, and everyone else should be as well. Parker was obnoxiously self-absorbed and had no sympathy for others experiencing the same adversity he'd managed to overcome. His hypocrisy knew no bounds, and I had rapidly tired of his bragging and right-wing religious certitude. Making matters worse, he wasn't a very good surgeon. I don't think Leighton thought much of him either. She always seemed happier when we sent him off to the ER to see consults.

The vaginal hysterectomy on Ms. Richardson went beautifully. I let Leighton do most of the case. Leighton and I had worked together in the OR several times, and we'd become a good operative team. The case went quickly and Leighton asked dozens of questions, which I enjoyed.

Our second case was Carly Jo Baker, a nineteen year-old student from the College of Charleston with an imposing pelvic mass. It had to be huge for the doctor in the student health office to find it. From our ultrasound examination, we were certain that it was a benign cystic teratoma. Our goal was to remove the cyst and not the entire ovary. Leighton was again the primary surgeon and she was brilliant. We removed a bowling ball-sized dermoid intact. We opened the cyst on a back table. It was a nasty one with dense black hair, greasy fat and some tooth fragments. We inspected the other ovary to make sure the dermoid wasn't bilateral. The cystectomy looked dry and we closed.

Our third case was Ms. Olivia Ravenell, who had several large smooth muscle tumors on her uterus that were causing excessive menstrual bleeding. At forty-five, most women would opt for a hysterectomy, but family and friends had convinced her that a hysterectomy would change "her nature," which is a polite term in the African-American community for sexuality. Ms. Ravenell also had a secret desire to have another child, but not even her family knew about that. So, our plan was to remove all the fibroids and leave her uterus intact. We advised her that the fibroids could return, or that their removal might not cure her heavy menstrual flow. She wasn't moved by these concerns, so we proceeded and hoped for the best. As it turned out, she had eight good sized fibroids. Two were on short stalks and were easily removed, but the rest were within the wall of the uterus. They proved to be more challenging.

I decided to let Parker take the lead on the case, but he wasn't good at finding the plane of dissection between the fibroid and the normal musculature of the uterus. If you can find that plane, you can shell out a fibroid like a butterbean with minimal blood loss. On the other hand, if you miss the plane, you can get into a lot of bleeding. Parker missed the plane on the first three fibroids he attempted. We lost more blood than necessary.

At one point, I laid my hands on Parker's as he was working. Confused, Parker looked up at me.

I asked him, "Why don't you just put a bullet in her head. It would be more humane."

Parker just said, "Huh."

I could see Leighton smiling behind her mask. I knew it was a bit cruel, but I didn't like Parker Weaver anyway.

Parker struggled through one more relatively superficial fibroid, then Leighton and I took over and finished up quickly. The uterus looked pretty worn out when we were done, but it was intact and there wasn't any bleeding. We closed and moved her to the recovery room. It was just after two p.m. After checking on my post-op patients, I headed down to the ER to see a surgical consult.

MUSC EMERGENCY ROOM

The ER is a horrid place. Miserable, desperate and damaged people were left alone behind partially drawn curtains. Inadequate partitions that allowed privacy and dignity to escape while failing to invite either comfort or compassion to enter. The ER is always packed, regardless of the day or time. Gurneys are parked haphazardly. The ER nursing staff never knows where anyone is. The ER staff jabbers endlessly about elaborate triage and prioritization protocols, but it's a ruse to make the routine four-hour waits seem justifiable. One of the great shames of the American medical system is that so many people seek care in such a dysfunctional place. This late afternoon road trip to the ER was no exception to my expectations, another brutal shift in the heart of darkness.

Bailey Clark, the chief resident on the gynecology service, ran it down for me. The patient was a thirty year-old white female named Janie Johnson. She had slipped and fallen getting out of a hot tub at a downtown bed-and-breakfast. She had suffered a straddle injury and had a large labial hematoma. She was in remarkable pain and Bailey concluded appropriately, "I think we need to take her to surgery. By the way, they were turned away from Roper Hospital because they didn't have any ID or insurance cards. Her boyfriend had a roll of cash and registered as 'Panama Red.'"

"No kidding," I said.

"Yeah, look at the ER registration form." Bailey handed it to me.

"Cool. Panama Red."

Ms. Johnson was an attractive woman with brown hair and blue eyes. She was wearing a faded beige Hog's Breath Saloon T-shirt over her bathing suit top and flip-flops. Her bathing suit bottoms were off and an angry hematoma deformed her right vulvar area. After introducing myself and doing a very brief examination I explained the situation to Ms. Johnson.

"I know you're really hurting, and I promise we aren't going to mess with you anymore. We'll get you something for pain in a moment, but we need to talk first. This hematoma is quite big and even if it's stable, it's going to continue to hurt badly. Left alone, it will ultimately reabsorb, but that's going to take weeks. I believe we need to take you to the OR, drain this thing, and relieve the pressure. You'll feel much better, much sooner. Otherwise, you're going to be miserable for a long time."

"Please, just take care of it as soon as you can," she said, pleading, but under control.

"Don't worry, we will. We need to make arrangements with the OR. Dr. Bailey will come back and get you to sign an operative consent. Then we'll be able to give you some pre-op meds with something for pain. The anesthesiologist will see you, but I don't know if it will be here or in the OR holding area. We can wait till you're in the OR to place a Foley catheter in your bladder, but you'll likely need it for a while after surgery. I'll see you again in the OR. Okay?"

"Come on, dude," Panama Red said. "Can't we get this show on the road? We've been in this dump for hours."

"I know. I'm sorry. We know this is very difficult. We'll get things rolling as quickly as we can."

About an hour later, Bailey and I evacuated the hematoma in the OR. The hematoma was prodigious. After evacuating the blood clot we weren't able to identify a specific source of bleeding. The hematoma cavity was raw, however, with a lot of oozing. We made the decision to pack the hematoma cavity with a roll of Kerlex. I insisted that the Kerlex be soaked in betadine. The residents don't share my belief in magic potions and believe using betadine is akin to placing a poultice. Having been raised in the South, my mother treated every cut, scrape, bruise, broken bone or emotional distress with tincture of methiolate. I knew its powers. There wasn't anything that couldn't be improved by the application of a little iodine. The only thing missing was for the entire family to gather around and blow on the wound as the iodine soaked Kerlex was applied. The residents' lack of faith in the power of a shaman would sooner or later be their undoing.

We walked out of the OR at a quarter of six. It had been a full day.

I hadn't fully realized how exhausting my week had been until I hit my couch. I had a Klondike Bar for dinner and went to bed. I decided to not set my alarm and to sleep in. As a result, I didn't get into the hospital to make Saturday morning rounds until almost eleven.

After stopping in at the nursing station, I walked down to the gynecology ward to see my post-op patients. My surgeries from yesterday were all doing well. I stopped by Ms. Johnson's room. She was sleeping soundly. "Panama Red" appeared to be asleep as well on the couch next to her bed. He had a faded Houston Astros baseball cap pulled down over his eyes and a pair of gigantic Bose headphones over his ears. If he was awake, there was no way he knew I was in the room. He had stacked his cassette tapes on the window sill. There had to be several hundred. I suspected that "Panama Red" was tuned out much of the time. Not needing to wake Ms. Johnson up, I told the nurse to let her know that I had come by. I would see her tomorrow morning. We'd take the packing out then. My plan was to leave her Foley catheter in all day while the swelling went down. Ms. Johnson could have a regular diet whenever she felt like it.

I completed my charting and was headed to the elevators when one of the Labor and Delivery nurses, Ferdy Eldenz, caught up with me.

"Dr. Murphy, did you know that the Virginia All-Stars were playing at Myskins tonight? Several of us are going. I thought you might want to come by."

"I love the All-Stars," I replied. "I'm pretty whipped from this past week, but the All-Stars don't come down from Charlottesville very often. I saw the All-Stars at Myskins a couple of years ago and they really tore the place up. If I can catch a nap this afternoon I'll try to make it."

Ferdy smiled. "That's great. I'll look for you. You've got to promise me a dance."

"Deal."

December in Charleston can be a beautiful month. The cool, breezy days make for a great walk home down Ashley Avenue past Colonial Lake, across Broad Street and down a few blocks to my apartment on Tradd. The idea of a forty minute commute to and from work was inconceivable to me. Unfortunately, today wasn't one of those days. It was gray and bitter. I was glad to have my bike and was home in less than five minutes.

I changed out of my scrubs and made the reluctant decision to light my space heater for the first time this winter. Not a decision to be taken lightly. The first cold day each winter is commemorated by someone blowing themselves up because of a defective space heater, kind of a Charleston tradition. Considering the impossibility of getting approval from the Charleston Historical Society for renovations such as central heating and air, these losses must be considered acceptable collateral damage. The old homes downtown, especially south of Broad Street, were protected like an endangered species. I ignited my space heater with eyes closed, using the twelve inch matches bought specifically for this purpose. Everyone knew those eleven extra inches of match stick were the difference between life and death. As the space heater glowed to life, I smiled. Once again, I had avoided becoming the lead story in the *News and Courier*.

Watching the Saturday afternoon football games, I thought about Ferdy's offer and wished I hadn't been so enthusiastic about the All-Stars. Ferdy was a good nurse, and I liked her. I also knew that she liked me. She was shorter than I preferred, but it was easy to tell she had an exquisite body underneath her labor and delivery scrubs. She was a hard partier and I'd heard more than one Monday morning story around the nurses' station about Ferdy and friends. A lot of the stories seemed to involve Jägermeister, after which, all bets are off. One thing was sure. If I went to Myskins to see the Virginia All -Stars tonight, I would end up back in this apartment with Ferdy after the show. I wasn't sure if that was a good idea or not.

With the space heater, my favorite quilt, a dreary day and a blow-out game, I soon fell fast asleep and woke up famished about eight p.m. I found a can of Hormel Chili in the pantry and made some chili spaghetti with diced onions and grated cheddar cheese melted on top. I ate in front of the TV without paying attention to what was on.

I still didn't know what to do about Ferdy. The All-Stars put on a great show. Even more, I knew I'd enjoy Ferdy's warmth against my chest. But what about Sunday morning? How would I handle that? What would happen the next time I was on labor and delivery? Would she be clingy? Would she tell the other nurses? Of course, she would. Would the residents find out? Of course, they would. Would my faculty partners find out? Don't be stupid. Sooner or later, they would. Did Ferdy and I have a future together? Was I willing to lie to myself? I also figured Ferdy would turn me every which way but loose, and that went in the plus column.

I knew that I could handle whatever might happen tonight. I was much less certain of how I would handle tomorrow or the day after. For me, tonight would just be a lark. I doubted that Ferdy saw it the same way. A lot of guys were good at pretending they didn't understand that fact, but I knew better. A transaction was being proposed, and it needed to be fair. You shouldn't take, if you aren't willing to give. I didn't want to be that guy again.

Ultimately, I decided that if I was going to go to Myskins, I would have to wash the dishes and make the bed. That tilted the balance. Now, I had to figure out how to explain not showing up. I liked Ferdy. Disappointing her tonight was surprisingly painful.

THE VARIETY STORE

Sunday morning, I got up early to make rounds. I'd had a good night's sleep, but not as good as it could have been. I went into the hospital and paged Bailey Clark to come help remove the packing on Ms. Johnson. While I waited on her arrival, I asked the charge nurse to give Ms. Johnson a couple of milligrams of morphine IV to help with the procedure.

Bailey had already been in to see Ms. Johnson and reported no significant bleeding through the pack. Ms. Johnson was afebrile and her blood count was stable.

We knocked on the door and went in. "Good morning, Ms. Johnson. Dr. Clark says you're feeling better this morning."

"Well, I'm a little dizzy and still pretty sore, but nothing like when I first came in."

"The dizziness is probably our fault. We had your nurse give you some morphine because it's time to take out the Kerlex . There is a small chance the bleeding could resume when we take the packing out, but it's very unlikely. It will hurt some, but once the packing starts to come out, it will be quick."

"Okay, let's get it over with." Ms. Johnson said.

I noticed for the first time that "Panama Red" was gone, as were all of his neatly stacked cassette tapes.

"Will your friend be back soon? Do you want to wait for him before we take the packing out?"

"No, I'm not sure where Red is. He left earlier this morning. We don't need to wait. I don't know when he'll be back."

"All right. Let's get your nurse."

Bailey and I put on some disposable gloves and we frog-legged Ms. Johnson so that we could see her labia. There was still some distortion from the Kerlex packing, but the swelling and inflammation were much improved. Bailey found the free end of the Kerlex and started to gently pull. It unpacked easily. I never saw Ms. Johnson wince, although she kept her eyes closed. Ms. Johnson's imperturbability was a testament to Bailey's skill and our friend Morpheus, but also, some toughness on Ms. Johnson's part.

Afterwards, I told Ms. Johnson, "You did really well and the wound looks healthy. I'll have one of the other residents come in and check on you in a couple of hours. We'll get your nurse to take out the Foley catheter. You should be able to pee, but if you can't in the next four or five hours, let your nurse know. When you urinate, you can probably expect some stinging. Just dry yourself off gently. You'll be surprised by how quickly this heals. If you feel better later today, it'll be okay to shower, but no bath for right now. Don't try to get up without help until the morphine has worn off. Any questions?"

"No questions. I just want to sleep," Ms. Johnson replied wearily.

"Okay, get some rest and we will see how you are feeling tomorrow. Call your nurse if you need anything. There is always a doctor on the floor."

I was done with rounds by 10:00 a.m. After making rounds on the weekend, I usually wandered by labor and delivery to see what was going on. However, I didn't feel like bumping into Ferdy, if she was on. Sooner or later, I would need to apologize for not showing up at Myskins, but later was better than sooner.

The Variety Store was just a couple of blocks from the hospital at the Marina on Lockwood Drive. The highlight of every Sunday was breakfast at the Variety Store. Not as much fun by yourself, but a great place to read the Sunday paper. It was not as crowded as usual. It was another gray overcast sky. Purple –black clouds were gathering out in the harbor and the wind blowing in off the Ashley River cut right through you. The sail boats at anchor were bobbing more than was usual. A winter rain was on its way.

Once seated in a booth, however, the dreary day disappeared with the arrival of a cantaloupe wedge, 2 eggs over easy, hash browns, and sliced link sausages. The *News and Courier* headline had the words "Operation Jackpot" in big print.

Reading the first two paragraphs, I immediately realized that Jackpot was going to shake-up Charleston, just like the 1886 earthquake almost one hundred years earlier. The Holy City was always near the top of any list of America's friendliest or best-mannered cities. Charleston cultivates its reputation as a charming tourist destination with the same ferocity that the Charleston Board of Architectural Review protects the historic homes. Any crime downtown is rapidly addressed or suppressed to make sure the tourism dollars keep flowing smoothly. Charleston was a regular All-American city selection. A trip to Charleston is supposed to be a trip back in time to a beguiling and genteel antebellum existence.

It turns out, however, that the swamps, marshes, deserted barrier islands, and secluded deep-water docks of the South Carolina intra-coastal waterways had become a forgotten backdoor left open. According to the *News and Courier*, Georgetown, Beaufort, and Charleston counties were the on ramp to a drug superhighway supplying the entire east coast. This was not going to sit well with the Charleston Chamber of Commerce or the Jim and Tammy Faye Baker Christian Conservatives and Family Values Republicans who had come to dominate politics in South Carolina. There is nothing better than a little scandal flavored with the right amount of hypocrisy. This was going to be good.

President Reagan had personally approved Operation Jackpot to root out drug smuggling operations in the Low Country. Operation Jackpot was a combined federal-state task force under the direction of U.S. Attorney for South Carolina Thomas Sheprow. Taking his cue from Deep Throat, Sheprow had decided to follow the money. With fifteen United States prosecutors on his staff, support from all state law enforcement agencies and the arm-twisting power of the federal government , Sheprow was turning over every suspicious financial stone he could find. Each large stone revealed new creepy-crawlers underneath. The smugglers were making the kind of cash you can't hide.

Old family money and new drug money both share the same weak link, the hired help. The hired help do all the grunt work and are never paid enough to keep them from giving up the bosses when they get their asses in a sling. The task force had an early breakthrough with a bust involving a misdirected shrimp boat captain and crew that pulled up to the wrong dock. They were more than willing to roll over on the middle men and the higher-ups for suspended sentences and time served. Shrimping was back breaking work for low pay, but it was a hell of a lot better than Federal jail time. With their testimony, a special grand jury was convened in Columbia. The grand jury had returned sealed indictments against dozens of suspected smugglers the previous Tuesday. The Feds swooped in and started rounding people up on Saturday. What made it salacious was that these folks weren't low-lives and thugs. They were real estate agents, tennis pros, lawyers, sons of state legislators and scions of prominent Charleston families. As I read down the list of the accused smugglers, some in custody and some on the run, a name made me pause. I went back and read it again. Among those in custody, Taylor Holmes, 32 years old of Mount Pleasant. "Clarence 'Don't Turn Nobody Down' McCants" Taylor? Oh, my lord!

According to the *News and Courier*, there were two separate smuggling operations working the Low Country coastline bringing in marijuana and hashish to docks on Hilton Head, Edisto Island, Pine Island, Datha Island, McClellanville and other sites unknown. Taylor was reportedly working for his older brother, Bryan Holmes from Columbia, and J. Ford Rhett of Hilton Head. They had both been arrested earlier in the week by the Australian Federal Police at rented residencies in the exclusive Whale Beach suburb of Sydney. Bryan Holmes and J. Ford Rhett were being held without bond and were fighting extradition. The Holmes-Rhett ring was charged in various indictments with smuggling 187,000 pounds of marijuana and 100,000 pounds of hashish worth about $180 million and $284 million dollars, respectively. That explained the Jaguar.

Indicted with Taylor, his brother and Rhett were a number of other gentlemen smugglers from Beaufort, McClellanville, Fripp Island and Frogmore along with a few distributors up the coast in Virginia and Massachusetts. I also recognized the name Powell Whitesides who was a well-known tennis pro employed by the city of Charleston. There were also a number of yet to be unsealed indictments.

Even though I knew Taylor and had heard of Whitesides, the other smuggling operation sounded infinitely more entertaining. That group was based in Columbia and read like a 4-H Club project gone horribly awry. A couple of entitled, bad-seed students at USC had grown their college fraternity pot selling operation into a mini-cartel, now accused of smuggling 160,000 pounds of weed and 30,000 pounds of hash into South Carolina worth collectively about $240 million dollars. The two jacklegs at the top of this second organization were Leon "Crafty" Croft of Columbia and William "Dollar Bill" Haley II of Branchville.

Croft was a hyperactive huckster who had grown up less than a mile from me in northeast Columbia. We had gone to the same high school, although he was a few years ahead of me. I vaguely remembered him as being a goofball, which was an unusual thing for a freshman to think about an upperclassman. Haley was the son of a South Carolina state representative from Jasper county. Haley had continued selling marijuana as a student at the USC School of Law before moving to Hilton Head and opening his new specialty practice. Ironically, Thomas Sheprow had been one of "Dollar Bill" Haley's USC Law School classmates. Some of the other major players in the Croft-Haley operation were Fraser Hawk, another lawyer from Hilton Head Island, Walter Gervais and Arthur Redding, two other friends from Columbia. There was also an impressive list of distributors in New York, Miami, and Orlando. Many of these suspects were already in custody, but "Crafty" Croft and "Dollar Bill" Haley were currently at large, whereabouts unknown.

"Anything else I can get you?" The waitress asked, as she cleared away my dishes.

"You know what, how about a slice of apple pie and a cup of coffee?"

"We've got a good apple-rhubarb pie if you'd like to try that. Are you reading about Operation Jackpot?"

"Yeah, this is amazing stuff. I know one of these guys."

The waitress looked from side to side and leaned forward, putting one hand on the table, and quietly responded, "We all do, honey."

I looked around the crowded Marina restaurant as well. I knew she was telling the truth. "The apple-rhubarb sounds great to me. Thanks."

Another article described the financial organization of the smuggling operations and how the Feds used the money trail to take them down. Besides the hired help, another weak spot in any crime organization are their lawyers. The lawyers always know how to get out when the getting is good. Fraser Hawk was another law school classmate of Sheprow's. He, along with another lawyer named Wilkes Fairchild, had constructed their law practices to serve the needs of a select clientele. They had both already rolled over for the government, pleading guilty to tax evasion and conspiracy. Each was now serving something less than they deserved.

They testified about jetting to the Caymans and London carrying suitcases stuffed with cash. Hawk had set up dummy corporations in both South Carolina and on the Jersey Islands. Baachus Properties Ltd of South Carolina purchased real estate and businesses on behalf of Croft and Haley, which were then transferred to the Jersey Island-based Agora Properties Ltd. With Hawk's help, Bryan Holmes and J. Ford Rhett established another dummy corporation in the Caribbean called Bahamas Leeward Ltd., which served the same purpose. These overseas corporations helped these new businessmen hide their smuggling profits and then reinvested it in new purchases. These blind trusts in the Grand Caymans where used to start insurance companies. From there it was simple. You set up a real estate business, with loans from the bogus insurance companies. The real estate businesses then purchased millions of dollars' worth of legitimate property. It was a sweet money laundering package.

Operation Jackpot was the first case to be made under the new Drug Task Force Program created by President Reagan as part of his and Nancy's war on drugs. It was also the first use of the new Federal racketeering laws. A key part of the indictment was that these smuggling operations represented "continuing criminal enterprises." That made the "kingpins" subject to potential life imprisonment without the possibility of parole. That gave me pause. I had played basketball with Taylor just a few nights ago.

The new law made it possible for the government to seize any assets purchased with the proceeds of the criminal enterprise. Following yesterday's arrests and seizures, the Federal government was now the proud owner of a fleet of cars, boats, shrimp trawlers, property and cash. On the first day, the Jackpot task force had seized two lots on the Intracoastal Waterway in Cassina Plantation outside of Charleston, six lots on Hilton Head Island, one with a house, and four on the ocean, a $160,000 COD seized in the Bahamas, $344,000 seized from an account in an attorney's office, $47,000 being held in an escrow account, and lastly, 82 Queen Street, which was one of the most popular restaurants in downtown Charleston. The FBI even nabbed a couple of well-known Charleston lawyers digging up coolers full of cash in the back-yard of a Hilton Head mansion in the middle of the night. The prosecutors estimated the seized property would have a value of almost $8 million dollars.

Betsy delivered my apple-rhubarb pie. It smelled delicious. "Thank you Betsy. It looks great." And it was.

I read on looking for more sordid details. Something didn't feel right about the story. Taylor had always been a bit mysterious. I was surprised, but not shocked, that he could be involved in drug smuggling. He was apparently a man of means without any apparent means. But he didn't feel like a "kingpin" to me. It bothered me that law enforcement now came with a profit-motive.

MUSC GYNECOLOGY SERVICE

Monday morning, I met Bailey Clark and Parker Weaver for rounds at 7:30 a.m. They had already been on the ward for an hour and a half pre-rounding. When I found them, Bailey and Parker were preoccupied with the drama unfolding outside Janie Johnson's room.

"So what's going on with Ms. Johnson?" I asked.

"There are two big dudes in cheap suits who say they're from SLED. They won't let anybody in to see Ms. Johnson. They want to talk to you," Bailey said. Her eyebrows danced with anticipation. "Something big is up."

"Well, let's go see how big this something is." Despite my glib response, I knew the situation called for caution. SLED was the South Carolina Law Enforcement Division, the state equivalent of the FBI, but with less adult supervision. SLED was not to be trifled with. It was never clear to whom SLED was responsible. With Bailey and Parker hanging a safe distance behind, we walked towards Ms. Johnson's room.

As Bailey had described, the two SLED agents were both ex-jocks and wearing identical off-the-rack black suits that reminded me of the Blues Brothers. They were both middle-aged and over six feet tall. Neither agent's left arm fell flush against his side, suggesting shoulder holsters. Standing on either side of Ms. Johnson's door, there was a noticeable lack of humor about them.

"Good morning. I'm Dr. Declan Murphy. I understand you men are looking to talk with me."

The older of the two agents replied, "Yes sir. I'm Agent Wrenn and this is Agent Lesher. We're both with the State Law Enforcement Division. We've been assigned to protect your patient until she is ready for discharge."

"Agent Wrenn, I wasn't aware that Ms. Johnson was in any danger. She hasn't expressed any concerns to me and her injury was reported as accidental. What sort of danger is she in?"

"Sir, I'm not in a position to define the specific threat. However, she has been missing for more than a year. The circumstances surrounding her disappearance are unclear. Her hospitalization here at MUSC was just discovered. Her family wants to make sure she remains safe until her return home can be arranged. We'll escort her back to Columbia when she is released from the hospital."

"So you're telling me that she was kidnapped? I find that surprising. She has not said anything to us to raise such a suspicion and she has had many opportunities to speak with us confidentially. I'm sympathetic to her family and I'm sure they're very concerned. However, unless Ms. Johnson is under arrest for something, I suspect she'll want to decide for herself where she goes when she leaves the hospital. And, by the way, these two people are Drs. Bailey Clark and Parker Weaver. They're on my gynecology team and are responsible for the care of Ms. Johnson. Please do not interfere with their access to her again. I'm certain that Ms. Johnson's family doesn't want you to compromise her recovery."

Despite being named, I could feel Bailey and Parker distancing themselves, not wanting to be drawn into this mini-confrontation. After an electrically charged pause, Agent Wrenn responded politely, "Point well taken. We'll not hinder their work again. We would like to be kept posted on her progress, if that isn't too much trouble. Before lecturing me again, however, you should know that the patient in this room in not Jane Johnson. Her name is Helene Eastland."

As Agent Wrenn had calculated, that news hit me like a hammer. Helene Eastland was a name I knew well. Bailey and Parker were slower on the uptake. Finally, Bailey picked up on the last name and asked, "The Governor's daughter?"

I nodded.

SESQUICENTENNIAL STATE PARK

Coming-of-age stories have always made great fodder for made-for-TV movies. They are usually romantic fairy tales. Rarely do those movies illuminate the darkness, pain and guilt that enters your heart as the price associated with coming-of-age. The first sexual experience for most boys is a shameful, disturbing transaction that is more hurtful to remember than gratifying. Most boys rationalize their behavior as being natural and manly.

As a grown man, I knew better. Young girls are buffeted by different hormonal winds. They search for affection and attention, not sex. Young boys have no innate ability to separate the two. The nexus of neurons in a boy's brain that spark in response to affection is found much deeper in the root stalk. Girls develop a sophisticated cortical surveillance program much sooner than their male classmates. For the boys, their supra-tentoria hall monitor is a substitute teacher taking a smoke break in the lounge. Countless Southern Baptist Sunday mornings are dedicated to building a fence around the unchained male id. Sunday school is filled with parables, some obtuse, but others crystal clear. Premarital sex is a sin for boys to seek and a sin for girls to provide. The psychic fall-out from those simple Sunday school lessons was immeasurable.

Those lessons did little to slow the pursuit of sexual self-awareness by adolescent boys. That search for pleasure often came at an ugly expense. Bullying, begging, unimaginable lies and promises became part of a sad sack of sordid memories. For some boys, the amount of personal misuse committed in search of carnal knowledge becomes a life-long challenge to their self-image. Those memories, more than being avoided, need to be sequestered where they cannot be consciously revisited.

As a physician, I wondered where the lock box for those memories might be. The heart didn't seem likely. It was far too unreliable and prone to injury. The brain was a possibility, but that left you open to disturbing dreams. I believed it was the liver. The liver functions to filter toxins from your body. Some men spend their adult lives trying to drown their liver with alcohol or poison it with drugs to make sure these disturbing coming-of-age experiences stay at arm's length. I could taste the bile rising in the back of my throat as the humiliating missteps I'd taken with Helene Eastland many years ago began to claw their way back.

Helene Eastland had transferred into Spring Valley High School when her father was the newly-elected Lieutenant Governor. That was two terms as Lt. Governor and two terms as Governor ago for Larry Eastland. Governor Eastland was the most powerful political figure in South Carolina, and the star of the Republican Governors' Caucus. It was no secret that he was planning a run for Earnest Hollings' Senate seat once he completed his second term as Governor.

Helene had been a year behind me in school, but was noticeable beyond being the Lt. Governor's daughter. She'd had long strawberry-blond hair, freckles, and a beautiful smile. I thought that she liked me, and I liked her. One Friday night after a big basketball win over A.C. Flora, I asked her if she wanted to go to Pizza Hut. The place was crowded with friends, but we took a booth by ourselves. She was a lot quicker and funnier than I knew. We went through two medium pizzas and covered a hundred different topics. I drove her home when the Pizza Hut closed. When we got to her house in the new Spring Valley subdivision, she sensed my anxiety and came across the front seat of my Camaro. She gave me a kiss that left no doubt she liked me.

Helene started waiting for me after basketball practice. We would go to my house where we did our homework together. I don't think Helene cared that much about her schoolwork, but my routine and my mother's watchful eye were good influences on her. Helene was artistic and I would trade her some algebra for an occasional poem or drawing. Helene became a regular at the Murphy dinner table and stayed as late as my mother would allow. My parents both enjoyed Helene's company, but mom would good-naturedly run her out when propriety demanded. Helene would feign indignation and had perfected a humorous, "Don't you know that I'm the Lt. Governor's daughter," speech.

For the first time in my life, I looked forward to basketball practice being over. I felt a calm when we were together. Helene seemed to love being with me and at my house. She laughed, told jokes with my dad, sparred with my mom and her eyes sparkled when we talked about what we would do tomorrow. However, her mood would darken whenever I drove her home. Her thoughts turned negative, her jaw would clinch and her lips would tighten against her teeth. I worried about what I had done wrong. Only later, did I realize that the changes I witnessed were not because of where she had been. It was anger over where she was going.

We group dated several more times after my basketball games. When we began to date alone we officially became a couple. I looked forward to meeting the Lt. Governor, but never did. Helene always met me at my car when I arrived at her house. When I brought her home, we never went inside. The make-out sessions in Helene's driveway became intense.

Tired of movies, Helene wanted to go dancing. I took her to The Copper Door on the Rosewood Drive strip where I knew the waitresses were indifferent to my fake ID. We shagged for several hours to Bill Pinkney and the Original Drifters and enjoyed a couple pitchers of beer. On the way home, I asked Helene if she would like to stop at Sesquicentennial State Park. There was no gate and the Sesqui picnic area was a favorite parking spot. Tonight, the parking lot was empty. Helene knew we weren't going on the playground swings.

I loved my '68 Camaro, but the front bucket seats were a challenge. I got her blouse unbuttoned, but was too clumsy to solve the eye-hooks of her bra. In an impatient compromise, I took her bra straps down off her shoulders. I reached my hand under her wool skirt and moved up her thigh. Helene did not resist, nor did she help. When I found the wetness of her panties, she made an unfamiliar sound. I wanted to believe it was a sound of pleasure, but I had the uncomfortable feeling it was a sound of loathing. I avoided looking into Helene's eyes. I didn't want to know what I 'd find.

With the windshield and windows fogged, I never saw anything until the moment was shattered by a tap on the driver side window and blinding illumination. I jumped back into the driver's seat. I wiped the steam from the window and saw a South Carolina Highway Patrolman tapping the glass with his flashlight. I rolled down the window and immediately began to sound stupid.

"Shut up, son. Helene, button up your blouse and get out of the car. I'm taking you home."

It took longer than it should have for me to register that the patrolman knew Helene by name. How did he know that? How did he know we were here? I had some time to process those thoughts because Helene wasn't moving. In fact, Helene had not even made a move to cover herself. She stared at the patrolman, her lower lip trembling with rage and tears streaming from her eyes. As I looked at her, the patrolman walked to her side of the car and opened her door.

"Come on Helene. Don't make this more difficult than it needs to be."

"Fuck you!" Helene shouted, no longer able to contain her anger.

"Let's go, Helene," the patrolman said calmly as he grabbed her arm and pulled her from her seat.

"Declan, please help me," Helene implored, as she was dragged from my Camaro.

"Son, move from that seat, and you'll be sorry you ever took your first breath."

I sat motionless as the patrolman dragged Helene to his cruiser and threw her in the backseat. Once in the cruiser, I could no longer hear Helene crying, but in my head, I kept hearing her calling my name. I'd pretended I was man enough to reach under her skirt, but as it turned out, I wasn't man enough to even get out of my car to protect her from a state-employed thug. I started crying alone in the darkness of Sesquicentennial State Park.

That night at Sesquicentennial is the ugliest memory I carry.

A coward, I was unable to call Helene on Sunday or face her at school on Monday. Whether out of anger or shame, Helene avoided me as well. She wasn't waiting for me after basketball, and I didn't look for her. I was a weasel again when I told my friends that Helene was a prude and had a personal bodyguard to protect her chastity.

Already new at school, I watched Helene become more and more isolated. We spoke occasionally in the halls, but never anything consequential. I never asked her out again. Gradually, we saw even less of each other as Helene began to hang out with the potheads who loitered on the fringes of the school. I choose to believe we were both moving on, although I knew better. Somewhere in my liver, I hid the memories of my boorish groping, chicken-hearted inaction, and wicked insensitivity to a girl who deserved none of it , and needed so much more.

For a moment, I wondered if I might have met Agent Wrenn before. I tried to remember the face in my window at Sesquicentennial years ago. I puzzled if he might be one and the same. I worried about what I was going to say to Helene. I had operated on her and taken care of her all weekend. How had I not recognized a woman I 'd once dated? I had abandoned her then, and now, I hadn't even remembered her.

It was a bountiful harvest of shame. I had amassed a mammoth debt to Helene Eastland, and she held my marker. Sooner or later, we have to pay for our sins.

I told Bailey and Parker to finish up with the other patients. I would go see Ms. Eastland by myself.

HELENE EASTLAND'S ROOM

I told Agents Wrenn and Lesher I was going in to see Ms. Eastland and I wouldn't need their assistance. I was pleased to see that she was awake and enjoying a hearty Medical University stack of pancakes.

"Good morning, Helene. How are the pancakes?" I watched for a response to my using her real name.

Helene smiled, "I feel fine, Declan. Thanks for asking." Helene's tone of voice was more familiar than in her prior conversations.

"Did you know it was me since admission?"

"Of course."

That made me feel even worse. "Helene, this is very embarrassing. I can't tell you how sorry I am for not recognizing you. In fact, it's inexcusable. I guess this confirms every cliché about Ob-Gyns not looking above their patients' waists. The brown hair threw me off, but even if it was purple, I still should've known it was you. Please accept my apology."

"Don't worry about it. I've been working at keeping my identity a secret for a long time. I outgrew my freckles years ago, and I've been dying my hair for so long I can barely remember my natural color. I was a little worried you might have been the one who dropped a dime on me."

"No, it wasn't me. I was clueless until your two new friends from SLED showed up. You know about the two SLED agents outside, don't you? They're planning to take you back to Columbia when you're discharged."

"Yeah. They introduced themselves yesterday when they arrived. They seem like real gentlemen. I got an anonymous phone call saying that SLED was on its way. The caller suggested that Red might be better off clearing out before they got here."

"Is he coming back?"

"No, I don't think so." Helene looked away.

"Why didn't you go with him?"

"I don't know that I wanted to. My relationship with Red is complicated. Plus, whoever called made it clear that wasn't an option. Leaving with Red would only delay the inevitable and make things worse for both of us. And, despite your fine work, I'm not really fit to be on the run."

"Of course, but you're going to feel much better soon. The only real worry at this point is infection, but you've been afebrile. Vulvar injuries heal very quickly." I was irritated at myself for sounding so clinical.

"Well, if it isn't already obvious, I'm not in much of a hurry," Helene said in a softer voice, as if SLED might be listening.

"I understand. There may well be some 'concerning' redness we'll need to keep an eye on," I said grinning. "By the way, would you prefer I arrange for one of my partners to take care of you? I don't want to make you uncomfortable."

"Don't be silly. I'm very pleased with my care. At least so far. I'll let you know if I think the quality is slipping."

"Thanks. I thought I needed to ask."

"No, we're good."

I wanted to know more about what was going on, but I didn't know how to ask. On one hand, it was personal, while on the other, it was affecting our care to have two SLED agents posted outside her door. I fished.

"What do you want me to do about these SLED guys? They seem anxious to haul you back to Columbia."

Helene knew where I was going. "Declan, I don't know how much you know about my father. If you know anything, you know he has bigger plans than being Governor. Everyone is expected to be on board with Team Eastland. He and I have never been on the same page. Rebellious, stupid, druggie, hippie, whore or just plain trouble-maker. And those are the good things he has to say about me. Eighteen months ago, I took off. He's been looking for me ever since. He believes I'm a loose cannon and, if the truth be known, I probably am. I'm less of a problem for Team Eastland if I'm under his thumb."

"You're thirty years old. He can't tell you where to go and what to do."

"Declan, don't be naïve. My father is the most powerful man in South Carolina. Those are SLED agents out there. They're walking around your hospital like they own the place. That should tell you something."

"You've been able to stay off his radar for the past year and a half."

"It wasn't easy. Red has a pretty remote place down in the Keys. We also spent time in Jamaica and Costa Rica where Red has business associates. It wasn't like we were Bonnie and Clyde. We just lived quietly down there and didn't advertise who we were or where we were from. I became Janie Johnson, changed my hair color, and we always paid in cash. My father didn't know Red, so it was easy to stay hidden as long as we didn't reach out."

I told Helene that I was sorry she'd been found. I would try to keep her in the hospital as long as I possibly could. Maybe she could work something out. I briefly examined her to make sure her wound was closing. I would be back that afternoon after clinic. She was to have the nurse page me if the SLED agents, or anyone else, gave her any trouble.

As I left her room, Agent Wrenn approached. He reminded me that the Governor wanted Helene to be transferred to Columbia as soon as she was physically able. Governor Eastland would be interested in an update as to when Helene might be able to travel. It was subtle, but Agent Wrenn was a little more aggressive than I was in a mood to deal with. My patience with Agent Wrenn had run out very quickly.

"Look Agent 99, why don't you get back on your shoe phone, and tell whoever is pulling your strings that I'm her attending physician. I will discharge her whenever I damn well feel like it, and not a minute sooner."

My little tantrum didn't seem to faze Agent Wrenn at all. Wrenn leaned in close to my face and spoke softly, "Calm down, Doc. You do your job, and keep your mouth shut. You're in the deep end of the pool without any swimmies."

I hadn't intimidated this guy at all with my "attending physician" bullshit. That was important to remember. I turned and left.

LABOR @ DELIVERY UNIT

Leaving Ms. Eastland's room, I headed over to Labor and Delivery for a scheduled Cesarean. Betsy Wingo was a brittle Type 1 diabetic. We had gotten her to thirty-seven weeks despite severe nausea and vomiting her entire pregnancy, one episode of diabetic ketoacidosis, and a lack luster attitude about controlling her blood sugars. We bitched at her about her non-compliance at every one of her pre-natal visits. I wondered how good I'd be managing a disease that had ruined every day of my life since I was eight years old. Obstetricians are experts at laying on the guilt, constantly reminding women that there is "a baby on board". For some women, there must be a big heaping spoonful of "who gives a shit" mixed into the equation somewhere. Betsy Wingo was one of those women. When you considered how much her body had let her down, I wasn't sure I could blame her for being a bit skeptical about the "miracle of life" story. We confirmed fetal lung maturity by amniocentesis and were thankful to be getting this baby delivered. Fetuses trapped in a metabolic maelstrom like Ms. Wingo sometimes just don't wake up one morning.

I was glad to be operating with one of my favorite residents. Rachel Lipinski was a talented third year from Cleveland, but she wasn't particularly popular among her co-residents. Most considered her a gunner. Rachel liked operating with me and had probably muscled one of the junior residents out of the Wingo Cesarean. She also said exactly what she thought without a lot of filtering, which isn't the Southern way. The faculty, on the other hand, loved her confidence and aggressiveness. We knew her to be extremely intelligent and a tireless worker. The residents assumed these last two characteristics were shared equally by all. That wasn't reality. Rachel's knowledge base and work rate exceeded most of her peers, and the faculty appreciated it.

Rachel also had an old-school attitude. The oldest joke about medical training is that "the only thing wrong with being on call every other night is that you miss half of the great stuff." This mentality had fallen victim to "life-style" considerations. Rachel Lapinski hadn't gotten the memo. She wanted to be involved in every interesting case and scrub on every challenging surgery. The other residents were pissed when they found out Rachel had asked the L@D nurses to call her at home for twin deliveries or a breech. While they were offended, none of the other residents asked the nurses for the same consideration.

On this particular morning, I was distracted by Helene Eastland and Agent Wrenn. I was letting Rachel do the case and assisting on automatic. The trouble was, the Cesarean was proving difficult, and Rachel was struggling. There were dense adhesions everywhere. The uterus and tubes were stuck to everything else in the pelvis. Rachel couldn't find a window to get into the uterus for the baby. It had been almost five minutes since the skin incision, and we hadn't made much progress.

After another minute of floundering, Dr. Lapinski finally looked up. "Dr. Murphy, I could really use some help. I can't find the bladder and I'm afraid to go any farther without identifying the bladder dome."

"Sorry. Let me take a look. This is a little embarrassing since I'm the one who operated on her before. If we take down these adhesions right here, we should get to an open space around the side of the uterus. Then we can work our way back towards the middle."

The advantage that attending physicians have in situations like this is the knowledge that there is no one else to turn to. Being reticent is a luxury that only the residents get to enjoy. As the attending, it's a buck-stops-here situation. It's my job to make tough decisions and pull the trigger. I believed the incisions we were about to make were safe, and I cut boldly. If I was wrong, we'd all know soon enough. If I was right, there was never any need for Rachel Lapinski to suspect that I wasn't absolutely confident of the scalpel strokes I had just made.

After cutting a few thick scar bands, a nice space opened up separating the bladder from the lower portion of the uterus. Rachel took down a few more filmy adhesions, and we were able to open the uterus safely. After an interminable fifteen minutes of surgery in a disastrous pelvis, we finally delivered a squalling infant. We closed the uterine incision quickly to get control of the bleeding before finally taking a moment to relax.

"What's the matter Rachel? You look stressed," I said, smiling beneath my surgical mask. "We had it all the way."

"Maybe you had it all the way, but I sure didn't. I've never been in a Cesarean where I couldn't find the baby. I've got sweat running down the middle of my back into my butt crack, and you're off gathering wool. I'm glad you decided to join me. Especially since you're the hack responsible for this mess. What did you close her with last time, crazy glue? Try to stick around with me for just a couple more minutes so we can get out of here.

I'm glad she signed for a tubal ligation because I'm going to do one whether she wants it or not. No one should ever have to come back into this death trap."

Like I said, no one could ever accuse Rachel Lapinski of not speaking her mind. She was absolutely right. I didn't give Ms. Wingo's Cesarean the focus it deserved.

That afternoon I dropped by to see Helene Eastland as I had promised. Agent Wrenn wasn't there. It appeared to be Agent Lesher's shift. He was seated in a chair, reading, by her door. He noticed me, but didn't speak or lift his eyes. He appeared to be the more mild mannered of the two.

Helene was feeling better and was standing at the sink brushing her teeth. I decided that sort of progress was unacceptable. I told her she looked "flushed" and took her temperature myself. It was a cool 97.6 degrees, but I documented 100.6. I wrote in her chart that she was "feverish, flushed, and attempts to increase her activity had been inhibited by pain and swelling." I added that I was "very concerned by her temperature of 100.6 degrees." My plan was to "watch her closely for a secondary infection." Fuck you, Agent Wrenn. Maybe I did have a problem with authority.

After checking in on Helene and documenting my concerns, I headed home. We had a Journal Club scheduled. I was one of the discussants and I wanted to pick up a sports coat. Leafing through my mail, I found the letter from the American Board of Obstetrics and Gynecology I was looking for. I never doubted I had passed, but as I opened the letter there was inevitable anxiety as my eyes searched for the "we are pleased to inform" as opposed to the "we regret to inform" sentence. Thankfully, they were pleased to inform.

I put the letter in my coat pocket and headed off to Journal Club. It was going to be at a nice Italian place on Market Street called Garibaldi's. A glass of their house Chianti before dinner would be my own quiet celebration.

MUSC GYNECOLOGY SERVICE

All of my surgeries had now gone home except Helene, so I slept in a little bit Tuesday morning. I didn't get to the floor for rounds till about eight a.m. and was immediately confronted by an agitated Bailey Clark.

"Did you order a Psych consult on Ms. Eastland?" she asked.

"Of course not. What are you talking about?"

"She says a Hispanic doctor came in to see her last night at nine p.m. and asked her a couple of stupid questions. How was she feeling? Was she looking forward to going home? Was she anxious about seeing her family again? She didn't know who he was and only talked with him for a couple of minutes. She said she was tired and needed some sleep. Then I found this on her chart. It's a psych consult that says she's manic-depressive. It's totally weird. You better look at it."

I stood at the nursing station reading the three typed pages with Bailey re-reading it over my shoulder. It was poetic, albeit complete fantasy. It took a few minutes to wrap my head around it. Finally, I asked Bailey, "So what do you think about this?"

"I don't know what to think. Ms. Eastland isn't crazy, but this is."

"There're several interesting things here. First, look at the header. This guy works at the State Mental Hospital in Columbia. I will bet you anything this doctor is a Cuban Mariel boat-lift refugee. There's nothing that indicates he's board certified. He may not even have a state license. A lot of the doctors working at the state hospital aren't able to get a South Carolina license for one reason or another. Something about working for the state protects them. Hell, he might not even be a psychiatrist. These guys don't do anything but pick up a paycheck. He didn't come down here on his own. He was sent. Moreover, this thing was typed on State Mental Hospital letterhead. How'd he accomplish that at our nursing station at nine p.m. last night? This consult was prepared before he ever left Columbia."

"How do you know so much about the State Mental Hospital?"

Bailey seemed surprised when I told her that I had worked there for a summer during high school. Everyone in South Carolina knew what it meant to be sent to "Bull Street." I had worked as a runner between the main administration building and the residential blocks. I dreaded the older residential wards. The stench permeated your clothes the moment you unlocked the door. It was a sour, eye-watering combination of body odor, urine, some unnamed industrial disinfectant, remorse and resignation. And that was the men's ward. The women's ward added more unpleasant variables. As a teenager, it was my first exposure to hopelessness. The doctors only visited these wards once a month to sit in on the "team meeting" as required by law. It was hopelessly forlorn and unforgettable.

One of my jobs was to attend "team meetings" and collect the names of patients to be discharged. I'd been on a lot of teams and these were the most dysfunctional I'd ever seen. No one was ever discharged off the chronic adult wards. Ninety-nine percent of the discussions centered on how to control the schizophrenics. The main thing I learned that summer was that while some guys may be big, no one is bigger than "the BIG T" which was what the aides called

73

Thorazine. I was never religious, but I prayed that no one on those adult wards would ever realize the horror of where they were or how they lived. Full-goose bozo insanity was preferable to any illusion of recovery. On those wards, neither hope nor help ever came through those locked doors.

The only ward I ever looked forward to visiting was the adolescent unit. If nothing else, we at least had age in common. Their problems were more understandable. Since many of them were under court order, some evaluation and treatment was required. During one of my first trips to the adolescent unit, I walked by a girl about my age standing by the fence in the activity yard. As I came down the walk, I managed to mumble "good morning." She smiled and lifted her tartan skirt to show me her private parts. It was the first time I'd ever seen female genitalia.

The team meetings on the adolescent unit were punctuated by revolting stories of parental neglect and abuse, physical, emotional and sexual. From my perspective, once again, the wrong person had been locked up. When there was a discharge, my responsibility was to bring that information back to the central administration building, process it, and arrange pick up. I remember calling a family in a rural upstate town to tell them their fourteen year-old son was ready to come home.

"The hell he is," his father said.

I explained again. Their son's triage meeting had gone very well. The whole team thought his progress had been impressive and he was ready to come home.

"Hell he ain't," his father said again.

Too young to understand, I explained one more time. "Sir, your son is doing better. The doctors all say so. He has worked hard to get better and he wants to come home. I'm sure you want to see him."

"The hell if I do."

I didn't know what else to say and finally blurted out, "You have to come get him. He can't stay here."

There was silence for a few seconds and then his father replied, "Well, if he comes home, we'll just chain him back up in the barn like we had him before." And then, he hung up.

The emasculation and soul crushing indignities that life had in store for that poor kid were unimaginable. It's not easy to make a socio-path, but that family was well on its way. That kid didn't have a chance, and the South Carolina State Hospital couldn't offer him one. Ken Kesey's cuckoo's nest only scratched the surface of the horrors offered up at the Southern gothic fortress on Bull Street. There were no boundaries to the violation of the human spirit. When I left Bull Street at the end of summer, I promised myself I would never return without a torch. Throughout my medical training I never overcame my bias against psychiatry. I frequently refused to let my residents consult them.

"What do you think about his conclusions?" I asked Bailey. "He calls her manic depressive, describes 'self-destructive and reckless manic behavior,' and later mentions 'elements of a psychotically depressed state in some of her answers.' Where do you think that's going?"

"Shit. They want to involuntarily commit her."

"Exactly. That's what this is all about. There's more to it, though. Notice that there aren't any treatment recommendations. Maybe my imagination is getting the best of me, but what do you think they're planning when they get a hold of her at Bull Street?"

"Sometimes electroshock is used for psychotic depression," Bailey responded with both revulsion and disbelief in her eyes.

"That's what I'm thinking. Have you ever seen electroshock? It strips all the wiring. Sometimes the circuits come back on line minus the shorts. Sometimes, though, it fries the motherboard and the circuits never come back at all. Do me a favor. Make a couple copies of this consult and get the original off the chart. Don't make any mention of it to the nurses or anyone else. If you referenced it in your progress note this morning, pull that paper out and rewrite your note. We never consulted anybody. As far as I'm concerned, nobody was ever here. I doubt this is going to change things very much, but it might slow things down a little. We need some time to figure out what's going on."

"Will do, boss. This is getting sinister," Bailey said as she walked away.

"No kidding," I said to myself.

As I walked down the hall to Ms. Eastland's room, I saw that Agent Wrenn was back on duty. He didn't get up or speak, but did give me a shit-eating grin, clearly intended to make me angry. He was good.

Ever since her admission, I had been impressed with Helene's composure. This morning, I could see the stress beginning to take its toll. Her hair was uncombed and her hands were fidgeting. Her eyes darted around like a trapped animal. In a sense, she was. Helene was fighting to maintain her composure. It was evident that she'd been under stress like this before and knew how to handle it. That didn't mean it didn't cause wear and tear.

"Who was that man who came in here last night? What was he here for?" Her voice was now more abrupt and shrill than I had heard before.

"First of all, tell me what you two talked about last night."

"Not much. It was brief. He asked how I was doing and if I was recovering well. He said you had asked him to come by and check on me since you were out of the hospital. He asked if the SLED agents outside worried me. I told him no. He said that was good because they were only there to look after my best interests and safety. I told him that was bull-shit. Then he asked me if I was looking forward to getting home and seeing my family."

"What did you tell him?"

"I told him there was no way I was going back to Columbia. I'll see my sister again sometime, but not right now. I told him my mother was a clueless drunk and that my father was a prick. The SLED agents could follow me around forever if they wanted, but they better like to travel, because I'm getting as far away from my daddy as possible. I'm not going to play dress-up and help him win any more elections. He suggested that I was worn out and would have a different opinion once I'd gotten some rest. That pissed me off. I told him he was right about one thing, I was tired. Then I rolled over in bed and faced the wall."

"Then what happened?"

"He took the hint and left."

"Are you safe at home?" I asked, again angry with myself for slipping into my doctor voice. "Did things happen to you at home that we should talk about?"

Helene did not respond immediately. She stared at me, considering her response.

"We're both safer if we don't discuss what may, or may not, have happened to me at home." If you could spit a word, that was how Helene Eastland had said 'home.' "I've put that stuff behind me. But I promise you, I'll never go back to the Governor's Mansion. They'll have to kill me to take me back. Are we clear on that?"

"Crystal. However, you know that anything you tell me is protected by doctor-patient confidentiality. I want you to take a few deep breaths. You're worked up, and I don't blame you. I need you to calm down and consider what I'm saying. If there's been abuse, we can get protection for you."

"Declan, you need to step into the real world. This isn't high school. You work for the state now. The police work for the state. Those SLED guys work for the state. The magistrates work for the state. My daddy is the state. The first priority of political power is to maintain it. My father pulls whatever strings are necessary in order to get what he wants. I'm safest keeping my secrets to myself."

"That's what all abuse victims think. Abuse doesn't stop until you expose it. We can talk with your mother and let her know what 's gone on."

Helene laughed out loud. "Oh, that's a great idea. I can't believe I never thought of that myself."

"There's no need to be sarcastic."

"There isn't? Let me tell you a story. My daddy started coming to my room to 'read me a bedtime story' when I was nine or ten. He would reach under the covers and pull off my underwear. He'd force my legs apart and finger me while he masturbated. He used my panties as a condom. I learned to close my eyes and go somewhere else. One night, though, we both heard my mother's footsteps coming down the hallway toward my room. That might've been the only time I ever saw my father really scared. My mother's footsteps stopped outside my door. I could feel her hand on the doorknob, but it didn't turn. She couldn't deal with what she was going to find on my side of that door. I hate her more than I hate him. He's a slobbering animal. She made a choice. She chose being the first lady over me. I heard her footsteps moving away down the hallway. They never came back."

Helene paused and collected herself. "For years, I was afraid of my father and ashamed of myself. I'm still afraid of him, but eventually I learned that I didn't have to give in to that fear. When I finally became able to see my father for what he really is, I gained some leverage. By high school, I wouldn't let him come to my room anymore. When I wouldn't let him abuse me sexually anymore, he just shifted gears to psychological. What he did to my head in high school was more hurtful than what he did to my vagina when I was little. Mom watched it all from a safe spot on the sofa with her martini. Don't suggest my mother again as an option. The only way out was to escape from his prison and that's what I did as soon as I could figure out a plan."

"I understand," was the best I could muster.

"So, who was the guy who came in here last night? I think he lied about you sending him."

"Yes, he lied. I didn't know anything about him until a few minutes ago. He's a psychiatrist from Columbia, and I'm sure that your father sent him. We didn't request a psych consult, but it showed up anyway. We've pulled it off your chart. He says you are manic-depressive with reckless and self -destructive behavior. He has tentatively diagnosed you as having psychotic depression."

Helene stared at me for a few seconds with her eyes widening and a fullness developing on the lower lid. "Where does he work?"

"At the state mental hospital in Columbia. This consult is total bullshit. No other psychiatrist would support that diagnosis."

At that point, all the accumulated defiance in her face and spirit evaporated. Desperate fear replaced it. Her tears were no longer containable and began to flow down her cheeks. "Don't let them put me in there. I won't survive it. Don't let them send me to Bull Street. Oh God, don't let this happen to me." She rolled over and buried her head in her pillow.

"Helene, listen to me. It's going to be okay. We're not going to let them commit you. The whole idea is ridiculous. I'll get our psych people here to re-evaluate you and confirm that you're fine. No one is going to believe this dip shit from Columbia. Trust me. It's not going to happen."

My thoughts flashed back to the boy whose father was going to chain him back up in the barn if we sent him home.

OB–GYN DEPARTMENT CHAIRMAN'S OFFICE

The situation with Helene Eastland was spiraling beyond my reach. I called down to the department to see if Dr. Templeton was in his office. Francie said he was, and I asked her to let him know I needed a few minutes of his time.

Dr. Preston Templeton is our departmental chairman. He came to MUSC during my residency, as a nationally and internationally known Reproductive Endocrinologist and Infertility specialist. Templeton had a bumpy first year. For most of us, Dr. Laurence L. Hester, the prior chair, was a king-like figure. In the South, particularly in Charleston, new things are not well received. Charleston likes things the way they used to be.

To his credit, Dr. Templeton eventually won over the department. He was an honest and fair guy, and one of the smartest academics you could ever meet. In contrast to Dr. Hester, Templeton was not very imposing. He was short and balding with pinched eyes and he wore thick wire-rimmed glasses. But when he gave a lecture, he came alive. He could dominate a room with his intellect. When he commented on someone else's work, it was always insightful, never demeaning. He had written several sentinel papers on reproductive endocrinology and had no peer in his knowledge of pituitary abnormalities. His writing made the most difficult concepts understandable.

Since my return to Charleston to join the faculty, Dr. Templeton had been supportive in all our dealings. When he promised you something, you could count on it. That sort of integrity was unusual in academic medicine. Although Preston was not embracing on an interpersonal level and always a difficult person to read, I believed he liked me and watched out for my career. Even if he wasn't much of a back-slapper, you couldn't ask for more in a departmental chairman. You could certainly do a lot worse.

Unfortunately, his relationships outside the department had not gone as well. The Dean of the College of Medicine and the University President both considered him a failure. Dr. Templeton had been expensively recruited from Washington University in Saint Louis based on his reputation as an infertility specialist. Infertility was a huge money-maker and every university wanted a piece of the action. No insurance company covered infertility treatment, so it was a cash and carry business. Infertile women were willing to pay thousands for just one round of in-vitro fertilization. Each round carried only a one in four chance of success. The desperation associated with infertility brought the customer back again and again, for cycle after cycle, until their savings account was emptied.

Charleston already had a private fertility center that attracted women from the entire Southeast. It was a fantastically successful money mill. Having come from a highly endowed private institution, Dr. Templeton never understood how difficult it would be to establish a successful IVF program in a publicly-funded state institution. Despite all his knowledge and clinical experience, Preston Templeton had no clue how to carve an efficient business operation out of an intransigent state bureaucracy and "can't-do" mentality. The state of South Carolina has no job description for a customer service representative. Ultimately, Dr. Templeton was the director of a new but unproven, under-funded, and more expensive fertility center than his local competition. The expectation was that he would capture a significant share of the lucrative infertility market. His lack of success was easily tracked by an accountant's ledger.

In retrospect, Dr. Templeton made several serious mistakes. One of his most significant was a consequence of a noble, but misguided loyalty to his staff. When Dr. Templeton came to Charleston, he brought Dr. Andrew Liu with him from St. Louis. Dr. Liu was responsible for the day-to-day operation of the MUSC Infertility Institute. Dr. Liu was talented embryologist and laboratory guy, which made him a superb number two man in St. Louis. However, he totally lacked the necessary interpersonal skills or charisma to front such a facility, especially in Charleston. His accent was so severe that he was barely understandable. His shortcomings were obvious to everyone. Despite tons of pressure from hospital administration, Dr. Templeton stuck with Dr. Liu until it was too late. Dr. Liu finally had the grace to resolved the problem for Preston by deciding to go back to Hong Kong to start his own fertility center. By that point, we were solidly at zero point zero percent market share.

It was an inspiring act of fidelity, but it cost Dr. Templeton all the good will he had with both the Dean and the President. They had invested several million dollars in Dr. Templeton and the Infertility Institute. After three years, they had nothing to show for it. The department was now on the outs with both hospital administration and the College of Medicine. Dr. Templeton, always bookish, was becoming increasingly reclusive in his office.

When I entered, Dr. Templeton was sitting at his desk, listening to National Public Radio and working on a new book chapter. He hated to be interrupted when writing, but I explained I had a very serious situation. I needed his advice and probably his help. Over the next few minutes, I related everything I knew about Ms. Eastland's admission and care, the revelation of who she was, the arrival of the SLED agents, the bogus psychiatry consult, and my suspicion she was going to be involuntarily committed to the state mental hospital. I told Dr. Templeton of her admission and that she had been the victim of sexual abuse at the hands of her father, the Governor and potential next U.S. Senator. I didn't think it was a good idea to let him know we had dated in high school.

I'd gotten his full attention with the words sexual abuse and Governor in the same sentence. When he spoke, he was using his intellectual, professorial tone. "What evidence do you have of sexual abuse?"

"Just what Ms. Eastland has told me."

Dr. Templeton nodded his head silently. "Admittedly, the unrequested psychiatry consult is highly unusual and inappropriate. From what you've told me, the sexual abuse occurred many years ago and she's never reported it before. I don't doubt Ms. Eastland, but the solution she chose was to get away from home as soon as she could. Creating a conspiracy to involuntarily commit Ms. Eastland to protect a secret she seems more than willing to keep to herself, seems extreme, and probably counterproductive. Is it possible that Ms. Eastland does have some mental stability issues? Have you considered the application of Occam's razor?"

Occam's razor is attributed to Father William of Occam, a fourteenth century English theologian, logician, and Franciscan friar. William of Occam wrote that, "Entities must not be multiplied beyond necessity" which expressed in Latin is *Lex parsimoniae.*

The Law of Parsimony, Occam's razor, implies that the simplest explanation is usually the correct one. When confronted with competing hypotheses, select the one that makes the fewest assumptions.

The early applications of Occam's razor involved theological debates as to the existence of God. In the Middle Ages, an all-powerful God was the simplest, logical explanation for the many mysteries of life. Centuries later, Occam's razor also found a home in the fields of evolutionary biology and basic probability theory. Occam's razor has also enjoyed acceptance in the field of medicine. Diagnostic parsimony argues that when assessing multiple signs or symptoms, physicians should search for the one diagnosis that best explains all of the findings. A common expression of Occam's razor heard on daily teaching rounds is, "When you hear hoof beats, think horses, not zebras." Occam's razor is an important medical rule of thumb. Dr. Templeton was correct to suggest that the simplest explanation of this entire situation might be that things are exactly as they are described to be. Some of Helene's behavior may be manic and reckless. Maybe, supervised, in-patient psychiatric care is exactly what she needs.

I acknowledged the uncertainty. I agreed with Dr. Templeton that it wouldn't be surprising for an abuse victim to have some emotional problems. However, the entire situation left me feeling that a rush to judgment was dangerous. The obvious explanation was not necessarily the correct one, especially when the situation was being manipulated. Despite the psychiatry consult, I couldn't believe that Ms. Eastland was manic-depressive, although admittedly, I had only cared for her for a couple of days.

"You know, Dr. Templeton, there is a counter argument to Occam's razor."

"And what would that be?" Dr. Templeton asked, raising his eyebrows and staring up at me through his thick glasses.

"Hickam's dictum."

"Ummm, I'm not familiar with it."

"Hickam's dictum says that patients can have as many diagnoses as they damn well please. Sometimes multiple symptoms might be better explained by several coexisting common diseases as opposed to a single, rarer, but more unifying, affliction."

"Interesting, but I'm not sure how applicable it is to this situation."

"I'm not sure either, but given the consequences of a misdiagnosis, I think it would be better to look at all reasonable possibilities, even if there is one diagnosis that appears most likely."

"A reasonable consideration. You go back to work, and I will make a few calls. Don't worry, though. I'm sure we can figure this thing out. I will get back to you later this afternoon."

"Thank you Dr. Templeton. As always, I appreciate your support."

HELENE EASTLAND'S ROOM

After lunch, I went by the Gynecology floor to check on Helene. The circus had come to town. From the nursing station I saw Governor Eastland standing outside Helene's room, huddling with his SLED agents and a couple of buttoned-down aides. Dwarfed by the two SLED agents, the Governor appeared to be no more than five feet four inches in height. Despite the numerous times I'd seen the man on TV, I had no idea he was such a runt. His expensive three-piece sharkskin suit and elevator shoes spoke to his vanity. The suit's poor fit and the ham-handed Windsor knot of his tie spoke to his white trash roots.

The Governor's instruction to the agents was interrupted by a tall black man who emerged from Helene's room. The African-American man also towered over the Governor as they shook hands. The two men had a brief conversation before the black man headed off down the hallway in the opposite direction.

Completing his conversation with Agent Wrenn, Governor Eastland was directed towards me at the nursing station.

"I understand you're my daughter's doctor?"

Up close, Eastland appeared even more distasteful. He looked as if he were exploding out of his undersized suit. A middle-aged beer gut could not be contained beneath his vest or above his failing beltline. A fleshy neck spilled over an unbuttoned shirt collar. His too short coat sleeves were made more obvious by oversized French cuffs and ostentatious cufflinks. He did not extend his hand.

"Yes, sir. My name is Declan Murphy, and I'm Ms. Eastland's gynecologist. There're a number of people involved in her care, but I'm responsible."

"That's all well and good, but Helene says she isn't doing very well."

I was momentarily taken aback, but quickly realized how Helene had played things with her father. "I'll certainly check on that, sir, but so far she's been recovering about as I had anticipated. She had a fairly severe accident, and some patience is going to be required."

"Son, patience isn't one of my strengths. Do I need to have someone else called in to consult on my daughter's case? I can have President Turner assign anyone to her care. I expect her to be home soon. We clear on that?"

I was surprised by the Governor's aggressiveness. His beady black eyes, salt and pepper comb-over, and short stature bore little resemblance to his statuesque, green-eyed, strawberry-blond daughter. I wondered how much this genetic dissimilarity fueled the Governor's lust and hate for Helene. Probably more than either of them knew, and maybe a good question for Helene's mother.

"Sir, I'm sure you can do almost anything you want. What you can't do, however, is make Ms. Eastland heal any faster than nature allows. We're taking good care of Ms. Eastland. With time, she'll return to full health and function. When that day arrives, I will discharge her and she'll be free to go."

"For your sake, son, you'd better be right, and that day better be soon. I've told you once already that patience is not my strong suit. I don't remind people of things a third time."

"I think I understand you, Governor."

"Also, when Helene is ready to be discharged, I expect to be notified immediately, so that I can arrange her return to Columbia." He turned to the ward secretary. "Darling, why don't you see if you can find me a cold Coca-Cola."

The ward secretary looked at me with an unspoken accusation to which I could only shrug my shoulders. Myrtle got up to embark on a half-hearted search, but cut her eyes at me as she walked away. I was going to be punished for this later.

Readdressing the Governor, I said, "I can appreciate your concern for your daughter's well-being, but your daughter is now an adult. I'm her doctor, and my obligations are to her. I can't report her condition to anyone unless she asks me to. Where she goes when she leaves this hospital is her choice."

The Governor's eyes narrowed to menacing slits behind his chubby cheeks. His voice softened with familiarity. "Don't give me any of this doctor-patient confidentiality bullshit. Helene ran off last year with a bunch of scumbags and has been leading us all on a merry chase. That stops today. Order is going to be restored. You work for me. That girl getting me a coke works for me. This entire hospital works for me. Don't you forget that. When it comes time to discharge my daughter, you will notify Agent Wrenn, standing right over there, and we'll handle things from there. Good day, Dr. Murphy. Don't disappoint me."

As Governor Eastland walked away, I couldn't help but think that despite his diminutive stature, Eastland was every inch a Southern peckerwood. After the Governor left, I went down the hall to see Helene. I walked past Agent Wrenn who remained seated outside her door. I ignored him and he ignored me.

Her father's visit had made Helene more frantic, but purposeful. She had a day planner open on her lap. The telephone was on the bedside table.

"Who are you calling?"

"I've been trying to get a hold of Red, but nobody knows where he is. I've also called a couple of friends who live nearby, but no one will come with those goddamn SLED agents outside my door. I don't care, though. I'm feeling fine. I'll walk out of here if nobody will come pick me up. I haven't done anything, and those guys can't stop me from leaving."

We were quickly coming to a point when we'd find out if Helene was right.

"I agree with you, although I don't recommend walking home. It would be best if Red came and picked you up. I don't know what Agents Wrenn and Lesher have been told to do if you try to leave. They're waiting for your discharge."

"I'm ready to get out of here."

"I went to see my chairman this morning to let him know what's going on. He agreed that this whole situation is outrageous. He's going to talk with the Dean or whoever else is necessary, so that we can get back to treating you like a patient rather than a prisoner."

"Does your guy have enough juice?"

"This has nothing to do with juice. This has to do with what's right, and how patients should be treated at the Medical University. Unless you have been charged with something, there isn't any reason those SLED guys should be on the other side of that door trying to intimidate all of us."

"I haven't been charged with anything."

I couldn't tell if she was asking a question or making a statement. "Who was the black man that was here a few minutes ago?"

"Another psychiatrist sent by my father. A little more suave than the first one. I told him I wasn't talking and to get the fuck out."

I was about to ask his name when my beeper went off. Dr. Templeton's number was illuminated. I excused myself and went out to the nursing station. This was too quick.

When we were connected, I jumped in, "Hi, Dr. Templeton, thanks for getting back with me so soon. The Governor was here ordering people around like he owned the place."

"You're welcome, Declan. Let me tell you what I know. I've talked to the Dean and to Dr. Stiles, the Chair of Psychiatry. I tried to speak with President Turner, but he's unavailable. There is definitely a lot of pressure being applied from Columbia. My advice to you is to back off. Do not become more involved. The governor's office has been leaning heavily on both the dean and the president. They have signed off on her being transported back to Columbia. The dean has already met twice today with Dr. Stiles. I think you know that Bertrum is a tough minded and principled guy. He believes this stinks to high heaven, but he's got a department to protect. Tomorrow morning, he's going to personally see Ms. Eastland and do another consultation. It's going to concur with the one from the psychiatrist at the state hospital. With two concordant opinions, they're going to get an order for involuntary commitment from a magistrate in Columbia."

"That's wrong, Preston. This can't be allowed to happen," I responded with emotion sneaking into my voice.

"I know it's wrong, Declan. Dr. Stiles knows it's wrong, and I've never seen him back down from a fight. Yet, he's bending on this and we have to as well. None of us are happy about it. That alone should tell you something about the influence that is being wielded. These are not suggestions being made. You're not going to be able to stand in the way of this. When there's a hurricane, the palmetto tree will bend all the way over to the ground and survive. The pine tree has a deep tap root and won't bend. The pine tree snaps in half."

"It's not right. We both know it."

"I beg you to let this go. Would you like me to assign another attending to the case? No one will think any less of you for stepping off. I will take over her care personally, if you prefer. Everyone knows who she is and what her father is capable of."

My face flushed with anger, but I realized Preston was only trying to give me a graceful way out. This wasn't easy for him either. Helene was right. Dr. Templeton didn't have the juice. Whatever juice he once had, he'd lost. If there was anything Templeton could do for Ms. Eastland, he'd already tried it. His advice was sincere and represented the last card he had in his hand.

In a subdued voice, I replied, "I will."

"You will what?"

"Think less of myself."

"This is not your fault."

"Preston, this young woman deserves better from me. I don't need to be relieved. I'll see this through. It is only fair to Ms. Eastland. I can handle it."

"That's fine, Declan, and I'm very sorry."

I knew he was.

I lingered for a minute at the nursing station to gather my thoughts, and then returned to Helene's room.

"That was my department head. There's nothing he can do. Your father has everyone by the balls. The chair of Psychiatry is coming tomorrow morning to personally do another consultation. It will concur with the dip-shit your father sent. With those consultations in hand, they're going to get an involuntary commitment order from a judge in Columbia. They plan to stick you in an ambulance headed to Bull Street."

The tears welled up again in her eyes, but with more defiance than fear. "Then I'm leaving right now."

"No, you're not."

She stared at me, wide-eyed. "What are they holding over your head? Are you going to give me up again?"

I tried not to let the sting of that question show.

"Your father has already given me a list of my do's and don'ts. But the governor isn't telling me what to do anymore. You're not leaving now because we're both leaving later tonight. I've got to go take care of some things. I want you to stay here. Don't act like anything is different or make any waves. Don't talk to the SLED agents. And no more phone calls. That's a state line, in case you don't already know. At some point, get together a small bag with your essentials and hide it in the closet. Take a nap if you can. It may be a late night. You won't see me again this afternoon, but I will be back for you sometime after ten o'clock. When I come for you, be ready to go."

"How are we going to get past the SLED agents?"

"I'm not sure, but I have all afternoon to figure it out, and I will. The only thing I need to know now is if you're sure that running is what you want to do. We've got the option to stand and fight. I'll do everything I can to make a stink about this and try to keep you out of the state hospital. But right now it doesn't look good. They're coming for you tomorrow."

"We have to run."

BIG JOHN'S TAVERN

I stopped back at the nursing station and pulled Helene's chart. The progress note I wrote said that she was doing better and would likely go home tomorrow. Her wound was healing exceptionally well, and she'd been afebrile for the past twenty-four hours. Given her stability, I ordered her vital signs be discontinued during the night shift. I also made two quick phone calls. On the first, I got the answer I was looking for. On the second, I got no answer at all.

I handed the chart back to Myrtle Rucker, who scolded me, "I ain't git'in that man no damn Coke."

"You know that's the Governor."

"I don't give a tinker's damn who he is. He can't order me around like he's God almighty. He don't own me and step'n fetch it isn't in my job description anymore."

"I hear you, Myrtle. You're the only person around here that's making any sense."

Our black nurses, ward secretaries, and staff had clarity about certain things that the rest of us lacked. I was positive none of my residents or medical students had any idea why the hospital was designed as a giant letter H. The black staff all knew. When the hospital was built in the 1950s, and through the 1960s, the two wings were black and white photo negatives of each other. The one hundred thirteen day Charleston Hospital Strike of 1969 had been one of the last significant events of the civil rights movement after the assassination of Martin Luther King. The strike brought Coretta Scott King, Ralph Abernathy, Andrew Young and other members of Martin Luther King's inner circle to Charleston to march with Mary Moultrie, Naomi White, Septima Clark , and other local leaders.

At the Medical College in the 1960s, African-American women like Myrtle faced segregated working conditions and a $1.30 per hour wage, which was thirty cents less than the federal minimum wage. They also had to deal with racist treatment and epithets from the white hospital workers. Ironically, the Medical College president at the time was Dr. William McCord , a native of South Africa. He must have found himself very much at home. South Carolina was South Africa without the diamond mines.

In February 1969, the local union's first president, Mary Moultrie, asked the Medical College Hospital to recognize their union, to establish a fair grievance procedure and to raise salaries by thirty cents to the federal minimum. When these requests were refused, 300 service workers at the Medical College Hospital walked off their jobs on March 19th. They were soon joined by service and maintenance workers from the Charleston County Hospital. Like most of the other public service strikes in the South during the civil rights era, violence inevitably followed. Strike organizers put up pickets around the Old Slave Market Museum, and young blacks began to skirmish with police. Naomi White was arrested after fighting with police officers, and Governor McNair ultimately placed Charleston under a curfew order.

On May 11th, more than 5,000 people marched through downtown Charleston in support of the striking hospital workers, including Southern Christian Leadership Council luminaries, the president of the United Auto Workers Walter Reuther, and five US congressmen. Mary Moultrie stirred the crowd when she famously declared to the governor that she was, "Sorry, boss," but she wasn't planning on "putting a handkerchief back on her head." Myrtle had just told a new governor the exact same thing. I was glad the spirit was still alive.

With the strike becoming a national sensation, Charleston was embarrassed. A month after the march, the South Carolina legislature voted to raise pay scales for all state employees. Governor McNair ended the curfew, and the Medical College Board of Trustees met secretly with strike leaders to hammer out an agreement.

All of those things had happened less than twenty years ago. In some ways, it was amazing how much things had changed, but it was also amazing how much had stayed the same. People loved talking about the "New South." The conditions that precipitated that strike were no longer imaginable to me. At the same time, I wasn't sure that same statement was necessarily true for Myrtle. After spending ten minutes with Governor Larry Eastland, I felt like I had a small glimpse into a world that Mary Moultrie, Naomi White and Myrtle Rucker knew much better than I.

Tuesday was our academic afternoon. There were several resident lectures, but I wasn't presenting any of them. I dismissed an idea about calling Jack. There wasn't anything he could do to help me. Involving anybody else was a mistake. I went to my office and grabbed my backpack, a couple of laboratory coats, a stethoscope and my car keys.

From the parking garage, I drove down to Calhoun Street and turned left. Halfway across town, I pulled into the Citizen's and Southern bank and went to the automatic teller. I had $130 in my wallet. I took out $350, which was the maximum allowed. I continued down

Calhoun to East Bay Street. I found a parking place on Pinckney within a block of Big John's Tavern.

Big John had played pro football for the New York Giants back in the 6os. His place was where everyone got their parlay cards for the weekend college and pro football games. On a Tuesday mid-afternoon, Big John's would be about empty. A friend of mine was working. I'd checked this out with one of my phone calls.

My friend behind the bar gave me a nod when I walked in. There were two college guys playing pool in the back, but otherwise, the bar was deserted. It was pitiful that I didn't even know the real name of the one "friend" I had decided to go to for help. He didn't know mine either. I called him "Massillon" because he had played high school football there in Ohio a decade ago. According to him, he was pretty good. I bought my parlay cards from Massillon and he was usually helpful with the point spreads. He was especially good at pro football and the Big Ten. He knew me as "Doc," which he was fine with as long as I paid up when I lost.

"What can I do you for, Doc?"

"Just a draft. Heineken if you have it." I knew they did. I thought twice about the beer, but only one wouldn't be a problem.

After pulling me a frosty one, Massillon asked again, a little more quietly, "Anything else I can do for you?"

"Actually, yes. You told me once you couldn't go back to Ohio because of some trouble you had. What was the deal with that?"

"I got into a bar fight and busted up a guy pretty good. Broke his nose and his jaw. Everybody there knew he was drunk and had started it. When he woke up, he signed out a warrant on me for assault and battery. I should've faced up to it. Instead, I decided to bolt."

"What did they do to find you?"

97

"I don't know. It's possible they didn't even try. For a long time, I was paranoid they were right on my ass. I rode a bike for two years before I worked up the nerve to go down to the DMV for a South Carolina driver's license. I was sure alarms were going to go off as soon as I stepped up to the desk. About a month later, I got my first speeding ticket. Nothing happened then either. I figured South Carolina was so backwards it wasn't plugged in to any interstate databanks. I'll tell you one thing, though, I always pay my tickets through the mail. I never go down to traffic court. No need to spit into the wind."

"Have you ever been back to Ohio?"

"Nope, never. Might be okay, but I don't wanna take the chance. Don't know if I ever will."

"If you did go back to Ohio, how would you keep from being arrested?"

"Do I look like a criminal mastermind ? Just avoid the obvious things. Don't get pulled. Don't speed, but don't drive too slowly either. Don't use your credit card. Use cash, but don't go to the automatic teller. You know, that machine takes your picture. I've also heard about sting operations where the police notify your family that you've won a raffle or lottery. All you have to do is show up at the mall to pick up your prize. The prize turns out to be a pair of cuffs. The best thing you can do is get some new IDs, a new driver's license and Social Security number."

"Do you know anybody who could get those things for me?"

"Sorry Doc. What you're talking about is a big step up from taking your parlay. Maybe Big John has connections like that, but I'm not going to ask. What's going on? Are you caught up in Operation Jackpot? That's a federal deal and a whole different ballgame.

Crossing state lines won't help you. Leaving the country won't help either if they really want you. Jackpot is reeling in a couple of big fish from Australia. They've been in here asking questions. They're serious trench-coat guys. If they're looking for you, I'd recommend that you ninety-six any plans to run. Get a good lawyer and walk in on your own."

"No, this has nothing to do with Jackpot. I know one of the guys they arrested, but I'm not involved in any of that. I'm jacked up a little bit, but nothing like the heat those smugglers are getting from the Feds. I appreciate the information, though. Don't worry about me, Mass. I'm fine."

"Sure," Massillon said. We both knew I was lying. "How about another beer?"

"Yeah, one more would be okay. I think I'll take a parlay card too. Do you have any good tips? I might need some cash money this weekend."

"No problem, man. You can't go wrong with the Bengals to win and the Browns to cover this weekend."

"Thanks, Mass."

After leaving Big John's, I went a few blocks back up East Bay Street to the new Harris Teeter. It's an old train station that had been renovated into a grocery store, but it retained the look and feel of an old train platform.

I gathered some can goods and dry goods that would keep for a while. In the produce section, I grabbed a bag of apples and a bag of oranges. I also picked up two twelve-packs of soda. On the toiletry aisle, I snagged a tube of toothpaste, a couple of brushes, a deodorant stick, shampoo and conditioner, a bottle of Motrin , a bottle of Tylenol, Iodine and a box of 4 x 4 gauzes. I checked out using my credit card in order to save cash. I packed the grocery bags into the trunk of my car and headed home with several hours to kill.

75 TRADD STREET

Pulling into my apartment at 75 Tradd Street, I decided to leave the groceries in the trunk. I stood in the driveway staring at my biggest liability. In front of me was a white 1976 Cadillac Eldorado with a navy blue rag top and a powder blue crushed velvet interior. I had bought it used for only $2,500. It got gallons per mile instead of miles per gallon. No one had ever made a car salesman happier. Abby called it my "land yacht." Whenever the department had a guest, I was always asked to pick them up at the airport. Guests felt like we'd booked them a limo. It had every electronic gadget you could imagine. It also had a huge V-8 engine that could rip up a highway when you let it unwind. Unfortunately, it was also easy to pick out of a line up. There's no way I could drive this boat around very long without being noticed.

There wasn't too much I could do about it, but I did have one idea. I went into the house and got some scissors and electrical tape. With a couple of strips and a few revisions, I changed my South Carolina license tag from "FBC 719" to "EBO 748." I knew my work wouldn't stand up to close inspection, but to a highway patrolman pulling up behind me, it'd look fairly legitimate.

Back inside, I wrote a note to my secretary telling her I was going to be away for several days for personal reasons. I wasn't on call again till Sunday, but I probably wouldn't be back by then. Dr. Donovan could help her adjust the call schedule until I returned. I asked her to call Bailey Clark and have her cancel all my upcoming surgeries. Last, I asked her to call Annette Lott, our Ambulatory Care Manager. Ms. Lott could reschedule my upcoming office patients. I apologized for ruining her day. I would put the note on her desk tonight.

The phone rang. It was Jack Brunson. He reminded me about our next basketball game on Thursday at Moultrie Middle School. He was certain our Taylor Holmes and the newspaper Taylor Holmes were one and the same. He had tried to call Taylor several times, but never got an answer. I told Jack I was going out of town and wouldn't be there either.

"What do you mean you're going out of town? We're going to need you. We're playing the Summerville Rec Department, and both of the Lawson brothers play for them. It's going to be a tough one. You sure you can't play?"

"I'm certain. I've got some family things to take care of. I'm heading up to Columbia tomorrow, and I'm not sure when I'll be back. I'll probably be gone all week."

It didn't feel good lying to Jack.

"All right, but you're killing us. Get your stuff taken care of and hurry back. I'll call you Sunday. Maybe we can go to the college and play some pickup."

"Sounds good. I hope I'll be back by Sunday. Talk to you then."

With a couple of hours to kill, I filled a back pack with some things I thought Helene might be able to wear. I tossed in a couple pairs of elastic gym shorts, some T-shirts, a dress shirt that was too small for me, a pair of sweat pants, and a Seton Hall sweat-shirt. I also packed a shoulder bag with a second pair of blue scrubs, a scrub cap, a lab coat and my stethoscope. I put on a pair of scrubs myself, changed into my tennis shoes, and sat down on the couch to think things through.

Reflection brought little comfort. Since college, I had spent twelve years working to advance my career. I was now a board certified Ob-Gyn. I had a letter to prove it. Was I getting ready to throw it all away? Was Dr. Templeton right? Would it be wisest to walk away and let the psychiatrists and lawyers sort it out?

No.

I had watched this scene play out before from the front seat of my Camaro. To completely fail someone you care about once is a horrible mistake. To do it twice is unredeemable. I was certain they were planning to give her electroshock. I'd seen more than one post-electroshock zombie wandering the grounds at Bull Street. Helene was going to be a liability when her father ran for the Senate. A mentally disabled daughter generated sympathy; a runaway daughter generated suspicion.

But it was still a no-win scenario. Years ago as fraternity pledges, we had to endure a Hell Night as part of our initiation. During Hell Night, the brothers took us in pairs, blindfolded, into a blackened room to stand before the fraternity. After eight exhausting weeks of pledging, we were desperate to get into the fraternity. The pledge class developed a very tight bond as well. They took the blindfolds off, but we couldn't see because of bright lights glaring in our eyes. They told me and Denny Ferelli that one of us had been black-balled. Allowing just enough time for panic to set in, they announced the person black-balled was Denny and jerked him out of the room. Immediately, they demanded to know what I was going to do. Was I going to stick with the fraternity or leave with Denny? If it was with the fraternity, then I was in. If it was with Denny, then I was black-balled too.

The situation was impossible. There was no option to stall. The room was an angry wall of noise yelling at me to make a decision.

"What, don't you care about the fraternity?"

"Don't you want to be a brother?"

"Where's your loyalty?"

"What's the matter with you?"

"Are you retarded?"

"Are you going to step up and be a brother or be a God Damn Independent?"

"Come on man, make up your mind!"

The second I said, "I want the fraternity," I was ashamed. I've been ashamed of that moment ever since.

Of course, the room immediately erupted again.

"What's the matter with you?"

"Where's your loyalty to Denny?"

"Where's your loyalty to your pledge class?"

"What kind of brother would you be?"

"You're a worthless piece of shit."

"Get him out of here."

"Guys like you would ruin the frat."

The brothers put the blindfold back over my eyes and led me out of the room.

Of course, there wasn't any right answer to that question. Whatever I said, I was going to eat a ration of shit. Both Denny and I were in the fraternity. That had been decided long before Hell Night. Denny was one of the most stand-up guys in the fraternity. I liked him, but I couldn't ever look him in the eye. He never once gave me any grief for selling him out. He never had to. I regretted that answer every time I saw him. I'd give almost anything to get that decision back.

I was in that situation again. There was no winning answer. But, there was one answer I couldn't live with. If I was going to lose no matter what I did, then I needed to make the move that would allow me to sleep at night. If that Ob-Gyn board certification meant anything, I couldn't let those state thugs drag one of my patients off to Columbia against her will.

About nine-thirty, I put on my white coat and my MUSC ID badge.

Along with my shoulder bag and back pack, I grabbed my dark blue Seton Hall Pirates baseball cap and pulled a pair of bandage scissors out of a drawer in an old dresser in the foyer. I headed out to the Caddy and drove up Ashley to MUSC. I parked on Sabin Street which runs behind the main hospital and is generally used for service deliveries. Since it wasn't a patient entrance, it was poorly lit. I hadn't seen any security cameras when I drove down it earlier in the afternoon.

MUSC WOMEN'S SERVICES

Women's Services had always been the red-headed step child at MUSC. The profit margin on Women's Services didn't rate the hospital's attention, and it was always the last floor in the hospital to be refurbished. We had the same carpet for years. It's interesting what becomes of a carpet after years of exposure to a busy gynecologic and obstetrical service. Hospital administration criticized Ob-Gyn for not having more privately insured patients. No carriage-trade patients were going to walk down a carpeted corridor whose stains made it look like a giant game of Twister. We called the entranceway to Women's Services the "Hall of Shame." On this particular night, besides the stained carpet, the "Hall of Shame" featured a gigantic red trash can labeled "Biological Wastes," a cart from dietary overloaded with half-eaten dinner trays, and a broken recliner. My heart swelled with pride.

The Antepartum unit, Labor and Delivery, and Gynecology were on the west side of the hospital, and the postpartum unit and the normal Newborn Nursery were on the east side. Helene Eastland's room was number 567 on the west wing.

Arriving on Labor and Delivery, I bumped into one of my senior partners, Helen Berger, sitting at the nursing station. "What are you doing here? Pretty sure I'm on call tonight, but if you want to take over, feel free," she stated in her matter-of-fact manner.

Helen was the antithesis of warm and fuzzy. She had come along at a time when Ob-Gyn was still a man's surgical specialty. She was a fantastic doctor, an excellent surgeon, and the unquestioned general when she covered Labor and Delivery. Sadly, most of the women pioneers like Helen, had endured a demeaning training gauntlet. As a consequence, Helen had sacrificed empathy and softness for a wary and bitter outer shell.

"No such luck," I answered. "Eunice Fogleson paged me and thinks she's in labor. I figured I'd come in and head her off."

"That wasn't necessary," Helen replied. "We could have handled her."

Helen never admitted she needed help with anything. Eunice Fogleson was a patient everyone knew and dreaded. This was her third pregnancy with us, and she was as crazy as a bed bug. She thought she was in labor whenever she felt two contractions within the same passing of the sun. It was rare for Ms. Fogleson to come in and not demand that I be notified of her "desperate situation." On more than one occasion, I'd come in to reassure her that all was well.

On this night, I hoped Ms. Fogleson was doing well. I silently thanked her for providing my cover for hanging around Labor and Delivery. I told Helen I didn't mind waiting around for Ms. Fogleson. It would be easier for all if I saw her. The ward secretary was to give me a page when Ms. Fogleson arrived. I also asked her who was the ward secretary tonight on the Antepartum-Benign Gynecology unit. She told me it was Susie Belton who was relatively new. I didn't know her.

As I walked back down the Labor and Delivery hallway, I almost bumped into Ferdy Eldenz as she came out of one of the labor rooms. "Hey, Dr. Murphy. What are you doing here tonight?"

"Ms. Fogleson is coming in. I thought it would be better if I hung around. She'll be over the top like always. How were the All-Stars? I'm sorry I didn't make it. I was too worn out. I laid down for a nap Saturday afternoon and slept through the night. I would have loved to have seen them."

"The All-Stars were terrific." Ferdy said. "We had a ton of fun, but it would've been better if you were there. They played two really long sets. They closed with 'Mean Old Train' and 'HooDoo Blues' and blew the roof off."

"Now I feel even worse," I said with a grin.

"They said they might be back in Charleston in the spring opening for the Nighthawks at Guillard."

"That would be an awesome show. You can pencil me in."

"So it's a date then?"

"A date then," I replied with a nod.

"Okay," she said, as she turned to walk away. There was an obvious twitch in her step. About twenty feet down the hallway, she turned her head back and gave me another smile. God, I hope I'm able to keep that date.

Leaving Labor and Delivery, I walked back down the "Hall of Shame." After dropping my note off on my secretary's desk, I walked over to the normal newborn nursery and rang the bell for entry. With my white coat and ID badge, they rang me in, but I was immediately confronted by a burley charge nurse. "May I help you?"

"I'm Dr. Murphy. I'm the OB who delivered Ms. Wingo. I'm getting ready to see her and wanted to check on her baby first. I heard it was having problems. Can you tell me which bassinet the Wingo baby is in?"

"The Wingo baby is in the back corner over there. Bassinet number twelve. It's not having any problems that I'm aware of. Some mild hypoglycemia early on, but that has worked itself out. Ms. Wingo is breastfeeding and we haven't had to supplement the baby at all."

I went to the bassinet and looked over the chart for a couple of minutes. The charge nurse was right. Baby Wingo was stable. The nurse taking care of the Wingo baby was busy feeding another child, so it was easy for me to take the bandage scissors from my pocket and cut the ID bracelet off baby Wingo's ankle. I slipped both the scissors and the ID bracelet back into my coat pocket.

After visiting the nursery, I went over to the 5 East postpartum unit. I needed to kill another fifteen minutes, so I went to see Ms. Wingo. At about ten-thirty p.m., I headed back to the Labor and Delivery unit using the access hallway, which avoided the main corridor and the view of Agent Lesher. Having Lesher on duty was an unexpected plus. Lesher was the younger of the two agents, and, hopefully, not as seasoned or as cynical as I knew Agent Wrenn to be.

I told the Labor and Delivery nurses that Ms. Fogleson had decided to not come in, so I was heading home. I waited for the main hallway to empty, and then I exited through the back doorway leading to the service elevators.

Baby Wingo's ID bracelet in my pocket immediately triggered the BabyNet security system. The alarm could be heard throughout the fifth floor Women's Service. I dropped the ID bracelet into the garbage can outside the double doors and quickly re-entered the Labor and Delivery unit. The security alarm barely raised an eyebrow among the regular staff. Every other day or so, one of the nurses walks a new family down to their car and forgets to deactivate the ID badge before exiting the unit. A security alarm late at night was more unusual, but was still assumed to be a false alarm by most of the staff. I picked up the hall phone and called the 5 West Antepartum-Benign Gynecology nursing station.

"5 West. This is Ms. Belton. May I help you?"

"Yes, ma'am. There's a problem on post- partum. A man in a gray sweatshirt and black jeans just left the unit with one of our babies, setting off the security alarm. He crossed over into the Children's Hospital. Could you please ask the SLED agent sitting over there to come to postpartum and help us find this guy? We've called MUSC security, but he's much closer than they are."

"Oh, my goodness," Ms. Belton said. "I'll get him right now."

"Thanks, Ms. Belton. We need him as soon as possible. We can't let this guy get too far away."

I watched from around the corner as Ms. Belton went to talk to Agent Lesher. As soon as I saw him get up and run toward post-partum, I headed to room 567.

When I got there Helene was up and ready to go. "When I heard the alarm I knew it was time."

"Here, put on these scrubs."

Helene immediately pulled her T-shirt over her head and was standing there unabashedly in only her panties. I had a million things racing through my mind, but they all slowed and pulled over to the side of the road as I admired how striking she was. Helene put on the scrub top and bottoms while I retrieved her travel bag. I gave her a white lab coat and cloth surgical cap. She tucked her hair up into the cap. While she was doing that, I stuffed some towels, an extra blanket, and her pillows under her sheet. I formed them, as best I could, into a human shape. It had worked for Clint Eastwood in *Escape from Alcatraz.* I draped a stethoscope around her neck and stepped back to check out the look. Satisfied, I peeked outside to make sure there was no sign of Agent Lesher. We turned off her lights, closed her door, and headed off in the opposite direction from the postpartum unit and the newborn nursery.

Sooner or later, Lesher would figure out he was on a snipe hunt. Hopefully, he'd think it was accidental and not put two and two together. Even if he did poke his head in to check on Helene, I counted on him being enough of a gentleman to not flip on the lights and roust her. Agent Wrenn probably would. Time would tell how long our deception holds.

Once in the elevator, I whispered to Helene to keep her head down and face away from the console. She looked pretty convincing until I noticed her flip-flops. Probably one of a dozen things I hadn't thought of. We left the hospital through the Barre Street entrance. The security guard never gave us a glance. Just two doctors leaving the hospital at a late hour. We walked quickly down Barre Street and turned left onto Sabin where my car was parked.

"Nice car," Helene said as we got in. Helene took off her scrub cap and shook out her hair. She laughed, "Thanks a lot, Doc."

"What do you mean?"

"This doesn't help my reputation," she replied as she handed me back the scrub cap.

For the first time, I realized it was a pharmaceutical company give-away that prominently advertised Terazol cream for vaginal yeast infections. I smiled and apologized. I marveled at how Helene could find humor in the middle of such a stressful situation. I turned right onto Calhoun Street and headed for the bridge over the Ashley River.

HIGHWAY 17 SOUTH

Highway 17 South crosses the Ashley River and runs about sixty miles through the heart of the South Carolina Low Country. During the day, it's a beautiful drive through small towns like Ravenel, Hollywood, Edisto, and Garden Corners. It crosses the Ashley, Stono and Asheepoo Rivers in succession and cuts across swamp and marshland that seep up onto the shoulder of the road at high tide and a full moon. You can't help but stop at one of several roadside stands to sample local jams, jellies, apple butter, or relishes and buy an ice-cold Ball jar of peach cider.

At night, Highway 17 becomes more ominous. The long dark stretches of two-lane blacktop are overhung by ancient live oaks. Their tangled, gnarly branches and gauzy Spanish moss provide shade during the day, but at night, they block out any hint of moonlight or starlight. There's a perpetual mist that arrives at dusk and hangs above the tree line. A black preacher once told me that the mist comes so God doesn't have to see what happens in the fen after dark. I'm not a nervous driver, but I always believed a wrong turn or a broken transmission anywhere along Highway 17 South between Charleston and I-95 might lead to me waking up on ice in a chipped, stained bathtub missing a kidney.

Just over the Ashley River Bridge, Highway 17 is all strip malls, fast food joints and car dealerships. Locals call it the Savannah Highway Automile and it was surprisingly quiet. I turned off the highway at the Citadel Mall and pulled up beside a Citizen's and

Southern automatic teller. I took out another $350 and we turned back out onto Highway 17 heading south. We continued to drive in silence. Helene was probably wondering how in the world I was going to help her. I was wondering exactly the same thing. About twenty miles south of Charleston, we hit Ravenel and I stopped at a Scotsman convenience store. I only needed about half a tank.

Through the open window, I told Helene, "You better stay in the car. Can I get you anything? I'm going to grab something to eat."

"No thanks. I'm not hungry. Maybe a Sprite."

"Sure, no problem. Anything else? I bought some toiletries this afternoon. I think I have all the basics." I stammered a little bit, but finally sputtered out, "Um, any kind of protection or anything like that?"

After traveling in silence for almost an hour, Helene finally laughed. "Are you asking about condoms?"

"No, no, not that, you know, I mean...Umm...."

"Feminine hygiene?"

"Yes, exactly. That's what I mean."

"No, I'm fine. I packed some pads at the hospital. They're in my bag."

"Great, good thinking. I'd much rather buy the Sprite."

At the check-out counter, I asked the attendant how much farther till Highway 17 hit I-95. I also asked her for a South Carolina, Georgia and Florida map. I put a Sprite and a Mountain Dew on the counter. Strategically placed on a rack next to the cash register was a beguiling display of Little Debbie Chocolate Peanut Butter Wafers. Twenty-five cents for a package of two. I was always sweet on my Little Debbie, one girl who never disappoints. I took three packages, two for me, and I was certain Helene would go for one. On an impulse purchase roll, I also picked up a can of Bar-B-Que flavored Vienna sausages. I paid with my credit card and thanked the cashier for the help.

I fired up the V-8 engine and pulled back onto the highway, making sure I scattered some gravel as I fishtailed out of the Scotsman parking lot. About a mile further on down the road, I turned into an empty bank parking lot, swung the car around, and pulled back out onto Highway 17 heading north. It was time to find out if SLED used Occam's razor.

"What are you doing?" Helene asked.

HIGHWAY 17 NORTH

"This is my big move," I told Helene. "If they're going to be hunting you, which I assume is a yes, I want to give them some misdirection. I used my money card at the automatic teller, and I paid for the gas with my credit card. I also bought a Georgia/Florida map. If these guys can follow the nose on their face, they'll head south. Didn't you say that you lived in the Florida Keys? What's best for us is for them to be swarming south Florida."

"I lived in Savannah for a while too."

"So much the better. Gives them someplace else to look. Your father has a lot of resources, but I'm not sure he can look everywhere at once."

"Where are we going to be?"

"Well, the worst place for us to be is on the road. This car sticks out like a sore thumb. If the highway patrol is alerted, sooner or later, we'll get stopped. We need a place to lay low."

"Where's that?"

"Garden City Beach. My parents have a condo there. Garden City is way off the grid."

"Are you sure? They'll pull everything they have on your family. I'd think a beach condo might be one of the first places they'd look."

"My parents own it with four other families. Old army buddies. It's under a limited partnership and my parents aren't officers. They rotate weeks. My parents don't have it again until New Year's. I don't know who has it this week, but lots of times people don't use it during the winter. Being early December, we might be lucky. I called up there this afternoon and didn't get an answer. If we get there and somebody's home, we'll say sorry, our mistake, and move on. But I think it's empty. Families take the condo Sunday through Sunday, so if no one's home, we'll have a safe place through the weekend. Anyway, that's my plan. Got any other ideas?"

"I'm thinking about it. A few days would be pretty good right now. Gives us time to develop some options. Are you sure it's a good idea to drive back through Charleston?"

"I'm not sure of anything right now. Hopefully, Lesher won't figure out you're missing till the morning. Even if they already know, I'd be surprised if they've figured things out well enough to put out an APB on my car. The first thing Lesher will do is turn the hospital upside down. He'll check with security for anything they might have seen. I think Lesher will put off calling Agent Wrenn for as long as possible. At least, I know I would, if I were him. I don't believe they'll think about me until Wrenn gets involved. Even if they know you're missing, I think it's going to take them a while to start looking for us in this car."

"It's a gamble."

"I know. Promise we won't linger. We're going through Charleston like shit through a goose."

Thirty minutes later, we crossed back over the Ashley River Bridge into downtown and headed for the Cooper River Bridge and Mt. Pleasant. We didn't hold our breath, but we were quiet as we drove through town. We were the only car on the crosstown.

"Hey, do me favor. Open these up for me," I asked, reaching into the bag from the Scotsman. "If I'm going to get arrested, I'm at least going to enjoy my Little Debbie first. I got a couple of extras if you'd like one."

Helene rifled through the bag, pulling out her Sprite.

"What the hell are these?" She had found my Vienna sausages and was examining them in the dashboard light. It was more of an accusation than it was a question. Helene hit the console button that rolled down the window. She unceremoniously tossed out my sausages.

"What are you doing? Those are good We don't need to get pulled over for littering."

"I'd rather go to the State Mental Hospital than open up those sausages. They're disgusting." There wasn't going to be any more discussion.

By the time we passed Snee Farm further up Highway 17 North, we both began to feel more comfortable.

"Want to listen to some music?" I asked.

"Sure. What do you have?"

"All Springsteen, all the time. Do you like the E Street Band?"

"The Boss is the best. Red took me to see him in Atlanta about a year ago. Best show I've ever seen."

"When I went up to Seton Hall for college, I'd never heard of him. In Jersey though, Springsteen was already a legend. He played the campus pub my freshman year and came back a few years later for a concert in the gym." I slipped the *Born to Run* cassette into the player. We laughed at the irony of "*Born To Run.*" The second track was called "*Backstreets*" and it wasn't as funny. I knew in my heart that we were tying faith between our teeth and as we headed up the highway towards the beach, I had a bad feeling that we were running for our lives on these backstreets.

We listened to the rest of the album as we drove through the desolate Francis Marion Forest between Charleston and Georgetown, South Carolina. The Francis Marion Forest is an impenetrable old-stand pine forest and black water swamp. During the Revolutionary War, General Francis Marion kept his troops hidden from the British in this forest and earned the nickname, The Swamp Fox. By the time we reached Georgetown, Helene had fallen asleep, so I turned down the music. As my adrenalin rush wore off, I was getting sleepy myself. I opened the window to get some brisk air in my face. Fortunately, north of Georgetown, Highway 17 held your attention with brightly illuminated beach bars, pirate-themed seafood restaurants, and putt-putt golf adventure lands. We passed DeBordieu Colony, which the locals called "DebbieDoo," Pawley's Island, Litchfield Beach and Murrell's Inlet. Finally, I turned off onto Atlantic Avenue, a mile long access road to Garden City Beach. It was about two-thirty in the morning. I prayed the condo was empty.

GARDEN CITY BEACH

Garden City Beach is a glorified sand bar, about four blocks wide, separated from the mainland by a narrow salt creek and a mile-wide mind-set. Atlantic Avenue crosses the tidal creek and dead ends at Waccamaw Drive. Six months earlier, the intersection would still be pulsating with the humid heat of a libido-driven summer night, crowded with the overflow from the arcade on one corner and the Garden City pier across the street. On this December night, the intersection was abandoned as we came onto the Island.

In the winter, Garden City has a less festive feel. Without the summer vacationers, the beach became a little shadier and seedier. The year-round residents were mostly retirees who weren't looking for anything other than to be left alone. The others worked around the fringes and lived in the rows of trailers that filled the space between Highway 17 and the Intra-coastal Waterway. I felt safe on this strip of beach. People who came to Garden City in the winter weren't interested in being found or in trying to find anyone else.

Directly in front of us at the Waccamaw Drive stoplight was the Kingfisher Inn. Garden City used to be entirely residential, with classic, low-slung driftwood and cinder block beach houses. The Kingfisher was the first condo built, and it created a firestorm. Over the next ten years, many more were added, despite protest. Oddly, everything to the right of the Kingfisher remained residential, while almost everything to the left was now condominium.

We turned left and drove about a mile to the Horizon East condo. Pulling into the parking lot, Helene looked up at the building. The Horizon East was built soon after the Kingfisher. It was a soulless, featureless, cement box about eight stories tall built to withstand a category five hurricane. Anyone who ever stayed there never doubted that it would.

"Looks nice," Helene said sounding half-asleep.

"Let's leave our stuff in the car. If anybody's here, we'll pretend we're coming home after a late night out, and got off on the wrong floor."

"And if somebody is here? "

"Plan B," I said. I wasn't convincing, since I had no idea what Plan B was if some of my parent's friends came to the door at three in the morning.

We took the elevator to the fifth floor and knocked on the door to Horizon East 504. When there was no answer, I slipped the key into the lock and opened the door quietly. The apartment looked empty, but it was dark. I checked each of the bedrooms.

I turned back to Helene and nodded that it was all clear. That relief, as well as the weight of the entire day, hit us both simultaneously.

"Can we get the rest of the stuff out of the car in the morning?" Before I could answer, Helene had found a pillow on a closet shelf and curled up on a bare twin bed in the second bedroom. She was asleep almost immediately.

"That sounds good to me," I responded to no one in particular. I covered Helene with a blanket from the same shelf, and then I laid down on the couch in the family room. I had no idea what tomorrow would bring, but I couldn't worry about it anymore tonight.

"Good night, Helene," I whispered under my breath.

Wednesday morning brought the familiar and comforting cacophony of the beachfront. From the sound of the breaking waves, I could tell it was high tide. Sunshine sliced in through the vertical blinds. After a quick trip to the bathroom, I went out to the porch. The chill off the ocean was invigorating. It was a low winter sun. Only a few folks were on the beach, and the back patio of the Horizon East was empty.

First on my list of things to do was moving the car. Horizon East had a surface parking lot. With the building almost empty, the land yacht was way too obvious. The Water's Edge was next door to Horizon East and had a parking garage. In the summer, it would be packed, and their security would be on patrol. This time of year, it wasn't busy either. No one would pay any attention to one more car. More importantly, the Eldorado would be out of the line of sight from Waccamaw Drive.

I got one of the grocery carts kept in the supply closet on the ground floor. After rolling it over to Water's Edge, I loaded our groceries and backpacks. Next to the elevators, I dropped a quarter into one of the newspaper stands and picked up a copy of the Charleston paper.

Back upstairs, I could hear Helene showering as I unpacked the groceries and fixed a couple bowls of cereal. I cut up some orange and apple slices and dropped some bread into the toaster. While I waited for the toast to pop, I inspected the pantry. Each family had their own shelf. The "Murphy" shelf was well stocked with bourbon, rum, gin and dry vermouth. Like a lot of former military families, Mom and Dad kept a regimented schedule. A Virginia Gentleman Bourbon on the rocks for my dad and a dry martini for my mom promptly at five p.m. I was probably responsible for the rum at some point. Over the stove, we had another shelf with salt, pepper, sugar, various other spices, and some unused canned goods.

I buttered the toast when it popped up, and put it on the table with some cinnamon and sugar. There were some tea bags on the Garrett's shelf. They wouldn't mind. Helene emerged from the shower as I was pouring the tea. She was wearing the scrubs I had given her last night.

"How would you like a bowl of Honey Nut Cheerios?"

"I'm starving."

Although we needed to have a long conversation, we weren't ready yet and ate in silence. After breakfast, we cleared the dishes and went out on the porch. We watched a young boy and his dog repeatedly chase out the tide, and then beat a hasty retreat back up the beach as the tide inevitably turned.

"Let's see if there is anything in the paper," I said, when we returned to the apartment.

"I'll make up the beds. Where are the linens?"

"Check the closet between the main bedroom and the master bathroom. Each family has a shelf with their bed sheets and pillow cases. Thanks."

"Anything in the paper about our big breakout?"

"Not that I can find. I'm not surprised. Even if they found out you were missing last night, it would've been too late to make the newspaper. Is this something that'll ever make the paper? Don't you think your father will keep it off the radar?"

"I've been on the run for a long time, and it's never been reported. SLED does my father's dirty work, and they do it quietly. They'll know who they're looking for. The local police and highway patrol will just get a description and a license number. They won't know who we are or why they're picking us up. They'll be told that you're dangerous and that I'm a victim. If we get stopped by the police, you need to keep your hands in the air and your mouth shut. Understand?"

Taken aback, I only managed to offer a meek nod of my head.

"If they find us, then they've found us," Helene continued. "Like you said, you've already made your 'big move.' If this doesn't work, it's my problem. We need to be in agreement on that. If not, I'm going to walk out that door, find the nearest police station, and turn myself in. Are we clear?"

"Crystal clear sir," I said with a smile and mock salute. "I can't afford to be simultaneously in trouble with work, SLED, and you."

"How much trouble are you in at work?"

"I'm not sure. It's not going to take them long to figure out what's going on. You missing, me missing. Someone might be able to piece the puzzle together. I feel bad about bailing out on my other patients and the residents. Today is my OR day. I had three cases scheduled."

"What will happen?"

"They'll make up a lie that I'm sick, and will offer for someone else to stand in. Two of the patients are private. They'll probably want to reschedule. One woman is from the resident service, and has a tubo-ovarian abscess. She was just added on yesterday. I'm sure the residents will find another attending for that case. I've never failed to show up for surgery before."

"Do you want to call in?"

"No. No phone calls. That'd be a big mistake. No calls out, and don't answer the phone if it rings. We need to keep quiet until we can figure out our next step."

Helene nodded her agreement, but said nothing. Neither of us was prepared to tackle the question of "the next step." I finished reading the paper, and Helene stretched out on the couch.

"Anything else in the paper?" Helene asked after a few minutes.

"Not much. Big fire in West Ashley last night. I'm surprised we didn't see or hear the fire engines. Most of the front page is still focused on Operation Jackpot. The chief Federal prosecutor is a guy named Thomas Sheprow. Sheprow says it is the biggest combined federal-state interdiction ever in the Southeast. Bigger than anything they've ever done in Florida. He says it's the first time they've used the new federal law to go after a 'drug smuggling enterprise.' He's calling the guys in charge 'Kingpins,' Looks to me like he's planning to run for something. There's an article on all the shrimp boats and property the Task Force has confiscated, and another one about the people they're still looking for."

"What does that one say?"

"The older Holmes brother and his partner Rhett are in custody in Australia, but extraditing them is going to be a challenge. Australia doesn't have a law analogous to our criminal enterprise charge. Australia can only hold them for another month. Holmes is being represented by a guy named Tom Hughes, who's one of Australia's most eminent lawyers and a former attorney general. Good to know that money talks worldwide. The other major players are Croft and Haley, who are still on the lam. The paper says Croft sent the police a taunting letter claiming he was in the jungle. No coppers would ever find him. He seems to have some big brass balls."

"Does it say anything about Red?"

"Red who?"

"Red who was with me. Panama Red. His last name is Redding."

"Arthur Redding of Irmo?" I asked, knowing what the answer would be.

"Yes, Arthur Redding. But he hasn't been from Irmo for a long time. I've been with Red ever since I left Columbia."

"It says they arrested him in Savannah Monday night. I'm sorry."

"I thought he might go to Savannah. We had a place on Tybee Island, and he had money stashed there. I was afraid he was busted. I couldn't get him at any of the numbers I had."

"This keeps getting better and better. Are you mixed up with Operation Jackpot, too?"

"Red was involved. Back in Columbia, we used to hang around with Bill Haley and Leon Croft. Bill is a redneck with a bad monkey on his back. If they want to catch him, all they have to do is stake out the luxury boxes at the next Carolina game. He never misses a home game. He will be drunk and coked-up by halftime. Croft is an ass-hole. I don't know where he might be, but the notion that he could be the 'mastermind' of anything is a joke. He ought to turn himself in. No jury in the world could ever be convinced he was the 'kingpin' of a criminal enterprise. To answer your question though, I wasn't part of anything. I just know things. Sheprow wants me to tell what I know to their grand jury."

"Jesus, when is that supposed to happen?"

"I'm not certain. I think Friday. I just got the subpoena yesterday."

"When?"

"The black guy who came to my room was from Jackpot. He gave me the subpoena yesterday morning."

"You told me he was a psychiatrist. That's not right. There's a big difference between SLED looking for you and having the Feds on your tail."

"I know," Helene answered quietly. "I'm sorry. I should've told you. I was so angry and scared. I felt like I was drowning. You were the only chance I had. I was afraid you might bail if you knew I was tangled up with Operation Jackpot."

"I should've known the score. If your father and the Operation Jackpot task force are collaborating, I don't think we have much of a chance."

"I don't think they're collaborating. My father doesn't collaborate. He takes advantage. Operation Jackpot is probably how my father found me. I've been thinking about it for a couple of days. The night before the SLED guys showed up, Red got a call in my room. Whoever it was, told him SLED was coming for me, and if he was smart, he'd clear out. If he tried to take me with him, they'd pick him up before he got out of the building. Red said he'd try to come back for me, but I never heard from him again."

"So who called?"

"I believe that Operation Jackpot was preparing to pick Red up. The Feds must have known that Red was with me, so they gave dear old dad a courtesy call. I think my father had SLED call to warn Red off. It's bad PR for the Governor's daughter to be in the room when a drug smuggler is busted. Even South Carolina newspapers will pick up on that nugget. So, Red gets

125

picked up somewhere else, and SLED shows up to whisk me back to Columbia. Neatly done, wouldn't you say?"

"What do you know that the Feds want you to testify about?"

"I know how Red makes his money, and where he hides it. Most of these guys are real fuck-ups. Smuggling is the only thing they've ever done right. They're always bragging about their big scores. If you hang around them long enough, you'll get a pretty good idea about how their operation works."

"Did you take part in any of the smuggling?"

"No, not really. Sometimes I helped Red take money done to the Caribbean. We took boats and private planes. Leon and Bill set-up an organizational pyramid for the smuggling. At the bottom were the boat captains and crews, the people who provided the off-loading sites and security who watched for Coast Guard and DNR boats. From there, you move up the chain to on-site supervisors, transporters, and distributors. As you get near the top, you have the project organizers, financiers, lawyers, and money launderers. At the very top, you have Leon and Bill. You'll never meet a prouder pair of CEOs."

"What did Panama Red do?"

"Red was involved in planning, and usually supervised the off-loading. Leon also liked to send Red to the islands to move cash and negotiate with the island banks. Leon thought that Red and I gave each other good cover. Leon said it looked like we were on 'spring break.' Red knew banking and was a pretty smooth talker."

"Didn't you worry about getting caught? At least, wonder if you're doing something wrong?"

"It's only weed, Declan. What was I going to do, apply to medical school? I was a hell of a lot more worried about staying out of my father's hands, than I was a pot bust. There was a lot of money being made. When you're on the run, cash is what keeps you safe. The corporation was thriving, and there were dividends and bonuses for everyone. We drove Jags, Mercedes-Benzes, and Volvos. We vacationed for months at a time in Jamaica and the Caymans. At times, there was so much cash, it couldn't be counted. They had to weigh it. I'm not going to say that I didn't enjoy it, because I did. But mostly, it was like living in Sherwood Forest. Being with Leon and Bill's band of merry men kept me safe from the evil king. I didn't have the luxury of taking a moral stand."

"I'm sorry. I wasn't making a judgment. I just wish I had known about the Jackpot subpoena. The FBI has a longer reach than even your father."

"I know. It wasn't fair to keep that from you."

"We might have been able to trade grand jury testimony for protection from your father."

"You still don't get it. My father would never allow me to testify in front of the grand jury. Commitment to the State Mental Hospital solves the grand jury problem."

"Then, that's how we beat him. We hide out here until it's time for you to testify. Once you've testified, there won't be any reason to have you declared incompetent."

"Having me committed for being mentally defective works whether it's before or after I testify. Don't try to think like my father. He doesn't think like normal people. What he wants to do to me comes from a lot of places. Besides, I don't have any intention of testifying."

"Why not? If they wanted you in jail, they would have arrested you yesterday. They only want information. The Feds might be willing to make a deal in order to get it."

"Then what? Testifying is a bigger risk than my father. The newspaper refers to Leon and Bill as 'gentlemen smugglers.' The stories make it sound like they're a bunch of fun-loving, beach-combing Parrot-heads, whose hobby got a little bit out of hand. Think about where the marijuana comes from, and how much it's worth. They started out smuggling Jamaican ganja, but that stuff is crap. The real money is in Colombian weed. Top-quality Colombian sells for two hundred fifty to three hundred dollars a pound, which is double what they got for their Jamaican grass. So Leon started getting his weed from Santa Marta, which is a horrid little shit-hole at the base of the Sierra Nevada de Santa Marta on Colombia's Caribbean coast. Santa Marta Gold is the best there is. To keep the Gold flowing, Leon only did business with the big-time Colombian suppliers. Leon also figured out that you had to grease the palms of local police and military. Smugglers who don't know what they're doing end up in Colombian prisons, which are brutal.

Despite his pea-sized brain, Leon somehow, kept the Colombians happy by spreading around a lot of cash, and by delivering huge runs. Believe it or not, most marijuana is sold on consignment. The weed only has value if it makes it to America. The Colombians don't get paid until the pot is successfully sold to distributors in the United States. If a shipment gets intercepted or lost at sea, it can be written off because the weed is so cheap to the suppliers. In that business model, smugglers who can reliably deliver large loads safely into the distributor's trucks are valuable business associates. Leon Croft and Bill Haley are highly respected in Colombia."

"You're afraid of the Colombians?"

"Of course, I am. Those guys protect their investments, and they are cold-blooded. Red told me a story about one of their runs. Their boat waited offshore, and the Colombians motored out in these long canoes filled with bales of marijuana. The Colombians recognized one of the crew as a police informant. They put him in a life vest, put floats under his bound arms, and attached big hooks to his belt. They cut his legs to draw blood and threw him overboard attached to a long line. They used him as shark bait all the way across the Caribbean. The screaming stopped after a few hours."

"That was down there. They wouldn't come after you up here. That's a lot of risk for an operation that's already fallen apart."

"The Colombians do business with a lot of people. People who want to get on their good side or stay on their good side. Hibben Leary from McClellanville is the captain of the shrimp boat *Gulf Princess II*. A couple of years ago, Leary successfully unloaded eighteen thousand pounds of weed for Leon Unfortunately, he and his crew were arrested after they were found washing marijuana residue off their deck in St Helena's Sound. One of his crew, a kid named Nick Duffy, turned government witness and testified to a Federal grand jury. On the eve of the trial, Duffy disappeared. He's not been heard from since. Hibben Leary spent a year in jail after refusing to testify before the grand jury. He's still alive. People think we're only talking about pot, but the money involved is serious."

"Kind of exciting to not know who might come through the door—local police, SLED, the FBI or Colombian assassins," I said with a grin.

"Yeah, really exciting. I don't want to talk about this anymore. What's done is done. I've got nothing to say to the grand jury. I'm going to make a list of the things we need."

After completing her do-list and laying it on the dining room table, Helene excused herself. She was tired and needed a nap. I could see the weariness in her eyes. It was equal parts physical and emotional. I turned off the television and tried to think of what our options might be. The solution had now become more complex.

Doctors always expect alternatives. If a patient comes in with a pelvic infection, we put her on oral antibiotics. If that doesn't work, we'll go to IV antibiotics. If that doesn't work, we can change antibiotics or add more coverage. If that doesn't work, we'll look for an abscess to drain. There is always another move to make. 504 Horizon East was only an intermediate move. We were going to need several more smart chess moves in order to avoid being checkmated.

SLED was out there looking for us. If the Feds were looking for us too, that was even worse. The Jackpot task force had resources available to them from five different Federal agencies, including the FBI. It was only a matter of time until they found us.

The police weren't an option. They would pass us along to SLED. The same was true for MUSC. The Dean was spineless. At MUSC, all the shots were called by the President, Gordon Turner. He was a career politician who had been Chairman of the South Carolina Republican Party prior to becoming the university President. Turner had been nominated to the MUSC Board of Trustees by Governor Eastland himself. There were few other people in the state more invested in Governor Eastland's political career than President Turner. Dr. Templeton would be sympathetic, but he'd proven himself ineffectual. The South Carolina Medical

Association was also fool's gold. If Governor Eastland snaps at them, the SCMA will roll over and expose its belly like a neutered dog. Helene's friends had either been locked up by the biggest federal anti-crime task force of the twentieth century or weren't taking her calls. If it weren't so desperate, it would be funny.

About five p.m., I made myself a gin and Wink and started on supper. We didn't have much, but that was okay. I didn't know how to make much. My specialty was Chili Spaghetti, which is Pop-Tart simple. Step one, warm up some Hormel Chili. Step two, boil some spaghetti. Step three; pour the chili over the spaghetti. Wanting to add a little flare, I found an onion in the pantry, diced it up, and put it on the chili with some grated cheddar cheese. I also put butter and garlic seasoning on some white bread, and put it under the broiler to make garlic toast.

The garlic toast brought Helene out of the bedroom.

"Smells good."

"Hope it's good. Get yourself something to drink, and I'll serve the spaghetti. Good nap?"

"Yeah, I always sleep great at the beach. What are you drinking?"

"My own concoction. Gin and Wink. Want me to make you one?"

"I would love a gin and Wink."

"You got it," I said, as I ladled the chili over the spaghetti.

We both enjoyed dinner. I made each of us a couple more drinks and we took them out on the porch along with a blanket.

"So what did you do all afternoon?" Helene asked. "I know you didn't sleep."

"I tried to think of somewhere we could go when we leave here. Someone who might be willing to help us.

131

How are we going to get more money? You know, just regular stuff."

"Come up with any good ideas?"

"Not really. We've got to get out of South Carolina. It would be best if we could get out of the country. Do you have a passport?"

"I do, but don't you think Immigration will be on alert?"

"Probably. I don't know about you, but I don't know anybody who lives in another country. Do you remember Bill Parsons from high school?"

"Just vaguely."

"Bill was my best friend in high school, but I haven't seen him in years. He's a banker in North Carolina. Lives in a small town called North Wilkesboro. I know he'd let us stay with him. He could also help us get some more cash. From there, we might be able to plan a way into Canada or Mexico, or come up with some other ideas."

"I don't know about Canada. Sounds cold. Most of the people I know are in the Florida Keys, the Caymans, and Costa Rica. With Jackpot, who knows how many are still around. My friends have little interest in attracting attention. Right now, I'm sure that I'm considered unwanted attention."

"I agree. We need to be very careful about who we talk to and where we go. It might be better to keep moving rather than to reach out."

Helene considered that last thought. "I don't know. If we can lay low here for a couple more days, let things quiet down, maybe I'll be able to find someone who can move us."

"Like I said before, don't call anybody using the condo phone. Let's talk over any ideas you come up with. I'm not sure I'm going to like all of them. No more secrets, okay."

Helene nodded.

We sat and drank our drinks till Helene noticed some fireworks down the beach.

No matter the time of year, or how desolate the beach, there are always fireworks along the Grand Strand. Little else is as beautiful as shooting off fireworks over the ocean. The ocean's reflection of each rocket made their illumination even more majestic. No matter how high the rockets flew, they never penetrated the endless blackness over the Atlantic.

The kids were having trouble lighting their fireworks in the wind. Every few minutes, they managed to get off another rocket or a flowering cone. We watched on the porch until the kids depleted their supply. Without the fireworks, we realized how cold we had become, despite the blanket.

"Can I get you some dessert?" I asked.

"Sure, what do we have?"

"Don't worry. You'll love it." I went to the kitchen and found what I was searching for. I returned to the family room where Helene had turned the TV back on. I opened the package and gave Helene half of a Little Debbie peanut butter wafer.

"It doesn't get any better than this," I said smiling. "Little Debbie never disappoints."

We watched a couple of sit-coms and the ten o'clock news. We didn't expect to hear anything about ourselves , but were still pleased when we didn't. After the news, we called it a night.

I had no idea what time it was, but I knew it was early. From the couch, I could see the sun lifting itself over the edge of the ocean. Helene was thumping me on the head with her middle finger.

"Come on. Wake up. The day's young. I want to go to the beach." She thumped me again.

"Hey, come on. Cut it out. I'm not sure that's a great idea. Especially not a great idea at the crack of dawn. If I wanted to get up this early, I could have stayed at the hospital."

"If I wanted to be locked up, I could have gone to Columbia. What's the chance of someone recognizing us at dawn on Garden City Beach? I checked it out from the porch. There's no one down there. I need to get out of this apartment and stretch my legs."

"What do you want to do?" I asked, wiping the sleep out of my eyes.

"I want to walk on the beach and look for shells."

"Okay, okay. Make some toast and I'll take a quick shower."

Fifteen minutes later, I returned from the shower in a pair of gym shorts, a long sleeve T-shirt, Docksiders, and a wind breaker. Helene was still in her surgical scrubs and flip-flops. I made her put on one of my sweatshirts so she wouldn't freeze her butt off. Helene appeared excited as we headed downstairs.

She was right about the beach being empty. Although it was cold, the sun was shining, the sky was blue, and it had the makings of a gorgeous day. The sunshine, solitude, and the sound of the surf all conspired to soothe my anxiety over going down to the beach.

Garden City had a minor reputation for good shelling. The shelling was best in the early morning, especially in the late autumn and winter. My family had been coming to Garden City for years, and my mother was the ace. Mom filled bowls with calico scallops, slipper shells, lightening whelks, cat's paws, and angel wings.

Biblical arks featured scallop shell decorations and seashells have been found on top of sacred grounds from ancient Jericho to American Indian burial mounds. The Crusaders used the scallop shell as a badge of honor on their coat of arms. Botticelli painted Venus, the Goddess of Beauty, arising from a seashell. The early settlers of the new world in Jamestown used seashells as jewelry. As far as I knew, South Carolina had the only state shell, the lettered olive. A lettered olive was a major find. I described it for Helene, about three inches long and usually tan in color with purple or brown markings. The body of the shell is elongated with a narrow aperture and, at the top, a short spire with four or five surrounding whorls.

Everyone knew, however, that the real shelling prize was the sand dollar. It's rare to find one intact, but when you do, it's a powerful good luck talisman. The sand dollar is also known as the "Holy Ghost Shell." The flat side is imprinted with a design that looks like the Christmas poinsettia. The full side has a design that looks like an Easter Lily with a five-pointed Star of Bethlehem. Religious fanatics in South Carolina, of which there are many, believe the five slits on the edge of the shell represent the crucifixion wounds inflicted on Jesus. When I worked at the State Mental Hospital, the first thing they taught you was to never talk with the patients about the Big Three, politics, sex, or religion. Nothing got the schizophrenics going faster than finding signs of the crucifixion in something. Further, when you broke the shell open, tiny teeth in the center would tumble out that resembled white doves of peace. Whatever you believed, the beauty of the sand dollar was inspired. Momentarily, I wondered what religion Helene might be. I quickly realized it wasn't important to me at all. My own religion wasn't that important to me.

You can wade out about chest deep in the surf and use your toes to feel around in the sand for live sand dollars. You usually find them in beds. In a few minutes, you might find a dozen or more. Live sand dollars are covered with little spines that look and feel like green or purple velvet. By dropping them in a bucket of bleach overnight you could produce a beautiful white sand dollar, exactly like the ones you buy at the Market in Charleston or any other low-end souvenir shop along Ocean Highway.

My mother believed that taking live sand dollars was reprehensible and a major violation of the shelling code of ethics. More than once, I witnessed her dress down an unsuspecting eleven year old coming out of the ocean, proud of their newly discovered sea treasure.

A skill my mother had honed over many years was the ability to find shark's teeth. Among South Carolina's Grand Strand beaches, Garden City, Huntington Island, and the south end of Pawley's Island were known for their shark's teeth. Shark's teeth came in many different shapes and sizes, reflecting the diversity of shark species found in the waters off the South Carolina coast. Nobody can say how old a shark's tooth is. The black and silver-gray teeth are almost certainly fossils. Fresh teeth are pure white, but those are rare unless you're picking them out of a wound. Most teeth are the size of a thumbnail, but I've seen shark's teeth as large as my hand.

As you walk down the beach, you go from areas of fine packed sand with only an occasional shell to broad fields of crushed shells. The shell fragments create a mosaic of colors and shapes which reminded me of emptying a five-hundred piece puzzle box on the floor. I could stare at the mosaic forever and never see the corner piece. My mother, on the other hand, was a savant. When we were kids, my younger brother made a small fortune selling home-made shark's tooth necklaces from my mom's discoveries. My mother was one-eighth Indian. I'm certain she had some kind of hawk-eye vision that had gotten lost in the genetic voyage to her children.

Helene and I brought a small plastic bag with us. We were doing well with calicoes and slipper shells. I enjoyed how much Helene was thrilled by each discovery. We were nosing around in a particularly large patch of broken shells at the base of a wash when Helene called me over.

"Take a look at this," she said, holding out the palm of her hand.

"That's a perfect shark's tooth." It was about an inch long and an ominous gray-black. The point was still sharp, and you could tell where the gum line had been. Where did you find it?"

"I was looking over here. I knocked over this shell with my toe to see if it was a slipper, and the tooth was right under it. It jumped out at me."

I thought to myself how mom would have said the same thing. "Well, great find. Keep an eye out, because when you find one, there'll often be several more nearby."

As we walked the next twenty yards, Helene celebrated the discovery of eight more teeth, while I didn't see one. We found a couple more pink and red calicos and a nice piece of driftwood before finally reaching the Garden City pier. Helene wanted to go up onto the pier, but it wasn't even eight a.m. The pier was still gated. She made me promise to bring her back.

About half-way back to the condo, we froze when we saw a Garden City police cruiser coming up the beach towards us.

"What should we do?" Helene whispered as she leaned in close.

"They aren't looking for us. Just smile and wave. The police come down the beach early each morning looking for drunks or maybe dead bodies. Who knows, but they aren't cruising the beach looking for us."

I could feel the tension in Helene's body as she wrapped her arm around my waist and pulled herself close. She shook her head a bit to put some hair over her face and leaned her cheek against my chest. Although it was affectionate, I knew she was only concealing her identity . We waved at the officer as he drove by.

After the cruiser moved on down the beach, Helene released my waist and turned to look out at the ocean. Then she knelt in the wet sand and dug out a perfect sand dollar about five inches across. She looked up with a huge smile and showed me the sand dollar, which she held in the palm of her hand like a police officer's badge. "I think this is a good sign."

When we got back to Horizon East, we washed off our feet with a hose and headed upstairs. We both felt like we had gotten away with something big. Helene cleaned all the shells and arranged them in a glass rose bowl. It was an attractive arrangement and she was well-pleased with her work.

I wondered how many things Helene had to be proud of. From high school, I knew Helene had a good heart. Home hadn't been a safe or happy place, despite its privilege. Had she even gone to college? She'd been a runaway for almost two years. Her only friends were drug smugglers who had used her to mule their cash to off-shore banks. Now, in the most desperate situation of her life, the only person she had to turn to was a guy she had dated a few times in high school and who had failed her once already. She deserved a moment to enjoy her sea shell arrangement.

"Helene. Where did you go to college?"

"I did a year and a half at USC. Why do you ask?"

"No reason. Just curious. Want to play some cards?"

I taught Helene "Spite and Malice," a card game my family played whenever we visited the beach. The game lived up to its name. After several hands, Helene proved herself sufficiently adept that I didn't feel like playing anymore.

"How about some lunch?"

Helene laughed. "Afraid to play me again?"

"No, just hungry. We haven't fought the final round yet. I've got a haymaker coming your way."

I went to the kitchen and made us a pretty nice lunch, given our limited supplies. I heated a pot of split pea soup and ladled out a couple of bowls. I crumbled up some Ritz crackers on top. I sliced some hard salami and sharp cheese, and paired them with Ritz crackers as well.

"Come and get it while it's hot."

During lunch, I asked Helene if she kept up with anyone from high school. I realized it was a stupid question as soon as I asked it.

"No, not really. There were a couple of girls who lived in my neighborhood. I kept up with them for a while, but not anymore. I saw people from Spring Valley every now and then at Carolina. I didn't hang out with any of them."

"Did you have a boy-friend in high school?"

"Other than you? I had a pretty bad crush on you. I was hurt when you stopped calling." There was no expression on Helene's face, but the tone of her voice was serious.

"I don't have any excuse for my behavior, but I'm sorry. Every time I think of that night at the state park, I'm ashamed of myself. I was a coward. I should have never allowed that patrolman to drag you away like he did. It was unforgiveable."

"What do you think you were going to do?"

"I don't know, but I should have done something. Being afraid to even try is unacceptable. I couldn't face you afterwards."

Helene looked at me and studied my eyes. "You know, it wasn't a requirement that I have a security detail because my father was Lt. Governor. Neither my mother or my sister had a security detail. I was the only one my father had followed. It never stopped, even when I went off to Carolina. You were only seventeen years old. There wasn't anything you could have done to change how things happened."

"Did you think about going away for college? Get out of town."

"He wouldn't have allowed that. Plus, by the time I graduated, there weren't many schools that were clamoring to sign me up. My senior year I blew off most of my classes. I made a point of getting shit-faced drunk the night before I took my SATs. I threw up halfway through the math, and I passed out before finishing the verbal. The only reason I got into Carolina was because my father was Lt. Governor. I didn't disappoint them either. They got exactly the student they thought they were getting."

"You never answered my question. Did you have a boy-friend in high school?"

"Well, after you dumped me, it took a long time for me to get over my broken heart," Helene said with mock seriousness. "Later that year, I dated Matty Rochester for a while, but it didn't last."

"Matty Rochester. I didn't know that. He was a hell of a football player. He would've been All-State if he could've remembered the snap count. He wasn't the sharpest tool in the shed."

"To my great disappointment. We went to see *Fiddler on the Roof*, and at intermission he asked me why they wore little caps. After figuring out he was serious, I told him it was because of their religion. I knew what question was coming next, and it was terrifying. When I told him they were Jewish, he was legitimately surprised. Halfway through *Fiddler on the Roof* and Matty didn't know they were Jews. Since they were Russians, he thought they must be communists."

We both laughed. "He was beautiful," she continued, "but maybe one generation of inbreeding too many. By the end of intermission, I had decided that Matty should never reproduce. At least not with me. On the bright side, he never caught on that we were being watched. My senior year, I started dating Dallas Taylor."

"I remember him from Student Council. He was pretty much a pot head, if I'm thinking about the right guy."

"Yeah, that's the right guy. I spent most of my senior year high as a kite. We used to toke up behind the visitor's press box at Harry Parone Stadium."

"What happened to Dallas?"

"Dallas was no match for my father either. Pops let it go on for a few months, hoping I'd break up with him. When I didn't, he had some of his SLED boys pull us over on Two Notch Road one night. They searched his car and planted a kilo of hash in the trunk. They gave Dallas an option. Walk away and never come back, or else spend the next ten years in prison. It wasn't a hard decision, and I didn't blame him. He drove away from the traffic stop alone and SLED drove me home. After that night, things got worse at home, and I didn't try dating anymore."

"What do you mean it got worse?"

"My father's obsession with controlling me. He wasn't that way with my sister. He didn't pay any attention to her at all. I guess, I was just the apple of his eye."

"Did your sister know what was going on?"

"I might've made a combined 545 on my SAT, but she's never figured anything out in her entire life. She loves being the Governor's daughter. Life is one big game of dress-up for her. She spends all her time trying to win Dad's attention, but he ignores her and everything she does. My sister has no clue what goes on in our house, and she doesn't want to know. Whenever he and I fight, she runs away and hides in her room. My sister and I have a weird relationship. I'm glad she hasn't had to experience what I've been through, but, at the same time, I resent her for it.

"Mom's another story. She knows and doesn't care. She's an alcoholic and hasn't dealt with any family issues for a long time. I don't know if she was an alcoholic before she married him or not. I've never seen or heard him physically abuse her. I've always assumed he did in the past, but doesn't need to anymore. She's already been emotionally gutted. Dad found a new fish to filet."

"Let's talk about something else," Helene said. It wasn't a request. "Did you play basketball in college?"

"No, I wasn't nearly good enough. I tried to walk on the freshman team, but I got cut. There isn't a big demand for six-four power forwards in college. Especially those that can't run very fast, jump very high, dribble or shoot very well."

"Well, you were great in high school. I watched you every moment, whether you were on the court or not. Then again, everyone watched you."

"Come on. Both Neil and David were better players than I was."

"Declan, you played like an animal. It was amazing how much you sweated. Half the rebounds you got were because the other players didn't want to get near you. When you pulled down a rebound, the sweat would fly off you and the other players would run away. Even the referees kept their distance."

"Come on. I didn't sweat that much."

"Come on, what. There was a manager whose only job was to wipe up the sweat puddles from underneath wherever you were sitting during time outs."

"Yeah, but I didn't know anyone noticed."

"Then, you're about as clueless as my mother. People called you 'Horse' and laughed about how you 'lathered-up' during the games."

"Shit, I never knew that. If I'd heard that, I would've beaten somebody up."

"Hey, don't sweat it. No pun intended. I loved watching you play. It's one of my few good memories from high school."

"Did you ever think about being a cheerleader?"

Helene exploded with laughter. "You're really a dumbass. My dad can pull a lot of strings, and, Lord knows, he would have loved to see me in a pleated skirt doing splits on the court. But even the Governor doesn't have enough influence to break into a high school cheerleader clique. Remember, I transferred into Spring Valley my junior year. I had a better chance of making the boys basketball team, than I did of making the cheerleading squad."

"I don't think you would've liked the basketball team. I would've gotten sweat all over you," I said with a grin.

Helene returned my grin. "I used to think a lot about you getting your sweat on me." She let that one sink in a little bit and then continued."Let's walk back up to the pier in a little while, and find a pay phone. I've got a couple of numbers I want to try. Plus, I want to go to the arcade."

"Are you going to kick my ass at Pac-Man too?"

"Ms. Pac- Man."

GARDEN CITY PIER

Later that afternoon, we walked back to the Garden City pier. The beach was colder than it had been earlier. There was a dark storm churning far out over the ocean and its winds were beginning to blow ashore. Ugly gray-brown foam was being whipped up at the edge of the surf. We walked at a brisker pace, and Helene leaned in close. I put my arm around her shoulder for warmth. Once we got to the pier, we walked up to the road and crossed the street to Eagles Beachwear. In more than a decade of coming to Garden City, I'd never bought anything at Eagles. It was fun to go inside and look at the soft-core porn post cards from Myrtle Beach, suggestive Big Johnson T-shirts, and live hermit crabs, but I'd never left a penny on the counter.

I wasn't worried about being identified. Eagles was run by high school drop outs hired for their expertise in shoplifting. Helene needed some more clothes. Helene picked out a Garden City Beach sweat shirt, Buffalo sandals and, best of all, a black and silver Oakland Raiders warm-up suit with "Pride" and "Poise" stenciled on each sleeve. At my insistence, she also selected a floppy beach hat and some dark glasses even though we had convinced ourselves nobody was looking for us on Garden City Beach. While Helene was picking out her clothes, I bought a shark's tooth necklace.

After paying cash for the clothes, we headed across the street to the arcade.

"You're due for a smack down," Helene said.

Helene had been kidding about Ms. Pac-Man. It turned out, we shared another passion. The Garden City

Pavilion had several old fashioned, hard-wood baseball arcade games. One button would fire a pinball from the pitcher's mound, and a second lever swung the bat. With successful hits, runners pop up from under the field and run the bases. No electronic crap at all. Above the row of machines was a wall of stuffed animals with a sign that stated simply, "25 Runs Wins Choice."

Helene was good, but didn't know the machines. Garden City was my home field. She didn't know which bounces led to the infield "out" holes. She didn't know that going for the "double" was a fool's choice due to the "out" holes on either side. She didn't know how much the machine could be bumped without tilting. Mostly, she didn't know which pitches you had to lay off of. The pitch down the middle was enticing, but was too often destined for the "out" holes in straightaway centerfield. The inside pitch could be lined up the left side of the machine to the "single" hole time after time. The ball that curved away from the right handed bat could be driven up the right side where it ricocheted off the home run ramp into a "single" hole on that side of the machine. The worry with an outside pitch was being a little slow on the batting lever and squibbing it off the end of the bat. That mistake usually spun the ball off into one of the infield "out" holes. The key was the patience to wait for the proper pitch. People, who knew me, knew that patience wasn't my strong suit. But when it came to arcade baseball, I was all steely-eyed discipline.

Helene scored eleven runs in her first game, which was respectable. She didn't do any better in her next two games and became frustrated. In my first two games, I scored sixteen and twenty runs respectively. I was now at twenty-four runs with two outs and a man on second.

"Not getting nervous are you?" Helene prodded.

"I'm as cool as the underside of my pillow."

"Okay. If you say so. I thought I was beginning to smell a little something. A whiff of fear maybe? "

"What you smell is the sweet aroma of victory."

I rifled an outside pitch up the right side for a single that put men on first and third. "Have you picked out your favorite stuffed animal yet?"

I let the next couple of pitches pass to build the suspense. Then, I took a cut at a slow pitch curving outside. Unfortunately, I was a hair slow and only topped the ball. It curled off the bat and wasn't going to make it to the top of the machine. It would eventually come rolling back down the right side. This was a dangerous ball, but I was ready. As the ball's momentum dissipated, and it turned to roll back toward the infield, I gave the machine a little hip check at the right moment. The ball bounced off the side wall and away from the infield "out" hole. I gave Helene a sly smile and called for the next pitch. It was an inside fast ball, which I lined down the left side, slamming into the "single" hole bringing home my twenty-fifth run.

Helene screamed and threw both fists into the air. She ran to find an attendant. Helene picked out a purple and gold alligator, which was a good choice. I would've gone with the gorilla. The attendant fetched it with a long hook. I didn't say anything for fear of spoiling the moment.

"Let's get something to eat," Helene said, with a huge smile on her face and an alligator left over from Mardi Gras clutched in both hands.

SAM'S CORNER

No one could remember a time when Sam's Corner had not been at the intersection of Waccamaw and Atlantic. However long it was, the place had never changed. The beach music on the jukebox was vintage 50s and 60s. The coffee cost five cents and the foot-long chili dog was a buck and a quarter. One of the lights illuminating Sam's signature sign had been burnt out for a decade. Nobody cared. The tip jar at the counter had a stained and faded note taped to it that said, "Beer fund." I doubted there was ever a truer advertisement. The people who worked there constantly changed, but were always the same. The cook was a grizzled white guy, almost certainly a Vietnam veteran, who looked like he had a problem with the bottle. He had replaced a Korean War veteran who had, in turn, supplanted a World War II veteran. Sam's Corner had successfully treated more Post Traumatic Stress Disorder than the Charleston VA Hospital. The waitresses were a couple years past their expiration date and a testament to the dermatological hazards of too much sun. The bus boys were killing time waiting for the carnival to come back to town. We couldn't be safer if we were sitting in a Moroccan cafe in Marrakesh. No one in the history of Sam's Corner had ever looked a patron in the eye.

"Be Young, Be Foolish, Be Happy" by the Tams was playing on the jukebox. We took a booth, and Helene looked at a menu. I knew what I wanted. When the waitress came over, I ordered the foot-long chili dog I'd been thinking about all afternoon. Helene ordered a patty melt hamburger. We both ordered chocolate malted milkshakes and beer-battered onion rings to share.

"Why the hell did you order a patty melt hamburger? No-body ever orders that. I'm not even sure what it is. You should have gotten the foot-long."

"I just felt like a patty melt. I haven't had one in a long time."

"Why ruin a good hamburger by putting it on greasy white bread?"

"Don't lecture me about greasy, mister foot-long chili dog."

When our food arrived, it was perfect. I looked over the menu posted on the wall and thought about coming back for breakfast. I wanted to try the fried bologna and egg sandwich. Eating at Sam's Corner everyday would certainly kill you within a month. Helene made a point of telling me how delicious her patty melt was.

Helene nodded at the pay phone next to the bathrooms and asked me for a quarter.

"I know someone who lives near here. He's got friends who can help us." With my quarter in hand, Helene went over to the phone and leafed through the yellow pages.

She dropped in the quarter, dialed a number, and then madly waved me over.

"Hurry, I need another dollar twenty-five for the call. Get some change at the counter."

After securing the necessary change from the cashier, I returned to the pay phone. As Helene was taking the quarters out of my palm, I looked down at the phone book. It was open to the Escort section of the yellow pages with numbers listed for Myrtle Beach. After taking the last quarter, Helene pushed me away before conversing with the person on the other end.

The last few onion rings were a private treat as I waited for Helene to get off the phone. I used my fork to unwrap the wire from around the shark's tooth on the necklace. Before Helene finished her call, I was able to replace the small Eagles shark's tooth with the larger one Helene had found that morning. Now it looked like something a warrior would wear. I used the last onion ring to scoop up some chili that had fallen off my dog.

When Helene returned to the table, I couldn't help myself. "Who did you call?"

"A not very nice guy, but someone who knows people. He's going to check on a couple of possibilities. I'm supposed to call him back this time tomorrow."

"So, how do you know him?"

"Red and his friends work the edges. They need friends who are willing to do whatever is asked, whenever asked, and who'll keep their mouths shut for a little piece of the pie. Sometimes they need women. This guy can arrange for women who aren't expecting to be asked on a second date. I don't know if he can help us or not, but I can tell you, I'm getting near the bottom of my list."

"I'm sorry. I didn't mean to pry. We'll call him back tomorrow."

It was darkening and getting colder, so Helene pulled on her new Garden City sweat shirt. We needed to get back before it started raining. Walking back down the beach, Helene surprised me when she grabbed my free hand and interlaced her fingers with mine. I slowed a bit and looked at her. She smiled back. We walked on silently, but neither of us let go of the other's hand.

When we got back to the condo, we made ourselves some drinks, watched some television, and eventually drifted out to the porch. There was a bright full moon and I pointed out a broad moonbeam painted across the ocean. "Did you ever see the movie *Breakfast at Tiffany's*? That's what is meant by a 'moon river.'"

"I think they'll let you come back to work," Helene said abruptly. "I saw how the young doctors listen to you. You're a pretty big deal at your hospital. Just like you were at Spring Valley."

"You're never as big a deal as you think you are. The measuring sticks aren't what they should be. A couple of months ago, one of the cardiothoracic surgeons got mad at one of the anesthesiologists over an intubation. The argument got heated. The patient is lying naked on the operating room table with a tube in her throat, and the two attending physicians get in a shoving match. The surgeon finally punched the anesthesiologist, and they ended up rolling on the floor. A bunch of other doctors had to break it up. The surgeon walked out on the case. It took an hour to find another CT surgeon. The surgeon was so far out of line, he should have been arrested. You know what happened?"

Helene shook her head no.

"Nothing. He got the afternoon off and was back in the OR the next day. Turns out, he's one of the biggest billers in the University. The anesthesiologist got written up and peer-reviewed because he kept bitching about the incident. If you make the big bucks, you've got a get-out-of-jail-free card. I might be pretty good at what I do, but Ob-Gyn is small potatoes. We work all day and all night doing thirty-five dollar prenatal visits and fifteen hundred dollar Cesareans. We can't match bottom lines with CT surgeons doing $50,000 heart cases five days a week or the Ophthalmologists who do eight cataracts per day at $2,500 per eyeball. Medicine is big business. They won't think twice about throwing me into the sausage grinder, as long as it doesn't hurt the profit margin."

"That's pretty cynical, Dr. Murphy."

"Cynical, but true. If the University doesn't want me, I can start over somewhere else. I know a good trade, and there's always going to be work. It does worry me that they might go after my license."

"I don't want you to lose your career because of me."

"You don't need to worry about that. Things are going to sort themselves out. We wouldn't be here if we had any other options. Your father did this to us once before. He isn't going to do it again."

We ate a couple of apples while we watched some fireworks starting up next door in front of the Water's Edge. I brought the shark's tooth necklace out of my pocket and put it around Helene's neck.

"Do you recognize the tooth?"

"Of course. It's the one I found this morning. Thank you."

Despite my fears, I was content with my decision to be standing out on this patio with Helene. I'd done the right thing in helping her flee.

The teenagers in front of the Water's Edge were now doing their mini-equivalent of a finale. I thought about "4th of July Asbury Park / Sandy," another of my favorite Springsteen songs. The fireworks were hailin' over our own little Eden tonight. I could see the pier lights and I could imagine the aurora risin' behind it. I could hear the longing in Danny Federici's soulful accordion. As the sky again got dark, we realized how cold it had become. Helene said goodnight and turned in. I stayed on the porch a few more minutes until the song was over in my head. In the final stanza the boy on the boardwalk asks his girl to love him tonight for he may never see her again. The lyric made me shudder against the chill.

I usually slept easily at the beach. The sound of the waves typically washed over my subconscious and smoothed out the bumps of the day. Tonight was different. Helene's question about my work was rattling around in my head. I kept trying to calculate how much this ill-fated rescue mission was going to cost me.

Suddenly, Helene was standing by the edge of my bed wearing only her Hogs Breath T-shirt and an inexpensive shark's tooth necklace. She lifted the sheets and slid into bed beside me. When I started to speak, Helene put her finger to my lips. She leaned over me and rested her hand on my bare chest. The first kiss was only tentative, a brush of the lips, but rapidly became more intense. The hand on my chest moved down my abdomen and over the front of my gym shorts. My erection betrayed me, although I doubted Helene was surprised.

She caressed me a few times through the fabric, and then hooked the waistband with her thumb. She pushed my gym shorts down over my hips. Helene raised herself up and began to straddle me when I caught her arm.

"Are you sure?"

"Yes. Aren't you?"

"Yes, but I don't want to hurt you."

"Don't worry, I had a good doctor."

"That's not the kind of hurt I was talking about, but it's a good point."

"Declan, you're not going to hurt me. It's been a long time since high school. I'm a big girl. I know what I'm doing."

I released her arm and she mounted me, using her hand to guide my penis carefully into her. She began to slowly rock, working me inside her. She was in no hurry and began our love making at a pace that was slow and controlled. It had been a while since I had last had sex. I was scared I would come too quickly, but Helene wouldn't allow it. She slowed the pace even more, removed her T-shirt, and then restarted with only the slightest grinding movement of her pubic bone against the base of my penis. It kept me completely aroused, but at the same time, allowed me to relax.

I ran my hands over her hips and the front of her chest. I opened my hands and allowed her nipples to barely touch my palms. I tried to match Helene's patience, but I didn't have her mesmerizing control. She leaned forward, sat straight up, and then stretched back, with each position creating a different sensation. She never broke rhythm. I could tell she was being satisfied by her sounds, the distant look in her eyes, and the flushing of the skin over her chest.

Again, Helene slowed to almost imperceptible movements. I tried to increase the pace, but Helene exhaled and said, "Slow, baby." Gradually, though, she allowed me to take the lead, thrusting into her from below. I felt her vagina begin to tent, and Helene urged me on with a breathless "faster now."

I could feel Helene begin to rhythmically orgasm. I followed moments later.

Completely spent, we laid together, interlaced for several minutes. Finally, with an effort, Helene rolled off me, averting her face. I could hear her crying.

"Are you hurt? I'm so sorry."

"No, I'm sorry. I don't mean to be crying."

"What's wrong then? This was a mistake."

"No, you didn't hurt me and it wasn't a mistake," she answered emphatically. After a few moments, she added more quietly, "I had forgotten how good it felt to do that with someone I care about."

I felt breath leaving my lungs.

Helene got up and out of bed. Illuminated by the moon light, she stood naked beside the bed with her hand cupped over her crotch. She gave me a momentary look over her shoulder, before walking to the bathroom.

Too often, people are oblivious to quicksilver moments. The arrogance of youth blinds you to truly extraordinary experiences. Too few have the perspective to recognize that the exceptional does not become common. I was grateful for the understanding that I had just experienced something that would never be duplicated in my life. A depth of intimacy I could not reasonably expect to enjoy again. It was unexpected and passionate. I had no idea what to do or say.

Helene return to bed and rested her head on my shoulder. Her naked body radiated heat.

She kissed my chest and lifted her face toward mine, "Promise me one thing."

"Anything."

"Take me to Brookgreen Gardens tomorrow."

"What?"

"Brookgreen Gardens. Just down the highway. I'd like to go there tomorrow. I went a long time ago and I want to go again."

"The Gardens aren't at their best in December."

"I know."

"Sure," I said, somewhat perplexed. "Brookgreen Gardens tomorrow." It wasn't like I had a choice.

BROOKGREEN GARDENS

When I awoke Friday morning, I was alone in the bed. I understood that the worm had turned. No matter how I justified things to myself now, I wasn't Brave Cowboy Bill anymore. I had moved well past saving a damsel tied to the railroad tracks.

It's a rite of passage for graduating medical students to swear an oath to the practice of ethical medicine written in the late fifth century B.C. by Hippocrates. Among the pledges that Hippocrates made to the multitude of healing Gods was, " In every house where I come, I will enter only for the good of my patients, keeping myself far from all intentional ill-doing and all seduction, and especially from the pleasures of love with women or with men, be they free or slaves." A week ago, Helene had been admitted from the emergency room to my service and had gone to the operating room under my knife. There wasn't a lot of wiggle room in that. It wasn't like the ancient Greeks were Puritans either. This was written by a guy who thought buggering boys was good sport.

I closed my eyes and tried to imprint the image of Helene's nakedness in the moonlight. Instead, I kept seeing the twice yearly newsletter from the State Board of Medical Examiners. A nasty little rag no one read except for the two middle pages that listed the Board's disciplinary actions. In a small state like South Carolina, you were bound to see names you knew. The gossip mill would have grist for weeks. Drug abuse or writing illegal drug prescriptions were the undisputed champions when it came to getting your license revoked or suspended. But a solid third place was the shameful "inappropriate sexual contact." We all knew what it meant when it was written next to the name of a pediatrician. It was also a common affliction for dentists and anesthesiologists who couldn't deal with the constant temptation of unconscious women. When it was written next to the name of an Ob-Gyn, it was a career-ender. As I lay in bed and listened to the ocean in the distance, I knew my own professional scarlet letter would sooner or later be in the mail.

I also worried that Helene would regret last night as well. Helene had been misused by men her entire life. Her father was a wretched man, and anyone who rubbed up against him was stained. I didn't want to be just another man in her life who'd taken advantage of her. It would be easy to conclude that I'd manipulated her. Had I seduced her in exchange for a safe place to stay? Was that the subtext to our relationship? I would probably know in a few more minutes.

I pulled on a T-shirt, rubbed some blood back into my face, and walked to the kitchen. Helene was dressed in her new Oakland Raiders warm-up and a pair of my gym shorts that hung loosely on her hips. I'd never seen basketball shorts look so good. Helene was drinking coffee and eating a bowl of Cheerios.

"Hey, sleepy-head. You look terrible."

"There's a lot of stuff flying around in my head right now. Any more coffee?"

"Come sit down. It's just a Friday." Helene poured some Honey Nut Cheerios in a bowl followed by cold milk. "You can't handle coffee right now."

"It's way more than just another Friday and you know it. Last night was unbelievable. I can't tell you how unbelievable. But last night changes everything. Last week, you were my patient. From the outside

158

looking in, I took advantage of a physician-patient relationship."

"Oh yes, a man in a dingy white coat, stethoscope dangling around his neck, speculums in each pocket, I get all jelly legged and can't be responsible for what I might do. You're a big dummy. Last night was important for me too. I've been unhappy for as long as I can remember. I needed you badly last night. Last night, I didn't need a doctor. I damn sure needed a lover. If it makes you feel better, you can consider last night a therapeutic intervention."

"I'm worried you might have felt obligated to come to my bed. You don't owe me anything."

"I know that. I came to you last night because I wanted to. Most of my life has been motivated by obligation. Last night, was desire."

"Well, that's heartening. In case you're worried, I don't feel used at all."

"Eat your cereal, smart-ass. We've got a lot to do today, so quit goofing off."

"Just one question Did I dream it, or are we going on an outing?"

"Brookgreen Gardens. You promised."

Brookgreen Gardens has been a Grand Strand oddity since 1931. Archer Milton Huntington was the step-son of railroad magnate Collis Huntington. The elder Huntington made his fortune by founding the Newport News Shipbuilding and Drydock Company and later, as builder of the Central Pacific Railroad. Archer Huntington had no desire to be an empire-builder. He was a scholar, poet, and a Hispanist. He was fascinated by Spain and Hispanic culture. He was the founder and builder of the Hispanic Society of America in New York City.

Archer Huntington's second marriage was to the sculptor, Anna Vaughn Hyatt, famous in her own right for her animal sculpture and equestrian statue of Joan of Arc that stands on Riverside Drive in New York City. In 1923, they were married on their mutual birthday of March 10th. The new Mrs. Huntington shared her husband's interest in Spanish culture and added numerous pieces of sculpture to the grounds of the Hispanic Society. She modeled the equestrian statue of Spain's medieval hero El Cid and presented it to the city of Sevilla in 1927.

Archer's poetry reveals sensitivity to the beauty of flowers and the natural grace of animals. While on a yachting trip to the West Indies, they docked at Georgetown, South Carolina for supplies. They were charmed by the great forests and swamps of the region, lush with waterfowl and vegetation. In 1930, they bought a huge track of land on the Waccamaw River, which had formerly been four rice plantations gone to seed after the collapse of the southern rice industry during the Civil War. Inspired by a magnificent avenue of live oaks and the remains of a boxwood garden on the site of the old Brookgreen Plantation, they decided to build an outdoor museum for the plants and trees native to the region.

Archer Huntington built a serpentine wall of open brickwork to separate the gardens from the woods, while Anna designed the butterfly-shaped walks, gardens, and pools. They believed that the gardens would be a perfect setting for the great American sculptures of the time. The first piece selected was a dramatic limestone statue by Robert A. Baillie, "Youth Taming the Wild," a group of spirited stallions dominated by a single young man. Archer and Anna chose each piece personally and selected the proper garden setting to best evoke the sculpture's beauty. As a result of the Huntington's generosity and imagination, the ten thousand acres of Brookgreen Gardens became the first public sculpture garden in the United States and home to more than a thousand pieces of classic American sculpture.

Besides sculpture, Brookgreen Gardens is also known for its magnificent live oaks, nature trails, creeks, aviary and native animal habitats. Every school-aged boy or girl in South Carolina visits Brookgreen Gardens sooner or later. None of them sufficiently appreciate the beauty that surrounds them. I remembered an eight-grade field trip. My most vivid memory was the halter top Susan Poole was wearing that day.

"So why are we going to Brookgreen Gardens?" I asked.

"We went there once when I was a little girl. That summer, we spent a week at Pawley's Island and we visited the gardens. It's the last time I remember doing anything with my family when we were really a family."

"You know, driving to Brookgreen Gardens is a little risky."

"You promised."

"I know, I promised. It isn't far. We'll be okay. Promise me we won't have to take a pottery making class."

"No classes. Just a walk around and maybe a picnic."

Helene went out on the porch to check the weather. I put some bread in the toaster. We were running low on provisions and would need a brief stop at the grocery store on the way back.

After breakfast, we finished getting dressed and made some feeble attempts at disguise. I had gone unshaven for a couple of days and had built up some stubble. That and some dark glasses made me look vaguely threatening. Helene also put on some aviator shades. She pulled her hair back into a pony tail and threaded it through the opening in her baseball cap.

We walked over to Water's Edge. My car was undisturbed. I had a fleeting thought that maybe it was under surveillance, but then dismissed it. If authorities could find my car, how in the world had they not figured out where we were? We got in and fired up the engine on the land yacht.

Brookgreen Gardens was about ten miles back down Highway 17. On the way, we pulled into a Kentucky Fried Chicken and picked up a picnic box at the drive through.

After getting our yard bird, we continued on to the gardens. The entrance was unmistakable with two giant "Fighting Stallions" by Anna Hyatt Huntington battling for dominance. We walked through the oldest part of the gardens, which were still beautiful despite the December chill.

Helene's agenda included several of the most famous statues, all of which she'd seen before. Her favorite was "Diana of the Chase" which stood in the center of Diana's Pool. I wasn't surprised that Helene related to it. Helene wanted to visit the Dogwood Garden but was disappointed they were scraggly and bare. We walked back up Live Oak Allee and saw "Saint James Triad" and "Don Quixote."At each turn of the path, there would be some cherub or a devil set back in the bushes or hidden in an alcove. You wondered how it got there. There was a feeling they had run out of places to put things.

With so few people around and the low hanging sky, the gardens were quiet and serene. I was happy Helene had suggested it. Figuring out what to do come Sunday was weighing heavily on my mind, but for right now, the gardens were helping to clear my head.

The Live Oaks were majestic and reminded of the old southern plantation to which the land used to belong. We followed the live oaks to their end where "Youth Taming the Wild" was located. After viewing that piece, we took another path by Jessamine Pond to the picnic area. As Helene set out our KFC on a picnic table, I walked over to the Welcome Center to buy a couple of sodas.

The Welcome Center had a local craft shop. I became infatuated with some beautiful wood carved puzzle boxes. They were all different shapes and sizes, and were made from a variety of different types of wood. I was drawn to the dark cherry mahogany. Each box had a hidden locking mechanism. You could spin it around in your hands a dozen different ways, and it wouldn't give up its secret. Even after the guy at the counter showed me how to open it, the steps involved were hard to duplicate. A critical part of the sales pitch was to get you completely frustrated, and beg to try it again.

The craftsmanship was magnificent. There were no locks, latches, springs, or any other evident mechanisms. There was a small rectangle of wood that had to be slid in one way or another. That movement revealed another sliding piece of burnished wood, which, when moved, allowed the two halves of the box to slide apart. Hidden away was a small compartment lined with velvet. It sounds simple, but it wasn't.

Moreover, every box was different. The opening sequence successful for one box was useless on another. It was a marvelous engineering feat. I wanted to talk to the artisan, but unfortunately, the pitch man wasn't the talent. He had already bull-shitted me about how the mysteries of the puzzle box had been passed down from old Indian folklore. The puzzle boxes were way over-priced, especially the dark mahogany ones, but I didn't care. I picked out the prettiest cherry wood box I could find.

While there, I had the unsettling feeling that the security guard was watching me. After purchasing the puzzle box, I hurried outside as quickly as I could.

Helene had pulled apart some chicken and put it on a biscuit with some coleslaw. It looked pretty damn good. I sat down and we began to enjoy our lunch. At least until Helene nodded at me from across the table. She tilted her head towards the Welcome Center. I turned and saw the security guard walking toward us.

Under my breath, I told Helene, "Let me do the talking. Be cool, but be ready to run to the car if I have to slug this guy."

The security guard did not seem agitated or on alert as he approached. He was within a few yards of our picnic table when he called me by name.

"Dr. Murphy?"

"Yes, I'm Dr. Murphy," I answered, not being able to think of any way lying could help us. I could tell that Helene was antsy and ready to run.

"I thought that was you. I'm Chip Burdette. Do you remember me?"

"I'm very sorry, sir, but I don't. I meet a lot of people."

"Of course. It was about two years ago," Officer Burdette said. "You delivered my wife Terri and our twins. We were transferred to you from Georgetown Hospital with preterm labor. When we got to MUSC she was already four centimeters. It looked like she was going to deliver. We were only seven months. You stopped her labor and gave her some steroid shots. You kept her in the hospital, and she made it another four weeks before she ruptured her membranes. The first one was coming feet first, and you did a Cesarean."

"Yes, I think I remember. Does Terri have red hair?"

"Yes, that's Terri. You did a great job doc. Terri recovered without a hitch and both boys came home in a couple of weeks. Let me show you a picture. This one's Luke, who was twin A, and this one's Ben, who was twin B. Good little guys, and they're both doing great."

"Officer Burdette, you've got yourself a pair of handsome boys. Congratulations. I can see they both have on their Clemson Tiger gear. Excuse me, I've been rude. This is my friend Phoebe."

"Phoebe, a pleasure to meet you. I'm sorry to interrupt your lunch. I wanted to say hello to Dr. Murphy. He's a hero in our house."

"Please give my best to Terri. I'm very glad your boys are doing well."

"Thanks again, Doc, and again, sorry for interrupting. Enjoy your lunch and the gardens. Phoebe, a pleasure. Go Tigers," Officer Burdette said with a grin.

Neither of us spoke till Officer Burdette was back inside the Welcome Center.

"Wow, that was intense. I was sure we were busted."

"Phoebe? Is that the best you could do? What the hell kind of name is Phoebe?"

"Sorry, it was the best I could come up with at the moment."

We finished the chicken biscuits and slaw, but I think Helene was still steamed that I had called her Phoebe. "I want to walk over to the nature area," she said.

We took the Low Country Trail over to the zoo and the native animal habitats. The nature area is not as active as it would be in the spring or summer, but there was still plenty to see. At the Cypress Swamp Aviary we saw owls, hawks and eagles, birds of prey native to the swamps. Moving on to other habitats, we came across a couple of wild turkeys, who we heard long before we saw. We also enjoyed the otter exhibit, from an underwater glass-enclosed space.

After the otters, Helene stopped and asked, "Can we please go to the Butterfly House?"

"Why not."

"It's two dollars extra to go inside."

"Call me crazy. Being at Brookgreen Gardens makes me feel like an early twentieth century robber-baron."

THE BUTTERFLY HOUSE

The Butterfly House was more than worth the extra two dollars. It was warm and humid inside, and the tropical flowers gave off an intoxicating aroma. The sound of water tumbling over rocks and rippling over stones was disarming. As soon as you entered the house, you were surrounded by hundreds of butterflies representing every color on the artist's palate. The butterflies would swirl and light and then arise again with any movement.

As I watched from the edge of the room, Helene moved to dead center where she stood statue still. Her eyes were closed and her arms rose upward like she was signaling for a touchdown. Dozens of butterflies had already landed on her with their wings still beating rhythmically. Hundreds of others seemed to be drawn in, circling her like an electron shell around an atomic nucleus. I moved a bit so I could see her face. You couldn't see any change in expression or even a muscle twitch. However, you could sense a restorative transformation. A subtle, almost imperceptible, illumination came across her face, coupled with the slightest trace of a smile. It was an intimate moment that was almost voyeuristic to observe.

I don't know how long Helene stood there, but it seemed like forever. Finally, she put her arms down, scattering the butterflies in an explosion of color. She did a small pirouette before opening her eyes. It wasn't the same Helene who'd walked into the Butterfly House.

"Are you okay?"

"They remembered me."

"Obviously," I replied with a smile. "But, I think it's time for us to go."

"I'm ready."

She was silent for most of our ride home, but startled me almost into an accident when she erupted, "Turn here." From her frenzied pointing, I discerned that she was directing me to a roadside fireworks stand at the edge of a near empty K-Mart parking lot. The stand was a discarded ship container with half of one side cut away, creating the impression of a store front. It had a garish, hand-painted sign announcing the availability of M-8os and Roman Candles.

The guy in the box was a gangly, undernourished twenty-year-old with frayed jeans, a camouflage jacket, unkempt hair, and a patchy beard that highlighted, rather than disguised, his bad post-adolescent skin and pock-marked neck. Despite these obvious misfortunes, he approached us with the attitude of a San Francisco waiter. He made it obvious we'd interrupted his graduate level study of the most recent Marvel comic. He stood silently in the acetylene cutout, daring us to initiate a dialogue in any language other than French. My hostility toward him blossomed immediately. I knew it was a mistake to get into it with him. We shouldn't even be out on the highway, much less, getting into a confrontation with a punk at a roadside fireworks stand.

Fortunately, Helene had much more life experience navigating her way through a world inhabited by fireworks boy. Sensing a deteriorating situation, she turned to the boy, flashed a beautiful smile, some cleavage, and turned on the charm.

"You have the best collection of fireworks we've seen anywhere along the Strand."

Surprised and a little confused, fireworks boy gaped back at Helene, dull-eyed, slack-jawed, and wordless.

"Do you mind if we look around for a minute? You have so many choices, and they all look so great."

"No, sure," the kid mumbled.

With the situation diffused, we surveyed the inventory for a few minutes until I tapped Helene on the arm and quietly reminded her, "We shouldn't be out here on the roadside very long." One local police cruiser had passed by already. I followed it with my eyes on down Highway 17. I thought for a second that it might have slowed, but it didn't turn around. Even if he had noticed the Eldorado, he probably couldn't believe that a couple of fugitives would be standing out on the side of the road buying bottle rockets. If he'd turned around I had no idea what we would've done. We weren't armed with anything but cherry bombs.

Helene nodded her agreement and we selected a modest display of aerials , Roman Candles, and whistling flying saucers. As we paid, we asked the boy for a couple of punks. He dropped them in our bag with the same disgusted condescension you'd get after sending back a bottle of wine at Café de la Presse.

As we drove out of the K-Mart parking lot, Helene exclaimed to no one in particular, "That was fun."

"Tons of fun," I replied sarcastically.

"Don't be like that. This is important. We can't watch the fireworks every night without contributing."

GARDEN CITY GROCERY

Helene reminded me that our cupboard had gotten pretty bare. We also had to call Helene's contact back after four p.m. Several large grocery stores dotted Highway 17, but those were too exposed. There was a small grocery store on the island. It didn't have much, but then again, we didn't need much.

Like when we first arrived, I turned off the highway onto Atlantic Avenue and followed it to Garden City beach. There was a parking space directly in front of the Garden City Grocery. To minimize our time on the street, we decided I'd go into the grocery store and Helene would go down the block to Sam's Corner. She'd use their pay phone again to call her "friend." Helene scooped a handful of coins out of the car's ash tray.

Walking into Garden City Grocery, I felt like I was in a documentary about the Russian winter famines. It was one big room with four rows of near empty shelves and one cooler box. I did a double-take to make sure that the place wasn't closed. I had my heart set on a sirloin steak and felt lucky to find one. Helene wanted a good salad, so I picked out a head of lettuce, a couple of tomatoes, and a cucumber. They had one bottle of Italian dressing. I found a bag of frozen Tater Tots in the cooler. Lastly, I grabbed a half-gallon of milk, a carton of eggs and a six-pack of Coors beer. The total came to a little over twenty-two dollars, which I paid in cash.

The woman behind the counter looked at me like I was the only customer of the day. Maybe I was. She was brown and leathery and looked much older than whatever age she was. The sun had lashed whip marks into her face, back and shoulders. The Marlboro that dangled from her lower lip had sucked all the moisture out of her skin. The smell of cigarette smoke and Tiger Balm liniment hung over her so heavily that it made checking out almost nauseating. She couldn't be very good for business.

As I handed her my selections I almost dropped the eggs.

"Jesus Christ, lord. Be careful. I just cleaned my mop."

"Sorry, ma'am."

"You takin' this feast on the road or you stayin' round here?" she asked as she dropped my groceries into a paper bag.

"Why you asking?"

"Dunno, just makin' conversation. The beach seems more crowded this winter than usual. Just a couple of hours ago a Myrtle Beach sheriff's deputy dropped by with a picture of two young desperados from Charleston they think might be in the area."

She reached underneath and laid a Xeroxed piece of paper on the counter without ever taking her eyes off the vegetables she was arranging in my grocery sack. It was my MUSC identification badge photo and Helene's high school graduation head shot. I studied the photos for much longer than was necessary in order to avoid eye contact with the cashier and to compose myself.

I responded without looking up. "Yeah, I guess there is some resemblance, but he's not nearly as good lookin' as I am. Would be nice to have that doctor money, though."

"Money don't help you none when you're in the slammer."

171

I raised my eyes to meet hers. She was staring right at me, yet her eyes revealed nothing other than complete indifference.

After a few moments of awkward silence I responded. "I haven't seen either of these people. Have you?" Her silence after my question made my throat turn dry.

She continued to study my face without expression. "Naw, I don't think I have. The only people I've seen all day are my customers. That sheriff never done bought nuthin' from here. It isn't good for business if you don't take care of your customers. Besides, he reminds me of a Johnnie Law who evicted me once from my house."

"You sure you haven't seen 'em?"

"I'm sure, boy. But I stare out this window all day. The beach has a funny feel to it. Like I said, too many visitors today. If you're plannin' on stayin' around here, you better keep an eye out for those two neer-do-wells. That lawman seemed to think they was around here and he seemed anxious to find them. Be careful where you go too. I got no use for the law, but you never know when someone might need something from the cops."

"I know what you mean. This beach does seem more crowded than I prefer. I'll keep my eyes open."

I thanked her and took the groceries out to the car. Helene wasn't back yet, so I started the engine and listened to one of the Myrtle Beach rock stations. George Thorogood's "*I Drink Alone*" was on. I kept my head on a swivel for any police cruisers. I was stupid not to park behind the grocery on a side street. I hoped that the staff at Sam's Corner had the same rebel attitude as the cashier at the Garden City Grocery.

Helene returned to the car as J.J. Cale's "*They Call Me the Breeze*" came on the radio. Helene jumped in, gave me a surprised look, and said, "I love J.J. Cale."

"I do too," astonished to have found someone else who shared what I considered a secret pleasure. "Did you know he wrote Eric Clapton's *'After Midnight'*"?

"Of course. He also wrote *'Same Old Blues'* that Lynyrd Skynyrd covered. I spent my entire senior year of high school getting lit to *'Crazy Mama'* and the rest of his *'Naturally'* album."

Satisfied that Helene knew her stuff, I shut up and let J.J. keep us roll'n and a roll'n back to the condo.

When J.J. Cale finished, I asked Helene what she had found out.

"He thinks he has something that might work."

"That's good news because the police are on the island passing out prom photos of us. We can't take any more field trips."

"You're shitting me."

"I shit you not."

Helene recounted her conversation. "He said driving out of here is not an option. Your Cadillac is too easy to spot. He had already told me that people were looking for us up and down the Grand Strand. He thinks getting out of the country is the smart move and he likes the idea of heading north."

"Does he have any suggestions how to accomplish that? We've got to get out of here right away."

"He says we should fly out. He'll get us two tickets leaving tomorrow from Myrtle Beach Airport. He will pick us up and take us to the airport so we don't have to go back out on the road in the Eldorado. Our flight will be to Cincinnati and then a connection to Detroit. Once in Detroit, we can rent a car and drive across the border into Canada. The crossing between Detroit and Windsor, Ontario is very lax. We can drive under the Detroit River through the Windsor Tunnel without having to show anyone a Passport. Once we're in Windsor, we can hop on the Canadian National Railway and go anywhere we want in the Great White North. I also asked him about some cash. He can front us whatever we need."

"How does he think we are going to get through the airport? There will be eyes on the airport."

"Yeah, I asked about that. Myrtle Beach is a third-rate airport that caters to weekend golfers coming in from up north. He'll buy our tickets under some names that he uses. If we don't check any bags, then all we'll have to do is just walk on the plane. We only have to present our tickets. No one checks IDs. He thinks it's unlikely anyone at the Myrtle Beach Airport will be looking for us, even if they did get a heads-up from the police. We're supposed to be in a car. We also took off four days ago. Their attention spans aren't very long. I think it'll work."

"It'll be a big gamble. Your friend said he would bring us tickets, cash, and give us a ride to the airport. Are you sure we can trust him?"

"I think so, but I can't be for sure. I know he doesn't have any use for the police. Turning us in isn't going to put him on anybody's 'good guy' list. More importantly, by helping us, he's doing a favor for people who can do favors for him. He's predictable. He's always going to do what's best for him."

"I hope you're right. What time is he coming to pick us up?"

"It's a late afternoon flight. We should be ready to go by three p.m. Myrtle Beach Airport is only ten miles up the road on the bypass. If we just pack a carry on and get there about thirty minutes before departure, we can boogie right through the terminal and onto the plane. No waiting around, no talking to anybody, never lifting our eyes off the floor. I think it'll be a piece of cake."

"Tomorrow should be exciting. Do you know anyone in Canada?"

"Not a soul," Helene said with a grin.

After dinner, Helene and I went out to the beach and fired off a few bottle rockets. Our meager display was put to shame by a group of teenagers fifty yards down the beach. Helene challenged me to a game of dueling Roman candles, but quit when a green flare came too close to her head. Helene chased me back to the condo with a barrage of flaming, colored candle balls. Safely returned, we popped a couple of beers and watched a movie. As we watched, I rested my head on Helene's lap. Helene absent-mindedly twirled the hair on my temples. It was incredibly sensual and a major disappointment when she tapped me on the forehead and told me to sit up. She needed a potty break.

After a minute or two of channel surfing, Helene came back from the bathroom wearing only her panties. Reflexively, I hit the power off button on the TV control. She reached over and turned off the lamp.

Helene knelt on the floor between my legs in front of the couch. She pulled loose the draw strings on my scrubs, which she pulled over my hips and down to my feet. I kicked them away. When Helene stood up and took off her panties, I slid down a little farther on the couch. Helene knelt on each side of my hips. I buried my face in her chest like a child until she lifted my chin with her hand. I looked into her eyes and followed with an intimate kiss.

Without interrupting the kiss, Helene guided me into her as she slowly lowered herself onto my lap. The sensation of her enveloping me took my breath. As she had done the night before, Helene controlled our lovemaking. At times, she would take me deeply into her. At other times, she would lift herself high over me till I felt like I might fall away, but she never allowed it. It was tantalizing.

Gradually, Helene's breathing became more rapid. Our passion grew simultaneously. For the second night in a row, we climaxed together. Helene grabbed me with both arms around my head and pulled me to her chest. Her chest rose and fell with the tightening and relaxation of her vaginal contractions.

When she released my head, I looked up at her face and again, saw tears streaming down her cheeks. I had never been with anyone with a more intense emotional connection to lovemaking.

"You're not starting that again are you?" I asked with a smile.

"Don't make fun," Helene said, as she popped me on the top of the head with an open palm. She raised herself off me and walked towards the bathroom. Halfway across the room, she stopped and turned back to face me. She was standing in a swath of moonlight slicing in through the sliding glass doors. She was totally immodest. She stared at me until I finally asked, "What's wrong?"

Helene was quiet for another long second and then answered, "You know, I love you, don't you?"

"I know. I love you, too. This plan is going to work."

That night we slept together. She laid her head on my chest, and we listened to the sounds of the waves beating against the sand a few stories below.

When I awoke, I could tell from the sun it was mid-morning, but Helene's head was no longer on my chest.

I went to the bathroom, washed my face, brushed my teeth and pulled on a surgical scrub top to go with my gym shorts. The condo is not large, so I was surprised when I walked into the living room and didn't see Helene. I called her name with no response and looked in the back bedroom. Helene wasn't in the condo. Did she go downstairs to get a newspaper? I had not seen her read the paper once since we'd been together. The keys to my Cadillac were still on the hook in the kitchen. I checked the front door to make sure it hadn't been broken in. It was closed, but not locked. What the hell was going on?

Walking back to the living room, I noticed the porch sliding glass door was halfway open. Helene wasn't out there, but a flashlight was on the porch table and a bath towel was draped over the railing. The towel had not been there last night. One of the most rigid condo rules is not leaving towels draped over the rails. They made the condo look cheap. I looked up and down a virtually empty beach. There was no sign of Helene. Finally, I thought to check the back bedroom closet where Helene had put her things when we first arrived. Her back pack and all her stuff were gone.

Befuddled, I sat down on the couch in the living room. The curio cabinet across the room caught my attention. Helene's shark's tooth necklace was hanging over the edge. The necklace was looped over a rose bowl filled with the shells Helene and I had pirated from the beach. Leaning against the rose bowl was a note.

Dear Declan,

I will never be able to apologize adequately for lying to you about us leaving together today. My way out was always obvious, but it wasn't for us to fly to Detroit. The people I know are able to move grass and hash into South Carolina by the ton without anyone being the wiser. They can move me out the same way.

If I had told you the truth, you would have either tried to talk me into something else or insisted on going with me. With the Operation Jackpot arrests happening every day, there isn't any way the people I know were going to bring you along. You might have talked me into making a run for it with you, but either my father or the Feds would have caught us. Then we would have both been ruined.

I want you to know that I'm safe. By tomorrow, I will be beyond anybody's reach in either the Dominican Republic or Trinidad/Tobago.

There is something poisonous in me. I had given up all hope that I would ever be able to cleanse it from my heart. But that was before I found you again. I know it might be hard for you to believe right now, but I was telling you the truth last night. Please take care of my shark's tooth. I don't know when, but someday, I'll come back for it.

No matter how angry you are with me, you need to listen to what I have to say next. The first thing you need to do is destroy this letter. Then go home. You are a strong- willed guy, and are cursed by an over-developed sense of right and wrong. But when you get back to work, you play deaf, dumb and blind. You don't know a thing about what happened to me or where I am.

Don't pay any attention to what they say they know. There's a big difference between what they know and what they can prove. All the men I've known in my life have either laid down or been rolled over. No matter what they threaten you with, stay on your feet and weather the storm.

I hated not telling you the truth. I hope you can forgive me. This was the only way I could think of that worked.

With all my love, Helene.

I read the letter a third and fourth time. No matter how many times I read it, I couldn't make it feel real. I thought I might throw up, so I went out onto the porch. The cold salt spray off the ocean and Helene's letter both slapped me in the face. I was frustrated to the

179

point of tears by my inability to argue with her or with her logic.

I said a silent prayer for her safety, and read her letter one last time. I tore it into small pieces and held the fragments out for the wind to catch and take down the beach. Before going back inside the condo, I pulled Helene's shark's tooth necklace over my head and tucked it down the front of my shirt.

It took all my energy to clean the condo. I searched for anything Helene might have left behind, but found nothing. The drive back to Charleston was going to be the worst of my life. I wasn't ready yet.

I sat on the porch for more than an hour with my eyes fixed on the horizon. Like a novice sailor, I needed its constancy to keep my stomach calm. If there was a breathalyzer capable of measuring your emotional suitability for driving, I would've easily blown the legal limit. I would have probably failed the field test too. I'd become more emotionally invested with Helene in four days than I had with Abby in four years. I'd meant it when I said I loved her. Is it possible I'd been played for a fool? Could the last couple of days have been a charade? Why hadn't Helene insisted that we leave together? Why would she ever risk coming back? Even though I tore up her letter, I could still see her words. It was going to be very hard to keep black thoughts from clawing their way into my head.

For the first time, I began to regret the damage I'd done to my career. I'd worked for years to become Board certified in Obstetrics and Gynecology. Had I given that accomplishment away? I had a busy and appreciative practice. I had won teaching awards. My curriculum vitae was already impressive. People said I was a rising star in Ob-Gyn. However, I wasn't delusional enough to believe those things counted for much. The Medical University could be a meat grinder. Its cogwheels were politics, power and big money. I knew what happened when you got caught in those gears.

As I sat and watched the ocean, I felt a gust of air and saw the hanging blinds billow into the condo. It was a cross-wind created by the front door opening when the sliding glass porch doors were also open. The Carveys weren't due to arrive until tomorrow. Helene had changed her mind. My guess wasn't even close.

Instead of Helene, I found three large men with handguns drawn. The options as to who these men might be were multiple. That question was answered by their Government Issue shoes and the stenciling on their blue windbreakers identifying them as U.S. Marshalls.

"What the fuck are you guys doing in my house," I yelled.

"We have a warrant for the arrest Helen Eastland," the lead agent responded.

"Well, she's not here and you can get those damn pistols out of my face."

The three agents were now joined by the same tall African-American man I had seen leaving Helene's hospital room earlier this week. It was obvious he was in charge, as soon as he walked in from the entrance hallway.

"We know she's here, Dr. Murphy. My name is Laurence Nodeen. I'm a U.S. District Attorney. You've made a serious miscalculation by assisting Ms. Eastland in this foolish effort to flee the judicial process. Ms. Eastland was subpoenaed to appear before a Federal grand jury yesterday. She has relevant knowledge regarding major drug smuggling operations occurring along the South Carolina coast. I'm sure you are familiar with the Operation Jackpot prosecution by now. Her failure to appear is a federal offense."

"I'm sorry that Ms. Eastland disappointed you, but, like I said, Helene Eastman isn't here. You're wasting your time, and mine as well."

"I'm certain you won't mind if we take a look for ourselves." It wasn't a request.

"Knock yourselves out boys."

I sat on the couch while the three U.S. Marshalls took an inexplicably long time to search a 1000 square foot apartment. I was crushed that Helene had left, but I couldn't help being a little happy. Helene deserved a win. She hadn't had very many. I gave no thought to the right or wrong choices involved. Somehow, Helene had seen this coming and had dodged another bullet. As I watched their search become more surprised, I couldn't keep a smile from my face.

After huddling with the three field agents, Nodeen returned to me. "You find this funny, Dr. Murphy?"

"No, sir. I don't find it funny at all when men break into my home, threaten me with guns and accuse me of things I haven't done. I told you she wasn't here."

"Cut the crap, Dr. Murphy. We know Helene Eastland was here. We want to know where she is. You are way out of your depth. Ms. Eastland became a federal fugitive when she failed to show up to testify yesterday. What little good will she had is gone. I have no problem rolling her up with all the other Jackpot miscreants if that's how she wants to play it. You have a choice. You can become collateral damage or not. If you don't tell us what we want to know, we'll charge you with aiding and abetting a federal fugitive. That, Dr. Murphy, is not an idle threat."

I stared back at the black attorney, but I didn't answer. I thought about the night at Sesquicentennial Park when Helene was dragged from my Camaro. I've been mortified by that choice my entire life. They weren't going to yank her out of my car again. I was done being bullied.

"You can do whatever the hell you want. Helene Eastland is not here. She's never been here, and I don't know where she is. If I did, I don't think I'd tell you. If you can prove that any of those statements are lies, then you better put the cuffs on me right now. Otherwise, you need to get out of here. I need to clean up the mess you've made and get back to Charleston. I've got work Monday morning."

The three field agents looked to the black lawyer for guidance. Nodeen finally nodded toward the door. He lingered as the other agents left, and addressed me one last time. "Dr. Murphy, you're playing a very dangerous game. You don't have nearly as many cards as you think. God help you, because I can't, unless you tell me where Ms. Eastland is."

I didn't reply. We studied each other silently for about a minute before the U.S. Attorney turned and left the condo.

The drive home was as confusing and defeating as I thought it would be. Crossing the Cooper River Bridge back into Charleston, I didn't have any better idea what to do next than I did when I left Garden City. Driving down East Bay Street, I began to notice Christmas decorations that hadn't been there the week before. They didn't lift my spirit.

When I got to 75 Tradd Street, I pulled into the driveway and emptied out the car. I emptied the trunk and pulled the electrical tape off the license plate.

In retrospect, I don't know why I was surprised.

My front door was unlocked and the house was completely trashed. My study was hardest hit. Papers were strewn everywhere. An early draft of a manuscript had been purposely ripped up. My bedroom closet and dresser drawers had been rifled.

Surveying the mess, it was hard to figure out what they could've been looking for. The kitchen stunk because all my food had been taken out of the refrigerator and piled on the counter tops or in the sink. At some point I realized, this wasn't really a search. I'd been vandalized. Most of the carnage had no other purpose than to fuck with me. Knowing that Agent Wrenn had been in my house pissed me off.

After cleaning up my second apartment of the day and bagging the spoiled food, I headed for the trash cans. After dumping the trash bags I checked my mailbox. I was surprised to find nothing. I wasn't expecting anything in particular, but, without fail, I get a slew of professional junk mail each day. The meeting brochures should be bulging out of the box. Someone was taking my mail. I knew it wasn't my neighbors.

I climbed in the land yacht and headed back toward the bridge.

BLUE HAWAIIAN

I drove back over the Cooper River to Mount Pleasant, took the Coleman Boulevard exit and stopped at the Blue Hawaiian for takeout. I had a mai tai while I waited. Armed with an order of sweet and sour chicken, I drove over to River's Bend Apartments where Jack lived with his girlfriend.

"Where the Sam Hill have you been?" Jack asked when he answered my knock.

"Some shit was happening with one of my patients. I needed to get away for a few days. I went to the beach and cleared my head. Sorry I missed our game. How'd we do?"

"We got massacred. You weren't there. We didn't have near enough money to bail Taylor out of jail. We haven't heard from Denny since Jeb threatened to kill him after Cannon Street. Frances got freaked out by all the Law Enforcement people that were there looking for you. I don't think he made a single basket."

"But you were there."

"Tommy Lawson ate my lunch. I can't handle that guy, and he knows it. But our game is old news. What the heck is up with you? A couple of guys came by here and wanted to know where you were. I think you might be on the FBI ten most wanted list."

"I'm sorry, Jack. Any serious hassle?"

"No serious hassle, but it wasn't a courtesy call. Those dudes were solemn. If I had to guess, I'd say they were pissed. They think you kidnapped that patient of yours."

"First off, I haven't kidnapped anybody. I've got no idea where the girl is. All I did was go to my parent's beach house. No matter what else you hear or whatever else I'm accused of, I want you to know it's trumped up."

"That's good enough for me. Did you bring any extra from the Hawaiian?"

"I just got a single order. I'll let you have half if you let me use your phone to call my parents. I might be a little paranoid, but I was scared to use the phone at my house. You should've seen my place. They really ransacked it. I think they even took my stash of condoms."

"Don't sweat it. It isn't paranoia if they're really after you. I met those muscle heads and don't think avoiding your phone is unreasonable at all. You're welcome to stay here if you want. I haven't seen any guys in dark glasses hanging around outside, but who knows."

"Thanks, Jack. I appreciate it."

After eating our Chinese, I called home and was happy to learn that no one from law enforcement had contacted my parents. After some probing, Mom mentioned they'd gotten a call early in the week from someone identifying themselves as being from the Ob-Gyn department. They said there was a question about call coverage. They wondered if I'd come home or if my parents knew where I might be. Mom and Dad didn't have any idea where I was, and gave them my home phone number. I reassured them it wasn't anything they needed to worry about. I had straightened it out.

We talked a little more and made some holiday plans. If I couldn't come up to Columbia for Christmas, I'd try to join them at the beach house for New Year's. The discussion of the beach house caught in my throat for a second. I told Mom and Dad that I loved them. I'd never said that to them with more sincerity.

Jack informed me that we had another basketball game on Sunday if I was able to play. I couldn't think of a better way to exorcize both some stress and anger. Win or lose, basketball provided a release I found in few other places. Jack was pleased and offered to drive. I thanked him, but said I would have to go home to get my stuff and would drive myself, "circumstances allowing." A grin accompanied that last remark.

Jack's drink was bourbon and after several rounds of Maker's Mark, my mood was improving. His girlfriend was a gorgeous Italian exchange student from the College of Charleston named Nicolette. She got me be a blanket and a pillow, and I made myself a place on their couch. Despite the Maker's Mark, I wasn't able to sleep. How different this night was, alone on Jack and Nicolette's couch, compared to the past two nights spent in Helene's arms. What would the next few days bring? Had I squandered my career helping someone who, long ago, learned how to play men for whatever she needed?

I finally fell asleep, but it was a restless night filled with chaotic dreams. I was still tired when Jack rousted me the following morning.

Neither of us were churchgoers, so Jack and I watched cartoons and looked through the Sunday papers. Nicolette was wearing one of Jack's tapered dress shirts and, as best I could tell, nothing else. I envied Jack, not for having such a stunning girlfriend, but for having an uncomplicated relationship.

Finally, I told Jack and Nicolette I'd better get going. I needed to get my basketball gear, and I definitely needed to shoot around before our two p.m. game.

After thanking Nicolette for putting up with me, I headed back downtown about a quarter till twelve.

This December Sunday morning was particularly bleak. Besides the cold, the sky was lifeless. The live oaks lining the streets rarely acknowledged either the season or the weather, but today they were heavily gauzed with nasty grey Spanish moss. The day perfectly matched my mood. Even with Christmas just a week and a half away, it was difficult to find anything joyous.

Most people have a hard time recognizing the source of their emotions, especially when they are ragged. It's tricky to know what is really under your skin. This time it wasn't hard. There were some real ass holes behind the carnage that I'd found in my apartment. It wasn't an accident either. As I got closer to home, I could feel a toxic bile of anger and frustration building up in me. Playing some basketball would be a good mental health break .

PRENATAL WELLNESS CENTER

There were several approaches I could take to my return to work. Some were bold; others were more tactical. Of no surprise to me, I chose the magical third grader approach. I'd just show up to my assigned clinic like nothing had ever happened. On Monday mornings, I was assigned to read ultrasounds at the Prenatal Wellness Center.

When I arrived at the Center, Katherine Donovan was already there. Kathy and I joined the Department the same year. She was my closest departmental friend despite the fact that she'd trained at Duke. Dookies were generally insufferable, but I'd learned to avoid Kathy on selected weekends between January and March. Having started at the same time, we fell into the habit of watching out for each other. That evolved into caring about each other. I was glad that it would be Kathy who I encountered first.

"Donovan!" I yelled from behind, making her jump as she was focused on reading an ultrasound. "What the hell are you doing here? Are you trying to steal my clinical dollars? If you don't pay attention every second around here someone tries to cut your throat. I never expected this from you Donovan. *Et tu Brute?*"

Kathy stammered for a second trying to regain her footing. Quickly, she realized I was yanking her chain. She gave me an irritated school teacher look over the top of her glasses and composed herself.

"No one told me you'd be back today."

"You must not have gotten my note. You need to pay more attention to your mail."

Kathy suspected I was lying, but decided to let it go. I'm sure she desperately wanted to know what had happened and where I'd been. I doubt she accepted any of the rumors that she had probably heard. Apparently, she decided that this was not the time to ask. Kathy had a faith in me that I wasn't sure I had in myself. I was thankful for that. I also knew there were few other people willing to give me that kind of trust.

"Well, maybe I missed the memo," Kathy said with some obvious sarcasm. "I'm more than happy to pass the baton back to you. You might find it hard to believe, but I actually have several other important things I need to do."

"You're right. I do find that hard to believe. You should hang around and see how it's done. This could be a great learning opportunity for you."

Recognizing I was being a smart ass, Kathy measured her answer. "Well, that would-d-d-d-d be quite the treat." She drew out "would" as long as possible. "As disappointed as I am that I cannot stay to learn at the feet of the master, I must attend to some other matters. Were that not the case, I'd certainly take you up on this very generous offer, you douche-rocket."

We both laughed. It was the first time I had laughed in a couple of days. "Hey, I brought you a sercy." I reached into my briefcase and retrieved the perfect sun-bleached sand dollar that Helene had found on the Garden City beach. "Does this get me out of the dog-house?"

"No, but it's nice. And, it's a start. Thank you." After gathering her stuff to head back to her academic office, Kathy stopped to talk with me once more. "If you have any trouble, you know you can call me, right?"

"I know. Thanks for not asking."

Kathy nodded.

Late in the morning, we scanned a thirty-seven year-old woman and found a fetus with a number of anatomic malformations including a heart defect. I suspected a chromosomal abnormality and asked our genetic counselor to speak with her. After many tears and a great deal of angst, the woman decided to have an amniocentesis.

I numbed her skin with Xylocaine and was using the ultrasound probe to guide the insertion of the amniocentesis needle. Arguing erupted in the hallway just outside the procedure room. Moments later, SLED Agent Wrenn entered the ultrasound room, followed closely by our exasperated charge nurse.

"Dr. Murphy, I need to talk with you immediately." Agent Wrenn's voice boomed in the small room.

"As you can see, I'm busy at the moment. If you wouldn't mind waiting outside, I'll be done here shortly," I said, as calmly as possible.

"Don't get all high and mighty with me, Doctor. I've waited long enough for you already. I'm here on a law enforcement matter. I want to speak with you at once."

Agent Wrenn's aggressiveness was startling. My patient was now visibly trembling. The amniocentesis needle was appropriately ominous protruding from her abdominal wall.

"Sir, I don't care what official business you feel you have with me. You're violating this woman's right to privacy. I'm in the middle of a potentially dangerous procedure. If she moves, or if my hand jerks, and I injure this baby, or she loses this pregnancy, I don't think anyone is going to care about your 'law enforcement matter.' Are you prepared to accept that responsibility?"

When Agent Wrenn hesitated, I added, "I didn't think so."

My momentary upper hand was supported by the woman's husky husband who was now on his feet and staring at Agent Wrenn. "As I said before, please excuse yourself and wait outside. I'll be with you when I'm done."

I could tell Wrenn was pissed, but there wasn't much else that he could do. The amniocentesis needle was ticking back and forth like a metronome as my patient hyperventilated. Wrenn knew he was in over his head. He mumbled, "I'm sorry. Excuse me, ma'am," before exiting back outside into the hallway.

Nurse Annette shrugged at me after Wrenn left. "I'm sorry. I told him not to come in."

"I know. Don't worry about it. It's not your fault. Tell you what though. Please call MUSC security. I don't know how much mayhem this guy is capable of."

I apologized to my patient and completed the amniocentesis. It was time to face the music. Agent Wrenn was hot to get his hands on me. Unfortunately for me, the ultrasound suite had no back door. At the end of the hallway, Agent Wrenn was waiting with Nurse Annette. She seemed to have him momentarily at bay. Wrenn was with another SLED agent I'd not seen before. I had a small amount of regret that it wasn't Agent Lesher. Knowing a confrontation was inevitable, I started walking toward the SLED agents. Believing that a good offense was the best defense, I addressed Agent Wrenn before I was halfway down the hall. "Sir, that was highly inappropriate. Your behavior put that woman's baby at risk."

Wrenn was not going to be cowed a second time. He met me with two strides and put a hard finger in my chest, "Doctor, you need to shut up and listen. You're in a shit load of trouble. We have questions for you. You need to have answers for us. We know you helped

Helene Eastland leave the hospital last week. We want to know where she is and we want to know right now."

I'm not sure how many nights' sleep Agent Wrenn had missed over the past week, but I could tell he was wired. His breath, clothes, and sweat all reeked of nicotine and caffeine, which made him even more dangerous than usual. Sleep deprivation had fairly predictable effects on both cognition and performance. What was unpredictable was its effect on mood. The burnout which comes with being sleep deprived can manifest as either apathy or anger. Agent Wrenn never struck me as the apathetic type. I could see in Wrenn's eyes that his wiring was frayed.

I used the outside of my left arm to brush his hand and finger away from my chest. I closed the space between us. The distance between our faces was merely inches. I forced myself to steady my speaking tone, "Sir, you don't know anything about me or what I may or may not have done. I don't know where Helene Eastland is. If I did, you'd be the last person on earth I'd tell. I've been away on a much needed vacation. And, by the way, you left my refrigerator door open. You owe me for a carton of milk."

Wrenn inched even closer and literally hissed, "Watch yourself, you son of a bitch. You're on thin ice. We're talking about kidnapping. Are you man enough to take that kind of weight? I don't think so."

Wrenn probably expected me to flinch at the mention of kidnapping. "If you had any evidence of kidnapping involving the governor's daughter, I'd already be in handcuffs. I'm also pretty sure those handcuffs would've been put on me by an FBI agent, not a local rent-a-cop who couldn't keep track of a post-op woman who could barely walk."

Wrenn was trembling with anger, but I didn't let up. "I don't know if I can take the weight of a kidnapping charge or not. But, I sure as hell would rather do that than be a trained Doberman running errands for the governor. Do you even remember when you used to be a real law enforcement officer?"

Wrenn's answer came in the form of a short right to the solar plexus that emptied my lungs of air. I dropped to one knee. My eyes watered from the pain, and I was gasping for air. I could hear Wrenn seething, "Get up, you son of a bitch."

I kept my head down, waiting for my eyes to refocus, but with every intention of obliging him. Undoubtedly, Wrenn had a lot more experience than I with dirty boxing. Like Butch Cassidy, if there weren't going to be any rules, then one, two, three, let's go.

Without looking up, I rose from the floor and lunged into his midsection. At the same time, I targeted his left kidney with a right cross. I felt him shudder as it connected. I was pleased he'd be pissing blood for the next few days. Even though my charge had taken him down, Wrenn was much too tough a customer to fold up after one kidney punch. As we crashed backwards onto the floor, he wrapped his arms around my neck and kneed me in the groin. His aim was good enough to hurt, but not perfect enough to incapacitate. I was able to get in another couple of quick punches to his left flank, and found his nose with my right elbow. I broke free of his grip around my neck. As I postured up, I blocked one right hand, but a left caught me on the side of the head.

I balled up my fist for another right ticketed for his chin. I let it go, but surprisingly, it didn't. MUSC security had arrived and had caught my punch as they were pulling me off him. Thankfully, they were also restraining him from tearing back into me. Wrenn quickly gathered himself. He and his new partner produced IDs identifying themselves as SLED agents. They were questioning me as a pertinent witness in a disappearance.

I expected the MUSC Public Safety officers to unravel like a pair of knock-off espadrilles. Fortunately, one of the security guys had notified their chief when called about the situation in the Ob-Gyn clinic. Someone had correctly surmised that things seemed a bit out of the ordinary over in Obstetrics. In what must have been record time, the MUSC Public Safety Director had located the hospital lawyer, Vincent Bellizia. Just when I was expecting the MUSC safety officers to throw me back to the lions, they instead addressed Agent Wrenn and his partner.

"Sir, the hospital attorney requests that you cease your efforts to question Dr. Murphy. The hospital will handle this situation internally. He would like you both to come to his office."

I liked the first part of that. Wasn't sure what I thought about the second part. It didn't appear that Agent Wrenn liked either part.

I was glad that the security guys were providing a buffer between me and Agent Wrenn. He looked hungry, and I was the red meat he wanted. I couldn't help myself and took another poke at the tiger in the cage. "You go tell the governor I couldn't come out and play today, okay. By the way, would you like Ms. Annette to get you an ice pack for your nose? Looks to me like it might be broken."

"This isn't over yet, you smart ass. We'll talk again." Wrenn emphasized the word "talk." "You can count on that."

"I'm looking forward to it."

OB-GYN DEPARTMENT CHAIRMAN'S OFFICE

Agent Wrenn and his new partner were shown their way out of the Prenatal Wellness Center. The public safety officers indicated they were to escort me over to Dr. Templeton's office. It was a bad day, rapidly getting worse.

Half-way across campus we bumped into Kathy Donovan heading back to the Prenatal Wellness Center. "Well, that didn't take very long."

"Doesn't look like I'm going to get to finish ultrasound today."

"Did you really get into a fist-fight with a policeman?"

"More of a wrestling match if you ask me. My new buddies here broke it up before I could pin him. And it was a SLED agent, not a policeman. I want my legend to be as big as possible."

"This isn't funny, you know. What the hell is the matter with you? What am I going to do when they kick your butt out of here?"

"I'm not sure I know the answer to that one. That isn't in my hands right now. He threw the first punch, but if they torture me, I'll have to admit that I provoked him." I was touched by Kathy's concern for me. "I'm sorry you got tabbed to cover for me again."

"Just do me a favor. Don't lose your temper, and don't use any curse words."

"That's two things."

"Don't crack wise with me, you dummy. This is serious stuff. You might want to play it smart and be a little contrite."

I could tell that Kathy was upset. I didn't want to rattle her chain anymore. "Yes, ma'am. I'll let you know what happens. I'll call you tonight. I doubt I'm coming back to clinic this afternoon."

Kathy raised her eyebrows and shook her head.

The remaining walk to the Clinical Science Building took about five minutes. That gave me an opportunity to think things through. Templeton would be pissed I'd left work without permission, and he had every right to be. That was a reprimand at worst. Templeton was too reserved to mention the accusations involving myself and Helene. If it weren't for the fight today, Templeton would probably have preferred no conversation at all regarding my absence.

Although nervous, I was curious to find out how far Dr. Templeton would go to stand up for me with his bosses. There was no love lost between my chairman and hospital administration. I wanted to think the best of him, but I knew Templeton was neither a strong nor a confrontational guy. When the shit-storm really started to blow in, could I count on Preston to have my back?

When I got to Dr. Templeton's office, his secretary made me wait about ten minutes. I could hear him talking on the phone the entire time. When I entered his office, my questions were immediately answered. Templeton and I were joined by our departmental business manager. His role was to be a witness for Dr. Templeton. Walking, talking confirmation that he had done as he was told. Not a good omen for me.

I initiated the conversation, mainly because I wasn't anxious to hear what Dr. Templeton had to say. "Preston, I want to apologize for the incident in clinic today. I think that all of the witnesses will tell you that the SLED agent initiated the confrontation and threw the first punch. However, it was still highly unprofessional. I can assure you nothing like that will ever happen again."

"Thank you, Declan. I appreciate that. It seems to me, though, that the first punch was probably thrown a week ago, figuratively speaking. Declan, my bigger concern, and the concern of the hospital, is that you've been AWOL since last Tuesday. No one knew where you were or how to contact you. You know that whenever you're away, you have to request the time off. For time off to be granted, you have to ensure all your clinics and patient care responsibilities are covered. You failed to do any of those things. Faculty schedules were disrupted. Office schedules were disrupted. I can't remember her name, but one of your patients was readmitted with a post-op infection. She was very upset that you couldn't be reached. All in all, it's been a pretty big mess around here, and it all could've been avoided. The rules regarding leave requests are in place for a reason. You had a responsibility to follow those rules."

"Dr. Templeton, I agree with almost everything you've said. I'm very sorry to have disrupted the office schedules. I will apologize to each faculty member. I'll also make things right with all of my patients. I disagree that it could've been avoided. I had personal issues I can't discuss right now. Those issues did not afford me the opportunity to call in and request leave through the usual process."

"Declan, did those personal issues involve Helene Eastland? I warned you right here in this office to back off that case. I'm told that you took her with you when you left. She was never discharged from the hospital. SLED believes that you took her against her will, against the will of her family, and against the advice of several different psychiatric consultants."

"Preston, that sounds scripted to me. None of those statements are true, and you know it. I didn't kidnap Helene Eastman, and I don't know where she is."

"I hope you're telling the truth, Declan. There are a lot of people who believe that you did," Templeton said, shaking his head while looking at a document on his desk. "They say you arranged a diversion to get her out of the hospital. You then took her to either Savannah or Atlanta. They're convinced you know where she is. They make a convincing case against you. You need to know this going in. My advice to you is to let the authorities know whatever it is that you know. "

I could hear Helene's voice in my head, warning me to be careful about what I said next. There's a difference between what they know and what they can prove.

"Preston, I don't care what kind of case they're making. I was in the hospital the night she disappeared, but I didn't kidnap Helene Eastland. Nor did I take her to Savannah or Atlanta. You and I talked about it that very afternoon. The whole situation was a Mongolian cluster. I finally realized I needed to get away from it. As you advised, I might add. I went to my parent's beach condo in Garden City in order to clear my head. I've been there all week."

"Declan, there's no way for me to know who's telling the truth. But, with you having gone AWOL and now, with the fight in the office today, I don't have any option other than to send you home till we can get some of these questions answered."

"Am I suspended?"

"No, but President Turner wants to meet with you tomorrow morning at nine a.m. Answers will be expected at that meeting. In the meantime, go home. Think this through. We all want you to come back to work. Nobody more than me. That, however, is going to depend on how things go tomorrow. Do you understand that?"

"Yes, sir, I understand. Please tell the faculty, especially those that helped out covering for me, that I really appreciate everything they did and, I guess, are continuing to do. Their support means a lot."

"I will certainly do that," Templeton said, with a formality that told me our conversation was over.

"By the way, there's one other way."

"One other way to what?"

"One other way to know who's telling the truth."

"How's that?"

"Believe what I tell you." I'd never spoken like that to Dr. Templeton before.

SULLIVAN'S ISLAND

I didn't know what to do with an afternoon off. It didn't seem like a good idea to go drink at Big John's, but I also wasn't going to sulk at home. I needed some fresh air. It was sad how infrequently I took advantage of the solace offered by the Charleston beaches. I could be on Sullivan's Island in about ten minutes.

Other than a small cluster of restaurants and bars as you came on the island, Sullivan's was completely residential. That gave it a unique feel, particularly in the winter. There were no tourists, despite some of the widest and smoothest beaches on the east coast. I parked on the street next to a public access, and walked through the dunes and sea oats out to the beach. The surf sounds louder during the winter which I think is due to the absence of any distracting man-made noise. It was the human quiet that made the wintertime beach special.

It was low tide and the beach was almost one hundred yards wide in some places. Small pools of trapped ocean were scattered here and there. I walked toward the surf, thinking about the shelling Helene and I had done last week. The wind whipped a shape-shifting cloud of sand down the beach that bit at my exposed ankles. Sandpipers and gulls raced back and forth over the sand as the waves rushed in and receded. Their search must have been of great consequence because their efforts were ceaseless.

I walked towards the Sullivan's Island lighthouse. There wasn't anyone else on the beach as far as I could see.

I wasn't confused about what was being planned for tomorrow. There would be promises, then threats. Some would be empty, and some would be real. It was going to be high intensity and high stakes. I needed to make sure my thoughts were straight before walking into the President's boardroom.

I didn't believe anyone had seen us leaving the hospital together or could place Helene at the beach condo. Helene had been with me at the beachwear shop and at Sam's Corner. I was confident no one at those places would remember us with their beer- and rum-soaked neurons, or if they did, would admit it to anyone of authority. Burdette, the security guard at Brookgreen Gardens, hadn't paid much attention to Helene. If he did, she had her hair pulled back under a baseball cap and was wearing dark glasses. He would remember her as Phoebe. The old crone at the grocery store only met me. She wasn't going to cooperate with anyone. The U.S. Marshalls hadn't found any evidence of Helene when they searched the condo Saturday morning.

As long as they couldn't prove Helene was with me when we left the hospital, they could push me around all they wanted. I hadn't done anything criminal. The medical school was another matter. They had me for leaving work without permission, patient abandonment, and for not fulfilling my academic responsibilities to teach residents, medical students, and whatever else the state pays me to do. My fight in the clinic today with Agent Wrenn was also a problem. When you set all the macho aside, it was pretty stupid. He might've even been trying to bait me into hitting him, although I didn't give him credit for being that clever.

The hospital didn't have to worry about what it could or couldn't prove. Hospitals worry about covering their asses and how things will look two weeks down the road

203

when one of their attending physicians is arrested for kidnapping the governor's daughter. That's going to look bad on the front page of the News and Courier. Even if it wasn't kidnapping, it would still be exciting to read about a university Ob-Gyn physician running off with the Governor Eastland's daughter, better yet, a post-op gynecological Governor Eastland's daughter, for a week of sex on the beach. The hospital was going to want to drop me like a bad habit. It would trump up whatever was necessary to get rid of me. Making the governor happy was a bonus. I could hear them talking now about the "win-win scenario." Hell, I might even be worth some supplemental state allocation for the medical university.

Although I didn't think I would be walking out of the President's boardroom in handcuffs, I was confident I wouldn't be walking out with a job. I was worried about my medical license. They had the ability to report me to the State Board of Medical Examiners. I doubted the governor would do it. The governor couldn't afford to be the complainant, because he didn't know what Helene had told me. He would need to stay above the fray. The hospital, on the other hand, could easily do the governor's bidding. How great to trumpet itself as a concerned health care institution, willing to even turn in one of its own in order to protect the public and medical profession from a bad apple. Two "win-wins" in one day would be administratively orgasmic.

I sat on the trunk of a fallen Palmetto tree at the edge of the dunes and watched a huge container ship get smaller and smaller before eventually disappearing. No matter what, I wasn't going to let their threats change my story and I wasn't going to give up Helene again. I also wasn't going to cadge for either my job or my license. If I had too, I would fight for my medical license at the South Carolina Board. The most important thing to remember is that they're going to do whatever they had already planned to do. Once you acknowledged that truism, there's no reason to be intimidated.

I thought about the possibility of contacting a lawyer. I was torn over that. Another faculty member's husband was a lawyer and had helped several people I knew. It was an option, but I didn't yet know what they were going to throw at me. I might need a lawyer at some point, but I couldn't imagine going to tomorrow's meeting with a lawyer in tow. It was also foolish to believe that having a lawyer would necessarily be helpful. I'd be asking some solo-practice, hand-to-mouth local barrister to go up against the governor and the Medical University of South Carolina. This isn't the movies.

South Carolina had been described as being too small to be a state, but too large to be an asylum. There're only a few million people who live in South Carolina, which is about the same number who live in Chicago. Moreover, only about a third of that number are educated. South Carolina is a "good old boy" state, and the good old boys protect the power they have. I doubt there is any other state where so much political and economic power is concentrated in the hands of so few people. Even when there is a rare change in state leadership, the jobs are just redistributed among the same old white guys. It's similar to the scene in *Casablanca* when Rick has shot the Nazi officer, and the Chief of Police tells one of his constables to "round up the usual suspects."

Having such an in-bred ruling class meant you had to be careful about where you looked for help. Every lawyer in South Carolina was related to, or owed something to, somebody in power. If they didn't, they were looking for a way to owe something to somebody in power. That might be cynical, but it's how business is done in the Palmetto state. Who's going to help me take on the state's most powerful politician? Not anybody I knew. If the shit hit the fan, it might be better to see who shows up to offer help, rather than making a random choice from the yellow pages. I didn't know them, who they practiced with, who their uncles were, or from whom their mother's father had bought his farm. I was better off on my own for now.

I finished my walk to the lighthouse and headed back. It was getting colder and began to smell like rain. No matter how hard I tried, I couldn't put out of my mind the festering concern that I'd been played by Helene. Had I been her only way out? Somewhere along the line, Helene had become skilled at getting men to do things for her. I could still see her standing in front of me in her hospital room, taking off her shirt and putting on hospital scrubs. Was that vulnerability or manipulation? If she was just using me, that was so much unnecessary icing on the cake. Although the thought seemed unimaginable, it kept coming back.

Shortly after returning to my apartment on Tradd the phone rang. I wasn't surprised when I heard Kathy Donovan's voice.

"What's up, K?"

"I knew you wouldn't call me, so I decided to call you. What did Templeton say?"

I didn't feel like rehashing everything, but I was grateful that Kathy would pick up the phone to call. She was calling out of true concern, not just morbid curiosity. Not many people have friends that good. She deserved my time.

"Great conversation. He gave me the afternoon off. He didn't want me to wear myself out after being gone for so long."

"Then what?"

"Tomorrow morning, I'm meeting with him and the Dean in the President's office. I'm not sure who else will be there. I'm only guessing, but I think the topic of conversation will be me."

"Is Templeton going to back you up?"

"I don't know. He didn't give me any reason to be optimistic. The words were coming out of his mouth, but they didn't sound like his. There was a Pontius Pilate-type of vibe in his office. I didn't actually see him washing his hands, but I think he was working a Handi-wipe when I left."

"Well, don't count on him. You know, the Dean doesn't like him. He's probably disappointed the President as well. I don't think Preston has much fight in him anymore. You're going to have to fight for yourself. Are you ready?"

"You know what, Kathy, I feel like I am. I've probably made some mistakes, but only venial sins. Nothing mortal. I can live with what I've done."

"That's good. You call me if you need anything."

"I know. Thanks, Kathy. I'll let you know how it goes."

After getting off the phone with Kathy, I made myself a rum and coke. I decided I was going to need several. About six-thirty p.m. I was startled when my beeper went off. It had been so long since I'd last heard it, I'd almost forgotten about it. I'm sure everyone was paging me the day after I left town with Helene, but by the time we were in Garden City, I was out of range. The beeper showed an MUSC number, and I was interested in who might want to talk to me.

When I returned the page, I recognized the voice of Bailey Clark on the other end. "Hey, Bailey. What's up?"

"Not much. Just wanted to let you know that all the residents are glad you're back."

"Thanks, Bailey. I appreciate that."

Bailey continued, "I don't know what you're doing, but if you're free, I was wondering if I might be able to drop by. I think you should know about some of the stuff that went on around here while you were gone. I can pick up some take out at China Palace if you haven't eaten."

"I haven't, and that would be great. I'll have their Chinese chicken wings and some lo mien."

"I'll pick it up and be over within an hour."

As I waited for Bailey, I thought about how much I disliked the China Palace, which is a "mom and pop" operation just across the street from the hospital. You never see "pop," but you see way too much of "mom." She's monstrous. "Pop" works in the kitchen and is subjected to constant harassment from his harpy wife who screams food orders and other invectives at him. Even though the food is pretty good, you can't enjoy it because of her screeching, which is even more annoying in Chinese.

The other irritating thing about Ms. China Palace is how cheap she is. If you order a soft drink, momma opens a can of Mountain Dew and pours it in an eight-ounce glass filled with ice. She puts the half-empty can back in the refrigerator. When you order a soft drink, you never knew if you're getting a fresh or used can. She also charges a nickel for each package of duck sauce. I don't know if I can tell pigeon from chicken, but I wasn't ordering the pancit.

Bailey arrived precisely when expected. She was happier to see me than I expected. I set the kitchen table and poured us both some ice tea.

"What's on your mind, Bailey?"

"Well, all the residents hope you'll be back to work soon. We miss you."

"Even Parker Weaver?"

"Well, maybe everyone but Parker. The only person he enjoys seeing each day is his own reflection in the mirror. He's moved on to oncology. He's a good fit with those guys. Seriously though, we've missed you."

"Nice to be missed. But that can't be the only thing. What's on your mind? Besides the charm of my company, of course?"

"Are you in trouble for that fight in clinic today?"

"Probably, but I won't know for sure until tomorrow."

"Well, we all thought it was way cool. That SLED guy was a real dick. Nobody minded seeing him get taken down. I thought it might help for you to be aware of what happened after you left town."

"I'd love to know what happened. Seems like my absence got everyone pretty worked up."

"First off, no one knew Eastland was gone until morning rounds. When Wrenn came in and found Eastland missing, he tore that other agent a new one. They thought she might still be in the hospital. Wrenn and MUSC security searched for quite a while, but eventually decided she was gone. Wrenn and some new guys showed up later in the morning and had a go at me for about an hour. They wanted to know where you were and figured I must know. Agent Wrenn wanted to know whatever I knew about you. Where you lived? Where you hung out? Who were your friends? He wasn't charming about it."

"I'm sorry Bailey. You didn't deserve any of that."

"No problem. I didn't tell him anything. I told him you were the boss, and your personal life was none of my business. He talked to a lot of other people though. I'm not sure what others might have said."

"Thanks. None of that surprises me. I hope they didn't make life too miserable for you."

"He didn't rattle me. The next day though, Dr. Templeton called me to his office. He leaned on me pretty hard about whether you helped Ms. Eastland get out of the hospital. He also wanted to know where you were. I was mostly honest. I told him you were upset about the Psychiatry consult you hadn't ordered and the plans to transfer Ms. Eastland to the State Mental Hospital. You and Ms. Eastland never talked about the possibility of sneaking out of the hospital in my presence. I told him I didn't think you had anything to do with her leaving and that I didn't know anything about Ms. Eastland's whereabouts. Ms. Eastland knew she was being guarded and that there were plans to move her to Columbia. I told Templeton that if I were Eastland, I would have bolted if I saw the chance."

I don't think Bailey expected me to respond to her theory. I think she was practicing a statement to see how it sounded when read aloud. I did think she was looking for some affirmation, so I nodded. "She was very worried about going back to Columbia. She'd spent much of her adult life trying to keep out of her father's filthy hands."

Some of the tension left Bailey's face. I realized she was probing to make sure her story was going to match up with mine without directly asking. She had some legitimate concern about being dragged into this. I valued her willingness to put herself in some jeopardy for me. I'd always liked Bailey, but hadn't appreciated the quality of her character quite as much as I did at that moment.

After a sip of iced tea, Bailey added, "They know you were in the hospital the night she left."

"How do they know that?"

"I'm not sure. They talked to a lot of people. Maybe they have some videotape. I told them you were probably here seeing Ferdy Eldrez."

"Why did you tell them that?"

Bailey blinked and looked a little surprised. "I don't know," she stammered. "All the residents think you and Ferdy are going out. I mean, Ferdy told Wrenn you had come to the hospital to ask her out on a date."

"I'm not sure about that," I said, again humbled that another friend had stepped up for me. "Any other things they told you?"

"Not really. But I can tell you they're convinced you took her. I got the impression they have something else. I don't know what it is."

"Well, I'll find out soon enough. I'm supposed to meet with Dean Funderburke and President Turner tomorrow morning. If they have something, I suspect I'm going to hear about it then. I don't anticipate a service award."

That made Bailey laugh, and we turned our attention back to our Chinese take-out.

"You know there was one other weird thing," Bailey added a minute later. "I'm not sure whether it's important or not."

"What was it?"

"I never had to dictate a discharge summary. I looked for her chart for a long time after they discovered her missing. It was just gone. Then I noticed her name never came up on my list of patients needing a discharge summary. I asked around. She didn't show up on anybody else's list either. Interesting huh?"

"It is. Don't know what it means, but I don't think either one of us is ever going to see that chart again."

"I don't think so either. So, I thought you might want this." Bailey dug into her purse. "You asked me to copy this." She handed me the psychiatry consult from the State Hospital. "I hung onto it."

"I'm glad you did. If they're trying to hide anything on her chart, this is probably it."

"That's what I thought."

There wasn't much left to say, and we had finished our Chinese. Finally, I let Bailey know how I felt. "You know, whatever happens tomorrow, it means a lot to me that you and the other residents have been supportive. I hope I'll be able to come back to work. Mostly, for you guys."

"You better come back. We've got cases piling up, and we need to get back to the operating room. You're not going to believe this, but I've found a couple of girls in clinic who say they bleed every month."

"No, shit." I laughed. "Sounds like a vaginal hysterectomy would fix both of them right up."

"That's what I thought, boss. You get back to work, and I'll get them on the schedule," Bailey said with a smile as she rose to leave.

After Bailey left, I watched a little television, but mostly I thought about Helene. I wondered if I'd ever see her again. I picked up the puzzle box I'd purchased for Helene at Brookgreen Gardens. I didn't know if I could still open it. After a couple of attempts the sequence fell into place. The cherry wood box revealed its dark blue velvet-lined innermost compartment. I removed Helene's shark's tooth necklace from around my neck, and placed it carefully in the secret compartment. I would save it there until I saw her again.

Sleep wouldn't come easily tonight. I put the brown album by *The Band* on my cassette player. I listened to *Whispering Pines*. I loved Richard Manuel's exquisite melody and haunted falsetto. Never until tonight, however, had I appreciated the heartrending desolation and engulfing aloneness of his "empty house." There was always something shaky and fragile in Richard Manuel's voice that I attributed to an effort to reach a note he really didn't have. Tonight, I understood. He was just another guy with a heart that had been broken. By the third stanza, when Richard and Levon Helm begin their call-and-response duet, I was sobbing uncontrollably.

Tuesday morning came too early and my sleep had not been restful. I showered, shaved and had a bowl of cereal with some blackberries. I had a choice. Dress in my best suit with a power tie or dress for work. I hated wearing the long white doctor's coat. Mine hung on a hall tree my dad had made for my medical school graduation. I walked past it every morning, but rarely put it on. On this day though, I decided to dress for work. The Spartan mother told her son, "Come back with your shield or on it." No matter what they tried to jam down my throat, they weren't going to make me choke on shame. If they're going to take my medical career away from me, I'm going to go down looking like a doctor, not like a Broad Street lawyer. I was pleased when I realized how stiff my white coat was from some long ago dry cleaning with extra starch. Too bad it wasn't enough starch to be bullet proof.

It was shaping up to be a magnificent Chamber of Commerce day. It was one of those crisp, clear winter mornings that showed up after a storm had blown through. The sky was sapphire blue without even a wisp of a cloud. It felt more like Indian summer than mid-December. When the sun hit your face it had golden, buttery warmth. If I was a kid, Mom would have made me put on a sweater, but I would've taken it off on the way to school. It was too fine a day for what was going to happen.

MUSC PRESIDENT'S OFFICE

The President's office was on the second floor of the administration building in the center of campus. Entering the reception area, I was greeted by the hospital's attorney, Vincent Bellizia. He was a rumpled little guy, perpetually sporting a second Sunday suit and tie. We exchanged pleasantries, but he gave away nothing of whatever thoughts were nesting behind his small bird-like eyes and pinched wire-rimmed glasses. After a few minutes, the secretary's phone rang and she waved us into the president's boardroom.

It was an impressive room by any measure. A large dark mahogany conference table dominated the center with overstuffed chairs around the periphery. Previous University presidents stood silent watch from the walls, imposing guardians of Southern medical tradition. It was a great home field advantage for President Turner.

One of the more celebrated events of the Charleston Hospital Strike of 1969 was a meeting between Medical College President Dr. William McCord and union representatives. That meeting was held right here in this office, around this table. However, when the union leadership arrived, Dr. McCord failed to show up. Having been manipulated, the union representatives staged an impromptu protest. The guardians of propriety watching from the walls were displeased, and the administration fired the twelve union representatives who had come to the boardroom for a parlay. The hospital workers walked off their jobs soon thereafter. The re-hiring of the union representatives became another of the major strike demands. There was a better than average chance that I was going to walk out of this conference room having suffered the same fate as the 1969 union organizers. This time, there wouldn't be any hospital strike demanding my reinstatement.

The first person I noticed was SLED Agent Wrenn slouching against the wall to the left of the door. Never one to avoid spitting into the wind, I winked in his direction. I could tell it roasted his oysters. If we were anywhere else security would probably be pulling him off of me again. A moment too late, I realized I might pay a high price for that wink if I ended up leaving this room in Wrenn's custody.

Standing around the table were some folks I expected and some I didn't. University President Gordon Turner was at the head of the table. To his right was the Medical School Dean, Dr. Colvin Funderburke. Dr. Funderburke was a psychiatrist by training and a wheeler-dealer by nature. To the President's left was Dr. Wilton Steed, the President of the Medical Practice Group. Steed was a bald-headed ferret who had failed as a surgeon because of his inability to convince anyone that he could perform a high-function task. Proving the Peter Principle correct, Steed had taken his inadequate leadership skills all the way to the Presidency of the medical staff. I couldn't figure out why Steed was here.

I was disappointed, but not surprised, that Dr. Templeton was missing. Had he been purposefully uninvited or had he just cut his losses? Either answer carried bad consequences. On the other side of the table, and separated by a few chairs from Dr. Steed, was Governor Eastland. I was surprised he was here alone, although his pit bull Wrenn was waiting by the door.

The hospital lawyer Bellizia was exchanging greetings with the other two men in the room. The white guy was Thomas Sheprow, the U.S. District Attorney for South Carolina, and the man directing the Operation Jackpot prosecution. With him was the African-American U.S. Attorney Laurence Nodeen whom I had met in Garden City. The presence of two U.S. Attorneys was disquieting. I noticed that no one offered to shake my hand. I also noticed that Nodeen was the only person not standing when I entered the room.

Bellizia directed me to a chair across from the Governor and close to the President and Dr. Funderburke. I suspected that President Turner would be the conductor of this symphony. As expected, he made the first overture.

"Dr. Murphy, thank you for coming in to talk with us. I know the past couple of days must have been upsetting for you. I know you share our desire to get this situation resolved."

"Well, I'd certainly like to get back to work." I was trying to be as non-committal as possible. "To be honest, I miss work a lot."

"And you're very good at what you do, Dr. Murphy. I've heard nothing but positive things about you from your colleagues. The Governor, however, is very concerned about his daughter who was under your care. We need your help to locate her."

"Sir, I appreciate the compliment, but I cannot tell the Governor where his daughter is. I've no earthly idea where she is." You could feel the warmth leaving the room. Now I was going to find out who the bad cop would be. It didn't take long.

Vincent Bellizia jumped in. "Dr. Murphy, I need you to understand the significant jeopardy you have created for the hospital. MUSC has a great deal of exposure having allowed the disappearance of such a high-profile

217

patient. What if something untoward were to happen to her while she is officially still an inpatient at our hospital? We need for you to do what is in the best interest of the Governor's daughter and the University. Resolving these issues will be necessary in order to preserve your future here at MUSC. Where did you take the Governor's daughter and who did you leave her with?"

"Maybe you weren't listening earlier. I don't know the answer to either of your questions. Why do you assume I'd know these things? I apologize for being argumentative, but Helene Eastland is a grown woman. What makes everyone think that finding her is in her best interests, if she doesn't want to be found?"

That didn't turn out to be a very popular question. It didn't appear that anyone was planning to offer a response.

Vincent Bellizia had been selected to apply the necessary pressure. As the hospital lawyer, I imagine they thought he added a measure of intimidation. My one time testifying in court as an expert witness probably gave me more actual trial experience than Vincent. He had long ago chosen to take the security of a corporate paycheck rather than hunt for live prey. He was certainly smart enough, and knew all the applicable rules, but he was a paper tiger. His threats would be hollow as well. On the other hand, I also knew he would be cautious. Anything he claimed to know would be well substantiated. If you were playing poker, you'd be a fool to ever think Vincent was bluffing.

"Dr. Murphy," Bellizia began again, leaning in for affect. "We know you were in the hospital the night Helene Eastland disappeared. We also know you were not on call. I'm sure it's not your habit to come into the hospital late at night on your days off."

"Mr. Bellizia, you have no idea what I do on my days off. But since you asked, I did come to the hospital that night, but it wasn't to see Ms. Eastland. I have a friend who is a Labor and Delivery nurse. I came to see her. We talked about a band we both enjoy. I invited her out on a date to see them. Her name is Ferdy Eldrez. If you want to check with her, I'm sure she'll confirm what I'm telling you. Correct me if I'm wrong, Vincent, but I don't think it's a violation of hospital policy for attending faculty to be dating members of the nursing staff. If I'm wrong, then the size of the medical staff just shrank by about a third, and you guys have a much bigger problem than one missing patient."

"Dr. Murphy, that's neither here nor there. We also know you were in the normal newborn nursery that night. The security alarm that went off later that night was for a baby you'd delivered."

"I deliver lots of babies. There were probably several in the nursery I'd delivered. I'm not responsible if the nursing staff walks through a door with a baby bracelet. Spend some time on the maternity floor. Baby alarms are a daily event. As far as being in the nursery, Ferdy told me that the baby of one of my patients with diabetes was having hypoglycemic spells. I wanted to check on how the kiddo was doing. It isn't unusual for me to go by the nursery to check on babies. I like to get an update before going in to see the postpartum moms."

I could tell that Bellizia was getting frustrated. I assume the others were as well. Did they expect me to cave because they knew I was in the hospital and the nursery?

"Doctor, the ward secretary believes it was you that called in the false child abduction and asked her to alert the SLED agent supervising Ms. Eastland."

"Unfortunately, she's made a mistake. I understand that she's new. I'd already gone home by then. By the way, nice word 'supervising.' A very sanitary selection."

Bellizia leaned back and looked at the others for support. Ferret-face Steed practically exploded. "That's a bunch of bull. You know it and we know it. We have you on video tape leaving the building after the alarm went off. We also know you left with someone."

Bingo. Steed showed their hold cards. They had us on video tape, probably from the elevator, but they couldn't tell who was with me or even if it was a woman. They didn't have a smoking gun.

"I didn't leave with anyone that night. Whether it was before or after the alarm sounded, I don't know. But I never heard the security alarms go off."

Bellizia tried to regain control of the conversation. "You are a clever man, Dr. Murphy, but you are lying to us."

"If I was so clever, Mr. Bellizia, I don't think I would be in this room right now."

Bellizia continued to probe. "If you left the hospital alone, where did you go?"

"I went to get something to eat and then I went home."

"You're lying to us again, Dr. Murphy. We know you did not go home. You took off down Highway 17 South. We believe you took Ms. Eastland to Savannah."

"You can believe whatever you want, but I did nothing of the sort."

"Then why did you lie to us about going to get something to eat?"

"I didn't lie. You've never been to the Edisto Motel in Jacksonboro? Best fried seafood platter and iced tea in the Low Country for only eight bucks. They were closed by the time I got there, so I ended up getting a drive through hamburger somewhere. Very disappointing. I didn't mind too much, though, because I needed a long drive. To be frank, I was upset with what was happening to Ms. Eastland. Things were messing with my head, and I needed some personal time. I decided to go to my parents' beach house. I've already apologized to my colleagues and to Dr. Templeton for my unexcused absence. They've accepted that apology. If Dr. Templeton were here he'd confirm that for you."

Wilton Steed lost his composure once again. "I hope you don't think this is going to be as easy as saying you're sorry to a handful of your Gyno friends."

Steed was flushed and his bald head was ridged with poorly suppressed anger.

Bellizia wrestled back control of the conversation. "I think Dr. Steed is saying that while the concerns of the Ob-Gyn department are important, there are also larger faculty practice and hospital issues which need to be addressed. When you disappeared, you left patients in the hospital, patients scheduled for surgery, and full slates of patients scheduled in the outpatient office. You left all these women and the medical center without pre-arranged coverage or notification of any kind."

"That, my friend, is patient abandonment," Wilton Steed interjected loudly.

"Wilton, as my friend, I'm hurt you never call."

Once again, Vincent Bellizia grabbed back the wheel. "Dr. Murphy, I don't think anyone here has anything but your best interests at heart."

Their hypocrisy, like Brussels sprouts, made me gag.

Bellizia continued, "We were very lucky that no one was harmed. However, your actions were irresponsible. That sort of behavior puts the entire medical staff and the hospital at risk. As a physician in South Carolina, you have an ethical responsibility to your patients. To not abandon them is near the top of that list. And..."

Here it comes. I could feel it.

"Despite your denials, we all know you took Ms. Eastland from the hospital. Sooner or later, she'll be found, and we'll be able to prove it. When we do, you'll need an explanation as to why you acted against her family's wishes and for why you're lying to us right now. Beyond that, I think you already know the consequences of having a sexual relationship with one of your patients."

That was a stab at the jugular. I could feel the color rising up my chest. I took several slow purposeful breaths to control myself. They were trying to provoke me. It was probably going to work. I needed to let it pass.

"As the hospital's attorney, I am responsible for protecting the hospital and University from having scandals like this explode in our face. In case you've somehow forgotten, we're talking about the Governor's daughter."

"Mr. Bellizia, I know exactly who we're talking about. None of these concerns involve me. In fact, I'm offended by the things you're implying."

I imagined they were having a hard time swallowing my hypocrisy as well.

At this point, Dean Funderburke decided he had heard enough. "Dr. Murphy, we need to protect ourselves from the fall out which is bound to follow when Ms. Eastland is eventually found. In our opinion, the only way we can protect the University and preserve your career is for you to tell us the truth. That truth includes the current whereabouts of Governor Eastland's daughter. Otherwise, we'll have no option but to report these ethical breeches to the State Board of Medical Examiners. You should also consider yourself suspended without pay until these matters are resolved."

The Dean probably didn't understand the slight smile that crossed my lips. Going after my Medical License meant either they didn't have enough evidence or big enough balls to have me arrested. It was probably the Governor's desire to use the relatively private application of regulatory pain and suffering as opposed to its public alternative.

"With all due respect, Dean Funderburke, I think your assessment is too dramatic. I appreciate that you must do whatever you feel is best for the medical center, but reporting me to the State Board seems excessive. I was away for a few days without permission to deal with personal issues. Ultimately, nobody got hurt. That's the bottom line. The State Board will view license revocation as a sledge hammer when all that is needed is a flyswatter. I can't imagine the State Board recommending anything other than a reprimand."

After almost eight years in the Governor's mansion, Larry Eastland was not very good at delaying gratification. He had long since grown weary of the verbal sparring between myself, Mr. Bellizia and "the ferret" Steed. Slamming both palms against the mahogany table, Governor Eastland rose from his chair and spoke to me with his slow, deep radio voice. "Son, you know damn good and well this isn't about you being absent without leave. This is about kidnapping the Governor's daughter, my daughter, and whatever perverse liberties you took with her. You don't strike me as a fool, but you are one, if you think you're walking away from this with your hide intact."

The Governor let that comment sink in for a moment, never taking his narrowed, menacing eyes off mine. He continued in an even slower, more guttural tone, "If you don't tell me where Helene is right now, I will make it my personal mission to crush your balls in a vise. Look in my eyes, son, and tell me if you think I'm making idle threats."

I didn't take my eyes off his. There was a deep well of malevolence that penetrated his core. I was certain of both his seriousness and ability to carry out his threats. At the same time, his use of Helene's name filled me with a disgust that made my stomach roil and heart pound. It took everything I could muster to maintain my composure.

"Mr. Eastland, Helene no longer considers herself your daughter. She's a grown woman who is free to make her own choices. As I said before, I didn't kidnap Helene, and I don't know where she is. Even if I did, I'd still keep it a secret from you. Do you want to know why? I also have an ethical and moral responsibility to your daughter. Helene is one of my patients, and I have a duty to not let you hurt her anymore."

"You son of a bitch," the Governor yelled.

"Whoa, whoa, whoa, there Governor. You probably don't want to say anything else right now that you might regret later." It was the first time Mr. Nodeen had spoken. Even now, and despite his words, he appeared disinterested in the entire tableau being played out in front of him. He slouched in his chair studying his finger nails and contemplating his cuticles.

"Excuse me?" the Governor said, turning his attention to the far end of the table with obvious irritation. "Thomas, I don't think I need any input from your people right now."

Without looking up from his nails, Nodeen, "Governor, I'm not 'Thomas' people.' Regarding the current federal drug interdiction that Mr. Sheprow is leading here in South Carolina, he would be reporting to me."

"Who the hell are you again?" Governor Eastland thundered.

"Governor, my name is Laurence Nodeen and I'm a U.S. District Attorney on special assignment. That assignment is the supervision of all drug enforcement activities along the southeastern United States coast. Mr. Sheprow is currently heading up a specific operation here in South Carolina that we are referring to as Operation Jackpot. God knows you need him. A large percentage of all the marijuana and hashish sold on the east coast comes ashore in the myriad of backwards, backwater tidal creeks that are so plentiful in your Low Country."

"Mr. Sheprow's primary job is the prosecution of these people. I hope you're not so naïve as to believe these men are all just coming forward to turn themselves in. The indictments you have been reading about in the paper are the result of more than a year of intense, multi-departmental investigation. To break down the financing and organizational structure of these criminal conspiracies, the Jackpot Task Force had to call on the collaborative talents of the Drug Enforcement Administration, U.S. Customs and the Customs Patrol, the FBI, the Internal Revenue Service, the Bureau of Alcohol, Tobacco and Firearms, the U.S. Marshals, and the South Carolina State Law Enforcement Division. The various offices of all of these agencies contributing to Operation Jackpot report to me."

"In short, I'm President Reagan's War on Drugs."

On cue, Thomas Sheprow chimed in, "We cannot be successful in taking down these large smuggling operations without a multi-agency approach. These smuggling operations have a fairly complex corporate-like structure. Targeting them for investigation is like taking on AT&T. They have their own lawyers, investors, and bankers."

Mr. Nodeen was now more engaged. He was sitting up in his chair with his arms folded in front of him on the table. He was probably in his mid-40s, but looked younger with sharp eyes and a smooth, milk chocolate complexion. He had short cropped hair, and his physique was that of a younger man. He jumped in when Mr. Sheprow had finished speaking, "The fact of the matter is that it takes a great deal of pressure to crack these criminal conspiracies. I'm the man responsible for applying that pressure."

"So what's your interest in Dr. Murphy?" Governor Eastland demanded, apparently still uncertain why he'd been interrupted.

"I have no interest in Dr. Murphy," Nodeen responded calmly. Then after a few seconds delay, he added, "I'm interested in your daughter, Helene Eastland."

Governor Eastland did not immediately respond as he processed the abrupt change in focus of the conversation. "Well, it's a lucky thing you're here then, because he's the man you need to be talking to. Dr. Murphy knows where she's hiding."

"No he doesn't," Nodeen said in a soft voice.

"What makes you so sure?"

"Because I'm hiding her. We have your daughter and she's safe. She walked into an FBI office on Sunday with a story to tell. We took her deposition yesterday."

"Then why didn't you say something sooner?" Governor Eastland bellowed, anger rising in his voice. "You need to deliver her to me right God-damn now."

There was an awkward silence as Nodeen pondered the demand and his answer. Governor Eastland was becoming physically more agitated as each second ticked by.

"First, I wanted to hear what Dr. Murphy had to say. Second, I'm sorry to inform you Governor, that Ms. Eastland is not a piece of lost luggage which needs to be returned to you or anybody else. She'll not be coming back to South Carolina anytime soon."

"Mr. Nodeen, you need to explain yourself."

"Helene Eastland is a material witness with knowledge of sophisticated drug smuggling operations in South Carolina. What she knows is pertinent to the ongoing Operation Jackpot investigation. She's not currently under arrest, but is in FBI protective custody. She'll remain that way for the foreseeable future. No one will be having any contact with her. And Governor, that explanation was complimentary. I have no need to explain myself to you."

"Mister, she is my daughter. I have every resource necessary to protect her."

Laurence Nodeen raised his eyes to meet the Governor's glare. Neither blinked.

"Governor, I've had several hours of conversation with Ms. Eastland. I have no doubt she is safer where she is right now, than she'd be returning to your protection. Unless I'm mistaken, you had her in protective custody just a week or so ago. That didn't work out so well did it?"

Governor Eastland was having none of that. "Son, my daughter was kidnapped and as a law enforcement officer your responsibility is to bring her safely home."

Nodeen wasn't having any of Governor Eastland either.

"Governor, kidnapping became a federal crime with the Lindbergh baby. Nothing carries more weight with the FBI or the Justice Department. We consider the kidnapper a bottom feeder on the criminal food chain. There isn't anybody we enjoy busting more than these scumbags. We put them into the darkest holes in the United States prison system."

"Then this must be a red letter day for you," the Governor interjected, "because you have a kidnapper sitting right over there." He pointed his finger in my direction.

Fifteen minutes ago, I decided to keep my mouth shut. It still seemed like a good idea.

"Governor, from our investigation, we are convinced that Dr. Murphy was involved in a kidnapping despite his unconvincing denials."

That was an attention grabber. I sat up straight and turned to face Nodeen and Sheprow at their end of the table. I waited for Nodeen to continue.

"However, we believe Dr. Murphy's involvement was in preventing a kidnapping, not in perpetrating one."

There was not a sound as everyone absorbed the last statement.

"What did you say?" Wilton Steed finally asked.

"Try to keep up, Dr. Steed. I think everyone heard what I said."

Nodeen's demeanor did not betray the tiniest bit of concern. There was no fluctuation in his baritone voice. He knew he'd just kicked over the hive, but he revealed no anxiety. This was a very cool customer. Whatever was going to happen next was going to be interesting. All eyes turned to Governor Eastland, knowing the next move would be his.

"Son, who the hell do you think you are and who do you think you're dealing with?" Governor Eastland waited a few seconds before adding, "Are you suggesting I was involved in a plan to kidnap my own daughter?"

"No sir, I'm not suggesting that. I know you were planning to kidnap your daughter. More importantly, I know why you were planning to kidnap her. Also Governor, I don't believe that we're related."

Nodeen let that hang for several second before he continued, "Governor, I want you to know that if I had my way, I'd be dragging your sorry ass out of this room in shackles. What you were planning to do to your own daughter is loathsome. Your Boss Hogg bluster makes me want to vomit. I don't have children of my own, but if I did, and I ever found myself thinking the way you think, I would lean into the strike zone and take a thirty-eight fastball in the temple for the good of the team."

For the first time, Governor Eastland's confidence appeared to waver. He looked around for support.

Agent Wrenn took a few steps forward from his position by the door. Nodeen stopped him in his tracks without even turning to face him.

"Agent Wrenn, you must be out of your mind. You'd better stand down. At this point, your only protection is your own stupidity. The next few minutes will probably determine whether you spend the rest of your life in prison or not."

The color drained from Agent Wrenn's face, and he returned to his place by the door.

Governor Eastland had enjoyed almost unlimited power for most of the last eight years. There isn't anything more pleasurable to have than power or as painful to lose. One thing I was sure of, Eastland wasn't going to give up without a fight.

"Mr. Nodeen, you work for Ronald Reagan. Operation Jackpot is a Presidential Taskforce, and you're nothing more than a political appointee. I've been friends with Ron Reagan for more than a decade. It's not going to be me who takes a fall here. After I speak with the White House, it might just be a fast-talking, smart-ass, affirmative-action Justice Department lawyer who gets the axe."

Without skipping a beat, Nodeen responded to Governor Eastland's threat. "Sir, the only reason you're not being lead out of here in handcuffs is that I've already briefed President Reagan."

Nodeen let that hot nugget burn into Eastland's flesh before continuing. "Among his many personal qualities, President Reagan is a devoted husband and father. Your daughter's deposition made his skin crawl. He understands you'll probably receive far less than you deserve for your perverse behavior. However, as President, he does not wish to sidetrack the Operation Jackpot prosecutions. He's also interested in making sure the state of South Carolina is spared the embarrassment this scandal will certainly generate. I suspect the President also does not want to be personally embarrassed by his long term association with a 'friend' such as you."

"We'll see about that," the Governor replied, but the swagger was gone.

"Governor, the President has asked that I convey to you, that you are now persona *non-grata* in the Republican Party. You will not be the Republican candidate for the South Carolina senate seat or any other political office, down to and including Richland County dog catcher. You should make no plans to visit Washington or the national convention. As soon as you complete your final year as governor, you'd better disappear faster than Nixon. Obscurity will be your insufficient penance for your sins."

A smile crossed Nodeen's lips. It was the first time I'd seen him change expressions. He was enjoying himself now. He'd checkmated the opposing king. Now he was going to take his time sweeping the rooks, knights and knaves from the board. I wondered if I was a white or black pawn.

Eastland slumped down in his seat.

Nodeen still had more to say. "Additionally, you're not to take any actions, directly or indirectly, to contact or influence Helene Eastland in any way. She's in FBI protective custody. That should be considered life-long as far as you're concerned. If you see your daughter walking down the street in Columbia, you should turn around and run the other way. The same holds true for Dr. Murphy. You'll be held personally responsible for any sanction, reprimand or discredit that comes his way. He has a get-out-of-jail-free card for all of his actions as they pertain to Helene Eastland and this investigation.

Nodeen continued to hammer away at the Governor. It didn't bother him that the Governor was done. "Since I know you're not a legal scholar, I'll explain this to you slowly and simply. There's no statute of limitations on kidnapping, nor is there one on scandal. Any deviation from these instructions given to you by President Reagan, this case will be re-opened by the Justice Department. Trust me, Justice will be pleased when that day arrives. Justice considers you a deviate and we're all offended that you're not in a box. The FBI has been given authority to use whatever surveillance is required to insure that you never hurt anyone else again. Do we understand each other?"

"Helene is a damn liar. She always been a liar. You can't believe anything she says."

"Governor, we considered that possibility. However, in our discussions with your daughter, we've found her to be extraordinarily candid and believable."

Now for the knaves, Mr. Nodeen rose from his seat and walked down to the other end of the table where President Turner, Dean Funderburke, and Medical Group President Wilton "Ferret" Steed were sitting. As he walked around the conference table, his stride was confident and purposeful. None of the doctors at the far end appeared to be interested in continuing the conversation with Mr. Nodeen.

"Let me finish up with this rag-tag collection of Renfields," Nodeen announced to no one in particular.

President Turner tried to deflect Nodeen's approach with some skillful white collar backpedaling. "We're pleased to learn that Ms. Eastland has been found safe and sound. That's all that really matters. You should be congratulated on the speed with which you've been able to bring this issue to closure."

Still coming forward, Nodeen was now standing directly above the University leadership. At six-foot six inches and looming over them, Nodeen must have looked eight feet tall. His positioning was purposeful, and gained him an advantage in what would be an interesting battle of jawbones versus sawbones. Nodeen smiled broadly and responded, "Thank you, President Turner. However, Ms. Eastland's safety should not be your major concern right now."

Dr. Turner answered with a half statement and half question, "And what should be our major concern? Dr. Murphy?"

"No, no, no. Dr. Murphy should be the least of your concerns. In fact, he *is* the least of your concerns."

Still at a vertical disadvantage, President Turner tried to recover by scooting his chair backwards, creating some horizontal relief.

"I'm afraid I must disagree with you on that point. While it's gratifying Ms. Eastland is in FBI custody, I personally still have serious reservations regarding the actions and behavior of Dr. Murphy over the past couple of weeks. As we discussed earlier, he has ethical obligations to his patients that he ignored. Even if your investigation has not revealed any criminal wrongdoing, we have to be concerned about possible moral failings. These failings may not be kidnapping, but they are serious breaches of professionalism. As a physician licensed to practice medicine in South Carolina, and as a member of our MUSC medical staff, lapses such as these are not tolerated."

I was amazed by how calm Nodeen appeared to be. I was a mess. I'd now been on this roller coaster ride for about forty-five minutes. I was getting sick to my stomach. One minute my stock was up, the next it was crashing, then a recovery, now it seemed ready to take another nosedive. President Turner was not inclined to let this thing go. He seemed intent on using me to score points with our beaten-but-not-dead governor. MUSC was still a state facility, and I was still a state employee. The University President was sending a message.

"You guys just don't get it," Nodeen said, shaking his head slowly.

President Turner answered, "What is it exactly we don't get? As a state hospital authority, we have certain obligations. Maintaining high standards of excellence is one of them. Part of maintaining our standards of excellence is performing peer review of our staff, including Dr. Murphy. Of all people, I think you should understand that."

Even though I was the subject of the conversation and should be self-absorbed, I couldn't help but think that sounded a bit condescending. Condescension was probably a mistake.

"Standards of excellence," Nodeen said softly. Pausing to let those words float around the room like an actor. "That's a very interesting phrase. Would one of those standards of excellence be a responsibility to maintain patient confidentiality? If so, please explain to me how Governor Eastland and SLED knew that Ms. Eastland was a patient on your gynecology service."

"Would another of those standards of excellence be a responsibility to maintain the integrity and confidentiality of patient medical records? If so, please explain to me why Ms. Eastland's medical records cannot be found despite a fairly exhaustive search by your medical records department."

"Would another of those standards of excellence be to certify and credential your medical staff, so that your patients can be confident they are being treated by competent and qualified physicians?"

He was rolling now. Each rhetorical question was being asked in a louder tone of voice. Nodeen reminded me of a Southern Baptist preacher.

"If so, please explain to me how Ms. Eastland was seen by a consulting psychiatrist who was neither licensed in South Carolina nor had medical staff privileges at MUSC."

Without taking his eyes off President Turner, Nodeen asked me, "Dr. Murphy, as the attending physician, did you order a psychiatric consult on Ms. Eastland?"

"No, sir, I did not. It was unnecessary and inappropriate."

"Dr. Turner, please explain how that happened."

"Is it a standard of excellence to establish a therapeutic environment for patients who present to your hospital for care? If so, please explain to me how Ms. Eastland was subjected to unwanted visitation and surveillance when she had requested no visitors?"

Nodeen continued without expecting an answer, "Would it be another standard of excellence to ensure that the civil rights of the patients are protected? If so, please explain to me how a woman recovering from surgery in your hospital was placed under twenty-four-seven law enforcement surveillance and detention without a judicial order, warrant, or indictment against her. Why didn't your hospital security know there was such a dangerous fugitive in their midst? Is it usual at your hospital to have gun-toting, private security roaming the hallways?"

Nodeen slowly looked from face to face of the MUSC leadership. "No, I didn't think you had good answers to those standards of excellence questions."

President Turner was stunned and in retreat mode. "Mr. Nodeen, if any mistakes were made in some of our internal procedures, we will address and correct those errors. I don't believe these problems are nearly as dramatic as you present them. We are fully JACHO accredited, and we provide care that is consistent with the highest standards of practice."

"Please spare me, Dr. Turner. Your problems are much bigger than a JACHO citation."

Under intense unspoken pressure to reverse the direction of the conversation, Vincent Bellizia tried to intervene, "Mr. Nodeen, I will personally look into each of these concerns and make certain that we identify any instances where the ball might have been dropped. Wherever problems are found, they will be corrected.

Let me assure you, we fully understand the significance of these glitches in our performance."

"I'm not so sure you do. You guys here in Charleston have a long history of thumbing you noses at federal law when you find it inconvenient."

Nodeen waited for his historical reference to register.

"So let me explain what you're going to do. Cleaning up this mess goes without saying. You will personally draft a collective letter of apology to Dr. Murphy for falsely accusing him of being involved in the disappearance of Ms. Eastland. Unfortunately, his role in preventing harm from befalling Ms. Eastland cannot be publically acknowledged at this time. Dr. Murphy will be allowed to return to full duties immediately. At no point will he be subjected to any poor performance reports or disciplinary activity. By my estimate, Dr. Murphy should be eligible for promotion to Associate Professor within the next three years. I'll be anxiously awaiting word of Dr. Murphy's good news."

Without turning his head, Mr. Nodeen's next question was directed at me, "Do you have any problem with those plans or that timeline, Dr. Murphy?"

"No sir."

"Very good, Dr. Murphy."

Nodeen turned his attention back to the MUSC leadership. "I know you guys are going to like this plan, too, and I'll tell you why. As long as Dr. Murphy's career continues to progress smoothly, I'll keep this file safely tucked away in my top drawer. If Dr. Murphy encounters any career impediments, I will gladly walk this report across the hall to my best friends in the Justice Department's Civil Rights Division. They'll be more than excited to investigate this institution's violation of Helene Eastland's civil rights. There is nothing the Civil Rights Division likes more than crawling up the ass of a bunch of hillbillies with a flashlight. It reminds them of the good old days."

Nodeen again looked from face to face, appreciating the impact of his threat.

"It's hard to know what they might find, but I'm sure Mr. Bellizia can confirm what would be at risk. First, there'd be that ugly newspaper article you all seem to be so afraid of. Second, would be the three hundred million in federal research dollars that come to MUSC each year. That money disappears if the Office of Civil Rights finds any evidence of discriminatory activity. Oh, by the way, good luck with future competitive grant applications with a federal discriminatory practices decision against you. Knowing you guys, and the history of this place, I don't think the OCR would have much trouble finding compliance problems with at least one applicable federal rule or regulation. Mr. Bellizia is that a fair statement of fact about what could be at stake?"

There was no response from Mr. Bellizia.

"Vincent?" questioned President Turner.

Bellizia looked up from whatever was holding his attention in his lap. "Mr. President, I believe Mr. Nodeen has offered us an attractive option for handling this unpleasant situation. It would be in our best interest to avoid a Justice Department investigation under any circumstances. I'm confident we'd ultimately be judged to be in compliance with all federal requirements, but such investigations can be subjective. Additionally, the investigation itself would be very disruptive to University researchers. Their federal funds could be put on hold for a year or longer while questions are resolved. It would also have a chilling effect on future research applications."

"An excellent analysis Mr. Bellizia. You should probably be in charge around here. If there aren't any further questions, can I assume we're all in agreement?"

Once again, Nodeen scanned the faces of the men he was schooling. No one spoke. Only the ferret had the mindless nerve to look him in the eyes.

"Gentlemen, an agreement?" Nodeen asked again.

Finally, President Turner spoke, looking directly at me rather than Nodeen.

"On balance, it appears that dropping this inquiry into Dr. Murphy's behavior is in the best interest of the Medical University. I will add that personally, I'm not pleased with how Dr. Murphy has conducted himself in this matter."

"Dr. Turner, there's a lot here to not be pleased with. Unfortunately, none of you know what any of those things are. You should probably be glad you don't."

"Dr. Murphy, I think you can excuse yourself at this time. I recommend that you return to work immediately. It sounds like the institution almost fell apart during the few days you were away."

"That sounds good to me. I feel like I've been here too long already. Umm, thank you." As I left the room, I realized Agent Wrenn would be my last gauntlet. He didn't look up as I passed him at the door.

MUSC HORSESHOE

It wasn't possible for me to head back to work as instructed. My thoughts were very chaotic at the moment. I needed to process all that had just happened. U.S. Attorney Nodeen had put all the pieces together. His diagnostic skills would have made Father William of Occam proud. He'd looked at all the disparate events and competing perspectives, and had made sense of everything. It was like the puzzle box. Once you knew the secret, breaking down the rest was easy. Helene must have laid it all out for them. The courage it took for her to do that was immense. She had overcome both her fear of the Colombians and the shame she carried from the sexual abuse inflicted on her by her father.

I had a lot of serious thinking to do about my own future. While I had been excused, I hadn't been vindicated. The hospital had been told to back down, but they were still in there talking. Was the hospital really going to let me walk away from this? The President and the Dean both had long memories.

I walked across the driveway to the lawn that filled the horseshoe in front of the Administration building. The area was nicely shaded by old crepe myrtles, and the walkways were lined by dozens of old Charleston benches. I'd frequently taken advantage of the horseshoe's serenity to eat a late lunch after a long-running morning clinic or between surgical cases.

I needed time to wind down after being in crisis mode for the past few hours and chose a seat under an old live oak. Everything seemed to be in hyper-focus. Earlier I'd noticed that it was a beautiful day, but now I saw the clouds standing out against the blue sky like they had been drawn and outlined with black charcoal. Every individual strand of Spanish moss was in sharp focus, loosely spun together and hung from the branch above my head. I saw the chipped brickwork on the façade of the old main hospital building fifty yards straight across from me. With perfect acuity, I heard the clanging of the rings on the flag against the metal pole in the middle of the common. I knew it was an adrenaline rush. It wasn't particularly exciting or unsettling, just a numb, disconnected feeling.

I felt very alone. Helene was in FBI protective custody. Coming back to South Carolina was probably not an option. In my head, I was glad Helene was safe from her father and the drug smugglers. They must be particularly pissed. After going through the hassle of spiriting her out of the country, she turns around and walks into an FBI office somewhere. From everything I know, the Columbians are vindictive bastards. But in my heart, I felt empty. I had no idea where to go with either my career or my personal life.

A brown-nosing medical student I knew from the last rotation, named George Staats, walked by and said hello. I usually had trouble remembering medical student's names. However, Staats had thick, curly black hair and a full black beard. Everyone called him "Cat" Staats after the singer. I considered failing him on the last rotation after Ferdy told me he was constantly hitting on the nurses, including her. When he told me he wanted to be a proctologist, I figured he had issues of his own, and decided to let him slide. I just smiled and waved.

There was a surprising absence of other activity on the horseshoe. It was mid-morning, which accounted for some of it. By about eleven-thirty, it would begin to fill, but right now, I was alone. The solitude helped me notice when the doors to the Administration building opened a few minutes later. Sheprow and Nodeen emerged. They didn't appear animated, but I imagined they were pleased with themselves.

They spoke together for a few minutes, and then Nodeen scanned the horseshoe until his eyes locked on mine. Nodeen turned back to Sheprow and they spoke for another minute before Sheprow shook his hand and walked around the side of the building. Nodeen ambled down the steps toward me.

"Dr. Murphy, I thought you were supposed to go back to work."

"Yeah, I know, but I needed a few minutes to decompress. It was too tense in there for my blood. You didn't make many new friends today, but I don't think that bothers you very much."

"Doc, ruffling a few feathers doesn't bother me at all. Especially here. MUSC doesn't have a very good track record when it comes to civil rights. It was before your time, but there was a historically significant nurses' strike here in the '60s over unequal treatment. MUSC found out quickly it couldn't get along without its black nurses and staff. With a little prodding, there was a non-violent settlement."

"You from the South?" I asked.

"Grew up in Atlanta and went to Georgia Tech. I stayed in town and graduated from Emory Law School. I've been dealing with crackers like those guys all of my life."

"How long have you been with the Justice Department?"

"I got out of Atlanta as soon as I finished Law School and headed to D.C. to join the Justice Department. It's the best decision I ever made."

"I'm glad you did. What do you think I should do?"

"What do you mean?"

"Other than a couple years in San Francisco, I've been at MUSC my entire career. There's a lot of bullshit here, but you'll find that everywhere. I love Charleston and would prefer to stay, but those guys in there don't like being embarrassed and, well..."

"They don't like being told what to do by a black man." Nodeen completed my thought for me.

"You've been around the block. You know those guys are dangerous. They're use to getting their way."

"Look, Dr. Murphy, you can count on everything I said in there. If you want to get out of here, I wouldn't fault you. It might be the smart move. Right now, those guys are highly motivated to write you a great letter of recommendation. Personally, I can't wait to get on a plane back to D.C. But if you want to stay, those guys won't give you any trouble. I wasn't kidding about keeping this file in my top drawer. MUSC has no interest in a federal civil rights investigation. The civil rights guys would enjoy tearing antebellum Charleston a new one even more than I do."

Nodeen reached into his suit coat pocket and produced a business card which he handed to me.

"Put this somewhere you can find it. If you ever have a problem or even a suspicion of a problem, give me a call. I'd love the opportunity to talk again with my new friends."

"Thanks," was my inadequate reply.

"You're not going to encounter any problems. This is just politics, and the politics of this are simple. Ms. Eastland has taken her father off the board. The Governor's career is over. All power is effervescent. You just got to witness his bulb flickering off for the last time. He gets to finish his term, against my better judgment by the way, but after that, he's done. The Republican Party won't even return his calls. Without power or position, Eastland has no leverage with Dr. Turner, the MUSC Board of Trustees, or anybody. He's going to become irrelevant quickly."

"What about President Turner? He's got to feel like he's stepped into a steaming pile of shit, and it's my fault. He can lay in wait for me for a long time."

"President Turner isn't going to be a problem much longer either. After you left, Mr. Sheprow and I informed the President, along with Dean Funderburke, that they'd be writing resignation letters to the Board of Trustees in the near future. As a courtesy, our taskforce notified President Turner and Dean Funderburke that we would be serving a federal arrest warrant on Arthur Redding at the Medical University Hospital. It was pretty easy to figure out that they alerted the Governor. The Governor warned Mr. Redding to clear out, and then sent SLED down to pick up his daughter. It was probably only President Turner, but why split hairs when Funderburke is such an asshole all by his lonesome. Best to just roll them up together. We didn't have any trouble finding Mr. Redding, but, if you want to be a stickler, and we do, President Turner and Dean Funderburke's actions represent obstruction of justice. The Department of Justice will inform the Board of Trustees that we'll defer prosecution if the University takes this opportunity to find more enlightened leadership. Knowing this place, I'm not particularly hopeful. They'll probably select that pinhead Steed."

"That would be something. President Wilton 'the Ferret' Steed." We both laughed.

"Can you tell me how Helene is doing?"

"I thought you barely knew her," Nodeen said with a grin.

243

"I think we both know better."

Nodeen continued, "You were very clever getting Ms. Eastland out of the hospital. You had SLED bamboozled. Your jaunt down Highway 17 convinced them you were heading to Savannah."

"I told you inside. I was going to eat at the Edisto Motel."

"That might work with the bozos in there, but don't try that crap on me. You got gas just south of Charleston at midnight. Ma and Pa Kettle who run the Edisto Motel close up at about nine p.m., and the entire town rolls up its sidewalks about thirty minutes later. Don't kid a kidder. Ms. Eastland has filled us in on the details of your time on the run."

"Point taken. Where did you find her?"

"In case you haven't already figured it out, she left Garden City by boat. We didn't find her. She found us. She called us from Costa Rica on Sunday. We picked her up and brought her in. Since then, she's been telling us what she knows about the Jackpot smugglers, her father, and about you. We moved her to another island where she's safe. Maybe bored, but safe. As far as our safe places go, it's much nicer than Oklahoma."

"Can you keep her safe? Will she have to testify?"

"I doubt it. The only stuff she has any direct knowledge of involves Arthur Redding. She's met some of the other guys who've been indicted, but her knowledge of what they've done is mostly second hand. Redding is stupid, and he's a punk. He's going to grab for whatever deal we offer, and then he's going to roll over on all his old buddies. We'll use Ms. Eastland for some leverage with Redding, but ultimately, his testimony will make whatever she knows, unnecessary. The dangerous guys are the Colombians. They're mean sons of bitches. But they aren't going to come looking for her. She doesn't have anything on them. Nor do they really care about what happens to Holmes, Redding, Croft or any of these other redneck gangsters. They're already lining up new associates at new ports o' call."

"Does she know all of this?"

"No, she still believes that she's the key to busting these smuggling rings wide open. She's very brave about it all. She's willing to walk into federal court and take on any and all comers. Helene Eastland is an impressive woman. I like her very much. She must be illegitimate."

"You know, I thought the same thing. Did you know we knew each other in high school? We dated."

"No, she didn't mention that. But, she cares for you very much."

"It's a long story, but her father was ruining her life even then. Did she tell you what he was doing to her?"

"Some things. They were hard for her. I don't think she would want them shared. She did describe how he isolated and terrorized her. When she got off the leash and ran away with Redding, the Governor became more than just sexually obsessed. Helene became a political liability, a loose end that could hurt his Senate aspirations."

"He's a son of a bitch."

"No, he's a pedophile and sexual predator who rose to a position of power with an appetite for more. But she stopped him, and she should be proud of herself. It doesn't usually go that way for victims of childhood sexual abuse. Many women who have experienced what Ms. Eastland has gone through end up taking a handful of pills or slitting their wrists in a bath tub. It's remarkable that she has remained strong enough to fight for her life."

"I agree. Thank you, for helping Helene. Are you sure that you can keep her father away from her?"

"I do admit to some reservations about the White House instructions. I would have preferred to put him in a locked hole."

"Why didn't they? Child molesters are never cured."

"Well, that question is bigger than the both of us. I can promise you, we'll be watching him, and he'll know it. The Governor isn't going to slip off our radar screen."

"I do wonder about one other thing This could have all been handled in Columbia between you and the Governor. Why come down here and put yourself in the middle of my problems. You could have easily burned me for taking Helene from the hospital and helping her dodge your subpoena. Don't get me wrong. I'm appreciative, but I'm not sure why I got to be part of this passion play."

"Do you remember what I told the Governor about kidnapping? Nothing is sweeter to the Justice Department and the FBI than taking down a kidnapper and getting somebody safely back. Sadly, it doesn't happen that way very often. As far as my boss is concerned, this is the second kidnapping you've thwarted. That makes you a superstar at Justice. Deputy Director Rosen wasn't going to allow you to be left out in the cold."

"Rosen?"

"Yeah, I think you know his wife and their daughter Lily. I have a lot of authority as the point person on the war on drugs. However, everyone has a boss, and mine is Martin Rosen. Mr. Rosen is the Deputy Director of the Justice Department immediately beneath the Attorney General. He seems very invested in making sure you end up on your feet. From a career advancement perspective, if you're Deputy Director Rosen's priority, then you're my priority as well."

"Please tell Mr. Rosen I thank him once again for helping me out of a jam. And give my best to Lena and Lily."

"I will. Mr. Rosen will want a full report as soon as I arrive back in Washington. What should I tell him about your plans?"

"I'm not totally sure, but I think I'll stick it out here in Charleston. It's been home for a long time. My family is in Columbia. I have friends in the department. It also seems I've got an angel on my shoulder. If I go somewhere else, I might not have the same get-out-of-jail-free card I have around here."

"He'll be glad to hear that."

"I don't know if you can tell me or not, but is Taylor Holmes going to come out of this okay?"

I immediately saw a shadow come across Laurence Nodeen's eyes. "How do you know Taylor Holmes?"

"Taylor and I play basketball together. He's a good point guard, but we didn't know anything about his smuggling. Some people say he was being used by his older brother."

"Bryan Holmes is certainly the brains of the operation, but Taylor is in it up to his neck. He's going down hard. There isn't anything anybody can do about that. The next team Holmes plays point guard for will be in maximum security."

"I'm sorry to hear that. A huge waste. We miss Taylor on our team."

"Not to change the topic from poor Taylor, but I used to play a lot of ball. I still like to find a game when I can. I'm not heading back to D.C. until tomorrow. Any chance of finding a good pick-up game tonight?"

"Are you any good?"

"I was the first African-American to play basketball for Georgia Tech."

"That must have been tough."

"Not so bad. Georgia Tech is in downtown Atlanta. There were shorter straws to draw. I played against the Mahaffey brothers in high school. I'm not sure what I would've done if Clemson was the only offer I received. I don't think it would've been so easy to have been the first brother to have laced them up for Clemson in Slim Pickens country."

"I'm sure they would have loved you," I said with a grin.

"So, any game?"

"Have you ever heard of Clarence 'Don't Turn Nobody Down' McCants?"

MOULTRIE MIDDLE SCHOOL

Our city league game was against the James Island
Rams and we were playing at the Moultrie Middle
School Gym. James Island wasn't very good. They were
mostly high school players whose eligibility had run
out. Their one threat was Emmett Mazyck. Everybody
knew Emmett. Emmett was a six-foot-nine inch bear of
a man who had once led James Island High School to a
state championship. Unfortunately, following a
storyline all too familiar to black Low Country athletes,
Emmett was failed by his school and community. By the
time he finished high school, dozens of major Division I
programs were interested in his basketball skills.
Unfortunately, he had nowhere near the necessary
academic credentials to make those dreams a reality.

After a year of community college in Kansas, Emmett
returned home, took a job driving a Charleston city bus,
and added fifty pounds to his already large frame. His
NBA potential had now been officially downgraded to
recreational league.

I got Nodeen a Clarence McCants T-shirt and
introduced him around as my lawyer and friend. That
was good enough for everybody. Most of the guys knew
I was in some kind of trouble at work and didn't want to
know anything more. It wasn't a good idea to mention
that Nodeen was the guy in charge of putting Taylor
Holmes in jail for the rest of his life.

We were lucky that Nodeen came to play. This was
our last game before the Christmas holidays, and our
roster was thin. I was glad Francis Bethea was there,
because I didn't want Nodeen to be the only black guy

249

on our roster. Even though Nodeen was older, it was clear during warm ups that he was in great shape and a good player. He ran the floor the way an elite athlete does and threw down several rim-rattling dunks. We listed him on the roster as Denny Williams, who was still missing in action. I found the roster substitution ironic.

As expected, Emmett Mazyck was a warrior in the first half, but James Island didn't have much else. Francis had taken over at the point since Taylor was arrested and was getting better with every game. He'd always been a slasher and a scorer, but once he took over the point, he transformed his game and orchestrated our offense beautifully.

Francis was distributing the ball with a craftiness that belied his age. If James Island loafed on defense, Francis didn't mind taking it to the hoop. When the drives weren't there, Francis got me the ball for open shots time and time again. I had sixteen by halftime and couldn't remember a shot I missed. I was glad that I was playing well in front of Nodeen. Emmett kept James Island close by dominating underneath. He was giving Jack and Jeb more than they wanted. Midway through the first half, Jack got into foul trouble and Nodeen came into the game. The first time down the floor, Nodeen hustled after a rebound and put back a missed shot by Jeb. The rest of the half, he battled Emmett hard and held his own with a couple of baskets, including a dunk on a fast break.

At half time, spirits were high as we knew we had the game in hand. Several of the guys were slapping high fives with Nodeen. I could tell he was pleased to be playing. At one point, he looked over at me and nodded. The second half was more of the same. Francis continued to carve them up, and Jack, Jeb and Nodeen took turns wearing Emmett down. By the middle of the second half it was over. Nodeen did tire a bit late in the game, but I'm sure he ended up in double figures.

After the game, Nodeen draped himself over four rows of stands. There was steam rising from his head.

I sat down beside him. "You okay? If you die, am I still okay?" I asked with a grin.

"No, man, if I stroke out, you'll be on your own. You better make damn sure I get home okay."

Francis Bethea came by and congratulated Nodeen on a good game. Nodeen asked, "Hey kid, how old are you?"

"I'm sixteen. I'm a sophomore, but can't play till next year due to school transfer rules."

"What's your name again?"

"Francis Bethea."

"Francis, you've got size and point guard skills. How are you doing in school? Are you taking college prep courses?"

"Yes, sir. I don't do well in Spanish, but I get good grades in everything else. My mom's a teacher. She'd kill me if I failed anything."

"You've got a smart mom. You keep working hard, because you can play major college basketball. I live in Washington D.C. and I see Coach Thompson fairly frequently. I'm going to tell him to come take a look at you."

"Coach Thompson at Georgetown?"

"That's right."

"Thank you, sir. I'd appreciate that, sir. I'd love to be a Hoya."

After Francis left, I thanked Nodeen for passing on the recommendation about Francis.

"Not a problem. He's talented and only sixteen. It's remarkable that he has the confidence to run a team of grown men. At six-foot-three and with his handle, he's a Division I prospect."

"Well, if he makes it, you can take the credit. He didn't even start until you arrested Taylor."

Nodeen laughed, "Well, this won't be the first time Coach Thompson has been accused of dirty recruiting tactics. Have you given any more thought to what you are going to do?"

"I've got a stubborn streak and don't like to be pushed around. I'm staying. I love Charleston, my job, my family, my team. If I have to fight for all this, then I'll fight for it."

"It or her?"

"Both. But I don't know if I'll ever see her again. Or if she wants to see me again."

"I can't answer that one. I don't know. She's a broken girl. I doubt her decisions always make complete sense. Any relationship with Helene Eastland is going to involve a lot of patience. But, I think she's worth it. She's smart and has a lot of guts. When she called us and said she knew about the Jackpot smugglers, she was putting all her chips on the table. She was already safe from her father. She didn't call us looking for her own protection. She was worried about what you were walking into when you got home. Everything she did was for you. To be honest," Nodeen laughed, "she didn't think you were very capable of watching out for yourself."

"I'm used to being underestimated."

"If it makes you feel any better, I thought you handled yourself well this morning. Ms. Eastland cares about you, and didn't want to see you get ground up by her father. She took a big chance in order to protect you."

"I'm going to be okay. I just think about her all the time. If you talk with her, or see her, please tell her that for me. If she wants to come back to Charleston, tell her I'm here, and I'm willing to pick things up. I miss her."

"No promises, but I'll let her know what I can. There are rules about our contact with witnesses. The most important thing is letting the Jackpot indictments run their course. As these guys plead guilty or get convicted, it will become clearer what witnesses we do and don't need. Arthur Redding is scared shitless of federal hard time, and, interestingly, Governor Eastland. As soon as his lawyer works out a deal, he'll go belly up, and tell us far more than Ms. Eastland ever could."

As we gathered our things to leave the gym I asked Nodeen one more question. "I was wondering, how were you able to find us in Garden City?"

"Come on, we aren't SLED. We knew Ms. Eastland had left the hospital, certainly with you, earlier in the week. However, we didn't become engaged until Friday when Helene didn't show up for her grand jury testimony. It took us a couple of hours to discover your parents' beach condo. We sent some local police by Friday afternoon, but they reported not seeing anybody at the condo. I sent one of my guys back Saturday morning. We found your big Cadillac in the parking garage next door. You can't hide a boat like that for very long."

"You were surprised that she wasn't there."

"We were. Probably less surprised than you were though. When we interviewed her, Helene told us that she left the condo at about four a.m., signaling the boat from the porch. She said that you didn't have any idea, but that she left you a note. You were smart to get rid of it."

"Surprised is an inadequate word. I was convinced that your guys were going to shoot me."

"Don't feel special. They always act like they want to shoot somebody. We didn't have any reason to be interested in you. Ms. Eastland was the only warrant we had. It was clear you didn't have any more idea where she was than we did."

"I was still in shock when you guys showed up. I do appreciate everything you've done for Helene. Keep her safe. And, I appreciate what you did for me today."

"Hey, tonight was a lot of fun. Thanks for inviting me to play. Their big man was a stud. I'll get the T-shirt washed and sent back to you."

"Don't worry about it. You keep it. See if you can get the Justice Department to look into what Clarence means when he says, 'We finance our own accounts.' Something doesn't sound right about that. I'll send you our game schedule. You played good tonight. We can use you anytime you're in town."

"Don't count me out. If I'm in town, I'll definitely play."

MUSC LABOR AND DELIVERY

Returning to work was good for me. My co-faculty and the residents wanted to know what had happened, but I decided keeping quiet was the best policy. Dr. Templeton called me to his office and wanted to be filled in on my meeting with the Dean and President Turner. Feeling more confident than the previous week, I responded by asking why he wasn't there. He said he was informed of the meeting, but wasn't invited. I probably destroyed whatever remaining relationship I had with Templeton by suggesting, if one of my junior faculty was being railroaded, I would have made a point of being there, invited or not. I wouldn't be receiving much more career guidance from Dr. Templeton.

Never one for conflict, Dr. Templeton appeared to lose interest in the conversation. His only question was, "Where does the matter stand?"

"Things were hashed out and they realized I didn't have anything to do with the disappearance of Ms. Eastland. There'll be a letter of apology coming to me from the President. When I receive it, I will forward you a copy for my file. As you already know, I was approved to return to work."

I didn't mention that the University would soon be rocked by the unexplained resignations of both its President and its Dean. I was hoping that enough time might go by that people wouldn't associate their resignations with my adventures. That was probably naïve.

I volunteered to take as many call days over the Christmas holiday as I could. We usually divide the time between Christmas and New Year's Day so everyone gets several consecutive days off over one holiday or the other. While the number of days is equal, nobody ever wanted the Christmas shift. I owed so many people. I thought taking call over Christmas would be a smart move. I was able to take Christmas day for Kathy Donovan, who had done the most to cover for me. Kathy had two young daughters and it killed her to miss Christmas morning with them.

As it turned out, Christmas call was a blast. Everyone felt like we'd been exiled to the island of misfit toys. The nurses all brought desserts, the residents brought some salads and I bought a couple hundred Buffalo wings. For what must be Biblical reasons, Christmas is always a low delivery day. There was only one woman on the board when we came in that morning. She delivered early, and the board stayed clear until the evening. It was a wonderful gift to have a quiet Labor and Delivery on Christmas day.

About six a.m. I was called stat to Labor and Delivery for a Cesarean. A woman had come in with advanced labor and heavy vaginal bleeding. We had no records, but one of the nurses recognized the woman with her as a lay mid-wife. They'd been attempting a home birth that had gone sideways. The fetal heart rate tracing was ominous. The initial assessment was a placental abruption and the baby looked like it was in serious trouble.

I met the patient and the residents in the OR. The patient was in agony and was being prepped for surgery. The Chief Resident was a solid but cautious young woman from North Carolina named Rory Henderson. Her husband was a know-it-all medicine resident who constantly belittled Rory. I often wondered if he damaged more than just her confidence. Rory never reached her full potential. She had all the tools. She was just afraid.

Rory updated me on the patient's status. She is thirty-nine weeks with two prior uncomplicated deliveries. She has been taking something called Black Cohash. I told Rory that mid-wives used Black and Blue Cohash to induce labor. They are supposedly uterine stimulants. Her abruption might be the effects of a Black Cohash overdose.

Rory suggested we go scrub while the nurses prepped. The fetal heart rate was decelerating again.

"Wait, let's examine her again. She was seven centimeters in triage and this is her third child. We might not need to section her."

"Dr. Murphy, the strip has been bad ever since she arrived. You always say the most dangerous strip is the one that is already bad when the patient walks in the door."

"I know, but doing a Cesarean might be a huge mistake. Look at her arm and teeth."

Rory inspected the lady's arm and found blood under the plastic skin guard covering the IV site. There was also a faint red outline around each of her front teeth. "She's got a coagulopathy," Rory said. "Do we have her labs back yet?"

"Exactly. Don't worry about the labs now. We don't really need them. Tell the nursing station to call the blood bank and order four units of O-negative blood, four units of fresh frozen plasma and a ten-pack of platelets. We need them stat. Un-strap her legs and get them up, so I can examine her."

As a result of the abruption, her labor was tumultuous. She was now complete. I asked for a vacuum extractor and applied it. Vaginal delivery was going to be much quicker than organizing even a stat

257

Cesarean. I guided the baby with the vacuum, and Mom unleashed the necessary instinctual fury to deliver the baby on her first effort.

As we feared, the baby was lifeless. We handed it immediately to the neonatal resuscitation team. They began to work, and within a minute we could hear faint cries coming through the small oxygen mask. Also, not unexpected, was the torrent of bright red blood that followed the baby out of the vagina. You know bleeding is excessive when you can actually hear it flowing.

Some of the blood had been hidden in the uterus behind the placental separation, but most was from shock to the uterus such that it now refused to contract. I began to massage the uterus while anesthesia administered some intramuscular methergine. After a few minutes of no response, we repeated the methergine injection and ordered some 15-methyl F2 alpha prostaglandin brought to the room. There was some response to the second dose of methergine, but the uterus was still boggy. When the 15-methyl F2 alpha arrived, we gave that as well. Within a few minutes of the prostaglandin injection, the uterine tone improved and the bleeding ceased.

The blood products arrived before the lab work. We started a two-unit infusion of fresh frozen plasma. Based on the bleeding we had heard and seen, along with a maternal heart rate of one hundred thirty beats per minute, we decided to start an infusion of O-negative packed red blood cells. With the excessive bleeding checked and the blood replacement started, I felt like the patient was stable. I went to evaluate the baby. I looked through the small window into the neonatal stabilization unit. My vision was mostly obstructed by various nurses and doctors, but I did see two small feet actively kicking.

A little while later, I was at the nursing station writing my delivery note when Rory Henderson came up beside me.

"I just wanted to say thanks. We might've saved two lives in there."

"You're welcome. But you don't need to thank me. The last time I checked, that's what they pay me to do. Everyone did a good job. When you have an emergency like that, everyone has to work together."

Rory studied my face a moment and asked, "How do you stay so calm? Weren't you afraid? I was scared to death that the baby was going to die."

"Of course I was afraid. It's normal to be afraid. If you're never afraid, you're crazy. What we do has significant consequences. But, I'll tell you what I've learned just in the past few weeks. What's really scary is being caught in the middle of something you don't understand. What keeps you calm in a dangerous situation is knowing what you're dealing with. There wasn't anything happening to that lady you didn't understand. There wasn't anything that needed to be done that you didn't know how to do."

"Well, I didn't see everything you did."

"That's why you're here, and that's why residencies are so hard. You've got four years to accumulate experience while old farts like me are hanging around to advise and help."

"If we would've done the Cesarean on her that I ordered, we would've regretted that decision."

"You know Murphy's rule. Good judgment comes from experience. Experience comes from bad judgment. Actually, I think Will Rogers said that. But either way, don't beat yourself up. You did a good job, gained experience, and everybody is going home happy and healthy. Next time, you'll be more aware, more confident, and less afraid. You'll encounter this same situation again. It's the nature of Obstetrics. You can run, but you can't hide from trouble. Trouble will find you."

"Well, I'm glad you were my attending this morning. We all missed you when you were away."

"Thank you, Rory. I missed you guys too. Merry Christmas."

"Merry Christmas to you too."

My beeper went off. The message said Laurence Nodeen was holding and wanted to speak with me, "caller request."

"Dr. Murphy, working hard this morning?" Nodeen asked, after we were connected by the hospital operator.

"We had a little excitement this morning, but it's all good. Nothing as exciting as the virgin birth of our lord and savior, but enough to get our blood flowing. By the way, Merry Christmas to you and your family."

"Thank you very much, Doctor. Same to you. How's everything going with work?"

"I was thinking pretty well until this call. I thought you were a government employee? It worries me that you're calling on a federal holiday. Maybe you should tell me how I'm doing."

"You're doing fine. Remember, my job description is to stamp out crime, save lives, and make America a more beautiful place for us all to live. It's hard to fit all that into the nine to five. Sometimes I have to work on the holidays too."

"I hear you. What can I do for you?"

Nodeen told me he would be coming back to Charleston on December thirty-first to prepare for another round of grand jury testimony and indictments. He wanted to know if there was a chance we could get together. I told him I wouldn't be in Charleston. I had the New Year's Holiday off and I would be staying with my parents in Garden City.

He thought that was funny and mentioned something about "returning to the scene of the crime." He said that was even better. He'd fly into Myrtle Beach and get in a round of golf before meeting with the grand jury.

"Do these new indictments include Helene?"

"No, I didn't mean to imply that. Ms. Eastland continues to be very cooperative, and we're convinced she didn't have any serious role in the smuggling operations. She might've muled some drug money to the islands, but we're going to put that weight on Redding."

"That's good news. Is she still in protective custody? Does she ever ask about me?" The first question was the appropriate one. The second, was the one I was more interested in.

"Those are some of the things I want to talk to you about when I come down. There're things I can tell you and some things I can't. However, what I can tell you is better said face to face. Will you have some time when I come down?"

"Yes, definitely. It'll be good to see you again."

"Great. I'll be in Charleston for about a week after the first of the year. I'll bring my Clarence 'Don't Turn Nobody Down' McCant's T-shirt just in case there's a game. By the way, we have a whole new task force looking into Clarence's financing. It looks like you've put us onto something big."

"What?"

"Just kidding. Thought I'd yank your chain a little. However, if there's a game I'd love to play."

"I'll have to check with Jack, but I'm sure we do. I don't have the schedule with me. I'll let you know."

"Sounds good. See you on the thirty-first. Have a good Christmas."

MYRTLE BEACH AIRPORT

That conversation was the explanation for my standing in the cold drizzle at the Myrtle Beach airport on New Year's Eve.

For the past two days, I'd explained to my parents the events of the past few weeks. As I'd expected, my parents were one hundred percent supportive. Always the ex-military wife, Mom was concerned that I hadn't cleaned the condo as well as I should've before the Carvey's arrived. Dad loved the part where Nodeen reamed out President Turner and Dean Funderburke. My dad knew Funderburke from the state board of the American Red Cross and thought he was a jerk. Mom insisted I invite Nodeen to dinner. I assumed Nodeen's news had to do with Helene. I felt like a school boy, wondering what her response would be to my "do you like me" note.

Right on time, a black two-engine Lear jet came in for a landing and taxied to the executive terminal. I imagined that it was the same Lear jet I'd seen before. Once waved to a stop and doors opened, U.S. Attorney Laurence Nodeen emerged and descended halfway down the stairs. When he saw me standing at the gate, he waved, but did not come over. Instead, he extended his hand to help Helene Eastland exit the plane. She was wearing the Oakland Raiders sweat suit and ball cap that she had worn on our last day together.

Nodeen escorted her half-way to the gate before she saw me and broke into a run. Helene threw herself into my arms and wrapped herself around me. It was a hard, silent hug that erased any lingering concerns. Finally,

263

she turned her head and kissed my ear. She whispered, "I love you." I pulled back slightly, so I could look into her eyes. "I love you, too. Welcome home." Then we kissed passionately.

After standing back patiently, Laurence Nodeen finally stepped forward and shook my hand. "Doctor Murphy."

"Nodeen, you cur. Would it have killed you to have given me a heads up? It's people like you that give the government a bad name." Then I replaced the handshake with an embrace. "Thanks for bringing Helene back safely. How long can she stay?"

"That's between you and Ms. Eastland. The federal government has concluded that Ms. Eastland does not have anything of relevance to contribute to our Jackpot investigation. She is free to do as she pleases. Although I can't for the life of me figure out why, she wanted to come see you."

"Very funny. How long have you been practicing that line?"

"Not too long. Mr. Rosen asked that I express his regret that he couldn't make the trip. He thought you'd understand. He wants you to know that he is available if you ever need him. Ms. Rosen and Lily also asked that I send you their love and thank you for their New Year."

"Tell them I understand. Please wish them all a happy and healthy New Year. Are you interested in some good eats? My Mom puts out a great spread on New Year's Day."

"No, I think I'll meet Mom and Dad Murphy in a day or two. There's already going to be enough excitement at your dinner table tonight. I'd love to be a fly on the wall, but my better half tells me not to intrude. Besides, I have a meeting tonight with Sheprow and a few other folks about the Governor."

"What's up?"

"Eastland tried reaching out politically to the White House and is making some threats. They aren't getting him anywhere. The South Carolina Republican Party has been given the word that he's toxic, so they're moving on to other candidates. We're going to meet with the Governor and re-explain his parameters. Everything he has is being stripped away. You'll be interested to know that the Director of the South Carolina Law Enforcement Division announced yesterday that SLED agents would no longer be providing security for the executive branch. That job is now the responsibility of the State House Security Office which, I believe, is a couple of retired, over-weight Columbia city policemen."

"No kidding."

"Your old buddy Wrenn has been reassigned to the prisoner transport service. That's the bottom rung on the SLED ladder of success."

"I have no idea why, but I'm glad he wasn't fired. He's probably a good cop. I know he's as hard as a bag of bricks."

"Don't go all bleeding heart on me. He should be the prisoner, not driving them around."

"No, Eastland is the bad guy in this drama. He's the one that needs to be in jail."

"I can't argue with that. Right now he has a pass. Eventually though, he'll go down. The great thing about the self-righteous is that they'll always fuck up again. They never believe they did anything wrong in the first place. We'll get another bite at this apple."

"I hope so, man. The idea of him walking around free is repugnant. Despite everything, I can't help but believe he's still a danger."

"Sooner or later, his bill will come due and we'll be there to collect. We can thank Helene for that. It would've not been possible without her stepping up. Now, you need to get her out of this drizzle before she catches pneumonia, and I have to write up an incident report. Ms. Eastland, it's been a pleasure. You're a great travelling companion. I hope your evening goes well. Declan, I'll call you in a day or two."

Helene's only bag was the same backpack I'd brought her when we left the hospital. I picked it up, and we headed for my car. "My Mom's going to be surprised. She was expecting a six-foot-six black man. I hope you have a big appetite."

"I'm starving. What do the Murphy's do for New Year's?"

"Well, tonight we'll go with tuna fish and pimento cheese sandwiches, Hoppin' John, and a variety of soups. Usually French Onion, Tomato Bisque and Split Pea with Ham. On New Year's Day, we usually do a lot of football and a big standing rib roast."

"Sounds delicious. I'm looking forward to seeing your mother and father again. It's been a long time."

"They're going to be excited to catch up with you as well. I hope you don't mind some questions. My mother won't be able to help herself. Dad's more laid back, but he's always listening. My younger brother and his wife are here too. She's a little prissy."

Helene hesitated a moment and then asked, "How much do they know?"

"I kept it simple. I told them you were mixed up with some of the Operation Jackpot smugglers, but just peripherally. I told them your father was trying to get you committed to cover up your involvement with the dope smugglers, so it wouldn't interfere with his Senate bid. They know we hid out at the beach house for a week until we could figure out what to do. Our solution was the FBI, and they've been protecting you, while you told them what you knew. My parents know I was in trouble with the hospital, but that is all smoothed over. Thank you by the way. They know you're estranged from your father, but I didn't elaborate."

"Thank you. Do they have a problem with any of that?"

"I don't think so. They can't stand the Governor. The Murphy's are all life-long Democrats. I thought that you knew that."

When we got to the car, I put her back pack in the backseat and picked up a small package and handed it to Helene. "A belated Christmas present."

As I pulled onto the highway, Helene unwrapped the cherry-wood puzzle box. She started rolling it around in her hands, exploring the lines and wood grains.

"Hold on a minute, and I'll show you how to get into it."

"That's okay, I'll figure it out."

"Sure," I said, grinning.

Helene continued to twirl the box in her hands and began to deconstruct it. Between my glances down the highway, Helene quickly opened the box and found the shark's tooth necklace in its velvet compartment.

"You found my necklace. I was worried it might be lost. Thank you for the box. It's beautiful. But mostly, thank you for saving my necklace. Our necklace, we found it together."

Smiling at me, she took the necklace out of the box and put it around her neck.

We turned off Highway 17 toward Garden City, then stopped at the light at Sam's Corner. I turned and looked at Helene as she reassembled the cherry-wood box.

"What's wrong?" She asked.

"Nothing. I just realized how good you are with puzzles. Tell me something, when did this thing change from being about me saving you, to being about you saving me?"

Helene smiled, "In the butterfly house."

If you enjoyed Roger Newman's *Occam's Razor,* please consider other recent Moonshine Cove books.

The Orphan Train by Steve Brigman—James is ten when he

is taken from a New York orphanage and sent out west on one of the infamous orphan trains, meeting a pretty little girl on his journey who will one day become the core of his existence and the source of his deepest despair.

Grandion by John A. Demarchis—Up-and-coming New

York City investor Salvadore Grandino always wanted to make a name for himself, but as the heir to a powerful mafia family — and its dirtiest secret — creating a new identity is more than a metaphor. With enemies closing in from all sides, he must fight for his own freedom, and for the chance to spend his life with the woman he loves. And it's a fight to the death.

Bullseye by Adam J Toci—After several successful years chasing counterfeiters, Secret Service Agent Terrance

"Dutch" Brown and his partner Harry Ludec have been fast tracked. The only problem? They are tasked with guarding a President who is quickly amassing enemies while pushing through landmark legislation on immigration reform. Her take no prisoners approach doesn't win her friends in Washington. But where are the enemies are coming from, beyond our borders or within?

CPSIA information can be obtained at www.ICGtesting.com
Printed in the USA
LVOW12s0543170914

404483LV00003B/5/P